Long Ride Yellow

Also by Martin West

Cretacea and Other Stories from the Badlands

LONG
RIDE
YELLOW

MARTIN
WEST
A NOVEL

Anvil Press Publishers Inc.
P.O. Box 3008, Main Post Office
Vancouver, B.C. V6B 3X5 CANADA
www.anvilpress.com

Library and Archives Canada Cataloguing in Publication

West, Martin, 1959-, author
Long ride yellow / Martin West. -- First edition.

ISBN 978-1-77214-094-1 (softcover)

I. Title.

PS8645.E75L66 2017 C813'.6 C2017-903381-6

Printed and bound in Canada
Cover design by Rayola Graphic
Cover photo by Ambrose + Wether
Author photo: M. Todor
Interior by HeimatHouse
Represented in Canada by Publishers Group Canada
Distributed by Raincoast Books

The publisher gratefully acknowledges the financial assistance of the Canada Council for the Arts, the Canada Book Fund, and the Province of British Columbia through the B.C. Arts Council and the Book Publishing Tax Credit.

Either he is occupied
or gone aside
or is on a journey, perhaps asleep
and needs to be awakened.

— 1 Kings 18.

1.

Nonni wore her latex dress, bronze shoes, and studded collar. In keeping with the fashion, the studs were chrome but the barbs were gold. She stood in a parking lot behind Seventeenth Avenue and watched a cottonwood weep its shadow across the road. Nonni didn't want the shadow to touch her shoes. They were new shoes. She had just bought them at Mindy's, off Eighth. Shoes were clean. Shadows were lonely. Wood was melancholic and parking lots were for plebes.

"I want the blond boy," she said.

A cigarette spark danced on the dashboard. The cherry blossoms slipped past the window and the neon strips dashed along the horizon. She was with her husband. They were on their way to the club.

"Which one?" Gerry said.

"The one who looks like a surfer."

"They're too young." Gerry had on his jeans and sports coat. His ascot, too. He didn't change until after they got to the club.

"They're easier to train that way."

“The young ones are trouble.”

“They don’t argue at least.” She blew menthol on the glove box until the fumes fled over the tachometer.

“Do you have to smoke those things?”

“They turn me on.”

“Everything does.”

“I hope Gwen isn’t there,” she said. “She doesn’t turn me on. She’s a bitch.”

“She’s the owner.”

“She’s always making up rules or saying people have called red when they haven’t. Maybe her husband will be there instead. What’s his name, Dan?”

“Don,” Gerry said. “His name is Don.”

The club was buried in the industrial quarter between a brass piping yard and a cement storage hut. The walls were stucco. The roof was tin. A neon oval with the word *Onyx* hung in the front window. The sign was the only thing that noted the location’s existence and that’s the way everyone wanted to keep it.

Nonni walked across the parking lot. The gravel crunched beneath her boots. She liked the sound of pebbles breaking on the concrete, the feel of concussion, the notion of rapture and wreckage.

Inside the foyer there was a wicket booth, just like a nineteenth-century bank. Gwen stood behind the wire with the member’s book open and a pen poised on the spine. She was a trim woman of forty who always wore a black evening dress and hoop earrings. The club had been registered in her name for over seven years and nobody got through the inner door without Gwen signing them in. Members only. No exceptions, no excuses, no unscreened guests. Memberships weren’t sold at the door.

“Is Don here?” Nonni said.

Gwen handed Nonni the pen. "He's upstairs."

A Bluebottle fly buzzed around the wicket. They were the first sign of summer. Soon the skylights would open to keep the club cool and the orange carbolic haze would settle under a warm moon. Gwen reached under the counter and hit the buzzer. The inside door clicked open and the weekend began.

The Onyx was a coliseum shaped cavern with rounded walls and dank light. There was a dance space, twelve tables, a metal cage, and a cocktail bar. On the second floor, open balconies ran around the perimeter where the players watched the newcomers file in through the foyer. Far up on the domed roof, an immense screen played German bondage porn in a never-ending loop. The club used to be a windshield repair shop before Gwen took it over.

Gerry wandered to the change room. Nonni went to the bar. She got a glass of Chardonnay, leaned back, and watched the screen. A woman coated in yellow rubber struck a man with a crop. There were sharp commands in deep garrulous tongues and Nonni liked to think it wasn't staged, but a real interrogation scene from some forgotten conflict, like Croatia or the Ugandan Civil War.

"Where's Gerry?" William said.

William was an overweight man of fifty who sported leather suspenders and polished wine glasses for the women who wanted drinks. His chest had an unusual amount of hair and his cheeks were puffed.

"He's getting changed," Nonni said.

"You don't make him wear his leathers here?"

"He runs things over."

"He needs discipline." William nodded as if it were a dictionary fact and handed Nonni a plate stacked with strawberries.

“He needs something.” She took a strawberry and pondered the room.

There were fourteen people on the dance floor and Nonni knew them all. There was Heidi and Randle, an anorexic couple in traditional leather who only got off with each other. Halfway through the evening Heidi would take Randle upstairs, tie him to the cross and flog him mercilessly. Every session, he would bleed, he would beg, he would cry, then finally go limp. Nonni liked the part when Heidi wrapped her flogger around Randle's neck. He'd beg to be choked, but it never happened. That was the only reason Nonni watched, hoping one day Heidi would choke his breath out, and make his face turn blue.

Shannon and Steve lounged by the metal cage. They were both thirty and both muscular. Shannon was Mediterranean, but had yellow hair. Steve was six foot, and unnaturally blond. Mostly the two sat downstairs and talked about their cruises to the Caribbean or Alaska. They were great to look at, but were always pontificating about the meals on the next cruise ship or complaining about the service on the last one.

Jim and Susan came in. They stored their gear in a set of airplane travel bags with wheels that they pulled behind them. The more excited they were, the bigger the bags got. Both of them were marathoners with smooth bodies and they looked like a couple out of a toothpaste commercial. Last month, she had put a plastic bag over his head and made him pass out.

There were a few others off the dance floor that she couldn't name. A gay couple who did bone piercing. An anthropology student into Fascism. A blond woman who sat in the corner, looking ill at ease, wearing too much makeup. Her face was Pro-Domme and Nonni thought of a mannequin in a fur salon near Banff. Gwen would never let her upstairs dressed like that.

Downstairs was where the common people talked and negotiated, but upstairs was where the savage grace happened. Upstairs were the racks and couches, broad clamps and wooden crosses. Upstairs was the screaming and the strict language of satisfaction.

"Who's the new one?" Nonni said to William.

"Never seen her before."

"She doesn't fit."

"Some don't."

Nonni filed the girl far down on the list of possibilities. In club language, a chokecherry slow. William examined a glass and put it up on the rack.

"Have you seen Daniel?" Nonni asked.

"Who?"

"The surfer."

"Never have."

She leaned over the bar and wrapped her hand around a cedar beam. There were grease stains engrained in the wood. Perhaps from an automotive spill. She liked the ancient scent. She had a theory. Everything erotic in the cosmos left an imprint and she was the one designated to measure the torque. She was the one to decipher the dead.

Nonni was thirty-three. She had no children. She was five foot eight, and one hundred and thirty pounds. She had platinum hair owing to her Nordic descent and it fell in two halves like clam shells on each shoulder. Her complexion was marble. Her nose was small and her face slender. She looked something like a china doll. In fact, her friends in school had called her China Doll because her skin resembled porcelain, but that was decades ago. She had new breasts that had cost Gerry eight thousand dollars and a lip puff that she had spent five thousand on. Once in a while she worked out, but most of her body had come to her through genetics rather than ardour. From time to time she thought she looked too docile, too obsequious — so after she had surveyed the crowd, she reached into her pocket, pulled out a tube of blue lipstick, and gave her mouth a thick coat.

Gerry came back to the bar with his tungsten chest harness made up like a Roman Gladiator and a pair of leather pants.

"Kneel," Nonni said.

"Wait until we go upstairs."

Nonni shrugged and tipped her wine glass for William to fill. Gerry sipped on his mango drink. "Where did Jim and Susan go?"

"No idea," Gerry said.

"They have the knives."

"What knives?"

"We said we'd do a knife scene with them."

"Right," Gerry said.

Gwen came over and put her hand on Gerry's hip. A sprig of lemon perfume hung on her shoulders.

"New outfit?"

"Nonni got it for me in Rome."

"Fabulous," Gwen locked her fingers together. Her teeth where square pearls and always looked wet. "What did you think of Italy, Non?"

"They speak Italian."

"She got it near the Trevi Fountain," Gerry said. "They took measurements. It took three months and I had to clear it with customs because the buckles are magnesium."

"What's the fantasy?" Gwen said.

"To have him gladiator fight in the Roman Coliseum."

"Imperial or senatorial Rome?"

"No clue."

"Thumbs up I hope."

"That depends on how he does tonight," she said.

Gwen smiled with one side of her mouth. Gerry inspected his buckle then gazed up at the wall. There were paintings and photographs. Black and white with pictures of stern dominatrixes and muscular men slicked with oil and rust. The new painting was an acrylic in decrepit orange. A couple from industrial Britain ascended through a thunderstorm in state of steam driven climax.

"Who did the new one?" Gerry said.

"Got it from a local artist for the price of a membership. Sort of the dirty-Victorian-nineteenth-century feel."

"Like what's-his-name?"

"Wardle?" Gwen said.

"That's him."

Nonni finished her wine. She wished she had gotten Okanagan over something from California.

"What's the show tonight?" she asked Gwen.

"Lisa and Terri are going to pierce Brian."

"They're going to do a man?" Nonni leaned back over the bar. A piercing might be good. She felt a quiver start near the bedrock of her heart.

"They couldn't find a girl."

"They'll castrate him."

"I'll make him sign a waiver."

"Why?"

Nonni imagined an uninitiated so horny he'd do anything without thinking, even if it meant getting pin cushioned by a pair who probably despised him. A heavy shape lumbered across the floor and the plumbing pipes in the attic bent over, and then there was a splash of red and chocolate on Nonni's boot.

“You dropped your strawberry,” Gerry said.

“It fell. I didn’t drop it.”

“Maybe you should have your blood sugar checked,” Gwen said.

“My blood sugar is fine.”

The chocolate dribbled over her laces. The strawberry followed and Nonni thought of lava chunks flowing down a volcanic slope. Will examined a wine glass and scraped off the detritus with a dental pick. Nonni snapped her fingers and pointed at the boot. Will came over, tucked the towel into his belt, then lowered his hulking frame to the floor. He bent down and his tongue lapped over Nonni’s toe while his chest hairs brushed the cement.

“Who’s the woman with the god-awful makeup?”

“She came with a blond,” Gwen said.

“Did she give you ID?”

“Driver’s licence.”

“New people make me nervous,” Gerry said. He shifted his weight from one foot to the other. The eagle icon on his shoulder strap tinkled.

“Don looked her up in the phone book,” Gwen said.

“The bathhouse raid last month made me nervous.”

“The police can’t raid bathhouses anymore. This is a private party.”

“Says who?”

“The Supreme Court,” Gwen said.

“Who listens to them?” Nonni said. She dumped the wine into the sink.

The minutes passed and another dozen people filtered in. Nonni recognized a few. There was a couple that they had been to a house party with the month before. She was dressed up like a geisha and he wore latex. Nonni couldn’t remember their names. Names didn't seem to matter much. Names came and went. Then there was the Spanish couple. The gay couple. No names there, either. A professional dominatrix came in with two of her boys. Mistress Marble or Goddess Granite. Those names she didn't want to know. Pro-Dommes were trouble. Gwen wouldn't let them upstairs for sure.

People lingered. The porn looped across the screen. Che Guevara foot worshipped an industrialist with black pumps. A woman was eaten by a plastic alligator. Then the air smelled of ozone. Nonni's nape prickled and she played a dozen scenes in her head: two girls getting perforated with swords, men choking on turbines, Gerry having his throat slit by a gladiator while she gave him the thumbs down.

"Let's go," she said and pulled down on his collar. This time he didn't mind. Maybe the mango drink was working.

Upstairs, the club was divided into four balconies. The first balcony had a row of crosses and hooks dangling from the ceiling, and looked like an abattoir. Basic industrial flogging. Beyond that there was the bedroom balcony with its red plastic sheets and vinyl pillows. That was for screwing. The medieval room had stocks and an ion machine that produced electric arcs in a film of humidity. But Nonni's favourite place was the fantasy room with its dungeon walls and vaulted ceiling. Here there was a padded electric garrote and a brick well. She liked to think of all the ancient souls that were stuffed down the well in the moment of pleasure and suffering.

Susan bound Jim to a Saint Andrew's Cross and lashed him with an elk-hide flogger. Every time she brought the tails down, he seized up, and his cries echoed down to the bar where William smiled and polished glasses.

"Give him a go," Susan said. Her face was pink.

Jim's body was too trim to leave unbruised, so Nonni picked

up the tails and counted out the strokes. The welts rose on his back, his mouth fell open, and she wished Gerry got like that when she beat him.

Nonni ran her hand over a dozen chrome instruments on the wall that might have been stolen from a dentist's office. Then the mood took her, because she wanted it too, and she grabbed her husband by the hair. He cursed. He sank to his knees. His face shattered in a grimace that looked like glass.

"What's your issue?" she said.

He lingered on the ground. Nonni swept that leaf aside and forgot. The party went on. Life was short. Terri tied up Brian with a length of Newfoundland fishing twine. Nonni found a metal pinwheel with spurs and rolled the darts over his scrotum. The blood formed such gorgeous pulpits. In the next balcony a domme had suspended her slave from a hook in the ceiling and shoved a ball gag in his mouth. It went on and on. Nonni marveled at what beautiful, still, wooden faces they all had in their moment of bliss, and she wanted a menthol.

Daniel leaned up against the door of the fantasy room. He was tanned and slender, with curly blond hair and the flat stomach of youth. A pair of rubber boxer shorts hung off his hips and exposed his beach-browned thighs. Beside him lilted the new girl with the plaster makeup. She was blond and bored. She surveyed the crowd for admirers. A man in a military costume asked if he could get her champagne. She smiled a coy yes and left. Daniel was alone and so Nonni went in.

"Hello," she said.

"Hello ma'am."

He'll do, she thought. "I've seen you here before."

"I come when they will let me."

"Now that you're in, why aren't you playing?"

"Can't find anyone."

His voice was detached and he spoke with a slight accent, although Nonni couldn't place it.

"Doesn't your friend play?"

"Not here," he said and glanced to the stairwell.

"That's too bad."

By the bar, the military man made large circles as if driving a tank and his new date seemed to be impressed.

"They're talking torque conversion," Daniel said.

Nonni adjusted her corset and moved the zipper down an inch. The bubbles that clung to the inside of Daniels' gin and tonic crept up and around the straw.

"So why did you bother?"

"A single man has to take what he can get."

Those were the facts. Single men couldn't get into these kinds of clubs alone. Single men needed a ticket to get into a club. The dating columns were filled with men wanting tickets. They were answered by women who knew what men could provide and so if events worked out, they both went as a couple.

"Now that you're in, what are your turn-ons?" Nonni tapped an unlit cigarette against his lacquered chest and consulted a distant star.

"I don't know."

"Ambiguity is a non-combustible."

He thought. His eyes were as green as quartz. A smell of singed wire crept through the room. Maybe the fuse box. "I'd like to be choked by an obscene creature."

"Might be dangerous."

"You asked."

Nonni pictured his eyes rolling back, egg white in their sockets, as his air ran low and his scrotum engorged. The singe smell grew and Nonni half expected a door to burst into smoke.

There wasn't a sprinkler system at the club, but that was life. She put her middle finger on the centre of Daniel's throat. For such a strong young man he had a very crushable neck.

"Let's go," she said.

"I can't here."

"Why not here?"

"My date would get angry."

"So?" she said.

"I'd never get back in."

"I'd let you back in."

"How?"

The pace of glaciers and men's cognition. Nonni pushed Daniel back against a wooden timber. A splinter stuck into his spine, but he didn't bleed, didn't bruise, didn't even notice. She kissed his cheek and his skin became rigid, a mask — high and opaque with a flat nose, wide eyes, and a small round mouth. She recalled her parents bringing something like it back from Bella Coola when they had been school teachers there in the 1960s. She twisted her hands around his windpipe and her knuckles calcified into his flesh. There were wind chimes. Chantal pushed her way back in with a pink martini clutched to her ribs.

"What are you doing?" she said.

"Talking," Nonni said.

"With your hands around his neck?" She threw her drink to the floor and the glass smashed on a pillory stand.

"This is a leather club my dear."

Gwen glided between the two women with a stilted smile. Her fingers were locked in the poise of a career diplomat.

"She's touching him," Chantal said.

"We do that here," Gwen said.

"She's choking him to death."

"You hardly gave me time to kill him," Nonni said.

"Do you want to brain damage him or what?"

"I wasn't interested in his brain."

Gwen put a hand on the girl's shoulder. "Do you mind if we have a word in the office?"

Chantal snatched her purse off the couch. Nonni tucked a business card into the boy's briefs. Gerry had his clothes on. His shirt was buttoned up and he had stuffed a peppermint candy into his mouth.

"Like I told you. The young ones are trouble."

"His face turned into wood."

"I didn't think you noticed his face," Gerry said.

Nonni put her hand on the timbers of the club wall. An Edwardian gaslight smell of boiler rooms. "Let's give it another go."

"I've had enough for one night," Gerry pocketed his keys.

"We just got here."

"I want to go home."

"I'm not tired."

"Your pupils are the size of donuts."

"That's because I'm having a good time."

He flipped the keys around his finger. "You hurt me back there, Nonni."

Your ass or your pride? she was going to ask, but when she rubbed her neck a patch of her skin had gone shiny and knotted like a burl of polished oak.

2.

Dr. Bertrand Sayer's office was on the twentieth floor of a green thirty-storey skyscraper in the centre of downtown Calgary which was devoid of natural green. The office was finished with light hardwood and leafy plastic palms, and Nonni went there every Thursday morning at ten. The hallway off the elevator had a strip of patterned carpet down the middle, wainscoted walls, and gas lamps by the office doors. This kind of doctor cost money and Nonni paid. There were reasons. The waiting room was large and always empty. Dr. Sayer booked his appointments with a ten-minute space in between so there was no chance that one patient would pass the next. Every once in a while, she would pass a worried looking person on the elevator, but there were accountants, marriage counsellors, and a civil litigation office on the twentieth floor, so it wasn't uncommon to see people cry about all kinds of problems. The doctor also never used the term "sexual aberration" and Nonni had been through three doctors before who did.

When Nonni went into the office, Dr. Sayer was sitting behind his desk with his hands steepled, gazing out the window. He did that often. He stared out over the skin of concrete that erupted from the black ocean of petroleum like it was his to own. He was a handsome man, tall and thin with a trimmed beard. He wore patterned ties and pressed shirts and was just what she thought a psychiatrist should look like, perfect and non-personable, and that is why, in the end, she had picked him.

"Nonni," he said. He smiled. His white teeth and his gold cuff links were always aligned.

There was a choice of two chairs in Dr. Sayer's office. The choice never changed. A big puffy white chair that came from Sweden on the left and a high fashioned uncomfortable chair with thin oak legs and an embroidered green cushion on the right. Perhaps it was a test. Everything was a test of sorts here. Sayer had once told her that the green chair came from Georgian England during the Age of Reason and Nonni believed him. She never sat in that chair.

On the far wall there was an acrylic abstract of pale yellows and brown stripes that looked like a bunch of wooden tombstones erupting from a meadow.

"That's new," she said.

"Do you like it?"

"It belongs in a paint commercial."

"What kinds of paintings do you like?"

"I'm off paint these days."

"Why?"

"Gerry and I had a disagreement on paintings. In fact, I hate them. He's into that stuff. Okay, whatever. But mostly I like ones with people in them."

"You don't see people in that picture?"

She looked. "Are there any?"

Sayer opened a manila file on the desk, pulled on his beard, and read through the papers. Sometimes they would talk about people and perversion. Other times they would talk about talking, like how in club language, a "birch bark green" was a newbie who came too soon when struck, or a "rectangle squeeze" was a date that just didn't work out. Mostly he wanted to talk about feelings. "How are you feeling?" he said.

She shrugged. Her coat was heavy and the vinyl was hot.

"You've been off the Paxil for fourteen days now."

"Fifteen." Nonni crossed her legs and gazed at the other paintings on the wall. There were a few photographs of people in row boats and walking down eighteenth-century streets, but nothing that she would describe as exciting. "And, I feel the same. Which is not so good. I sleep the same, which is not much. My mood pattern is the same. That's below average. I feel poorly in the morning, better in the afternoon, and best in the evening. I like the night."

"Moods tend to increase during the day."

"Why?"

"The chemicals that make us happy aren't produced as much when we sleep."

Nonni wanted a menthol. Maybe an Aspirin. The burl of wood that had hardened her neck crept around her jaw to initiate a migraine and so probably that is what she would get. "That's why I stay up all night and feel shitty the next day."

"Insomnia and depression go hand in hand."

"Is there a prescription for that?"

"How do you feel otherwise?"

"Like a chunk of Arborite."

"Always?"

"Almost always."

"When not?"

"When I'm aroused."

"Sexually?"

"Of course, sexually."

Sayer nodded. He always appeared to be on the verge of some great conclusion that he was willing to share if Nonni could only squeeze it out of him. His tie clip was on a bad angle.

"I don't want you to get the wrong idea," she said. She opened and closed the gold clasp on her purse but couldn't recall if it were a Gucci or Gabbana. "It's not just screwing. I'm not that shallow."

"Are you and your husband still going to the clubs?"

"To the SM club. We don't go to the swinger clubs anymore."

"Why?"

"The people are too straight."

"Too straight?"

Nonni thought of the discos and night clubs and holidays in Jamaica with husbands reviewing their golf clubs and wives reliving their high school years, and she remembered how much she despised them. "They think they're so moderne and hip. They buy records by John Coltrane. They vote for the Green Party. And sometimes they screw. Mostly they like complaining about how much tax they have to pay and how there aren't enough classic rock stations on the radio. So we just go to the SM club now. We were there last week."

"How was it?"

"I think Gerry might be losing interest."

"In SM or the clubs?"

"In going out altogether. In any kind of action. In me, maybe."

"What makes you say that?" he said.

Beside Sayer's wall painting was the westward facing window. A venetian blind hung halfway down the pane. The blinds rattled on and on, and Nonni couldn't decide if they were a cue or a code she was supposed to decipher, or maybe just the plastic slats babbling into nothing at all. A tiny red beetle lighted on the glass and Nonni thought of scarabs, or at least scarification.

"The other night, there was a painting on the wall," she said. "Nobody famous. Gerry got into this conversation with the owner about how it was realist or impressionistic, and they went on and on. God, it was endless. They talked about shadows and form. Cubism versus minimalism and I thought: who cares? We're here to play. Not to be talent scouts for the National Gallery."

"People like to talk about art."

"Why?"

"Aesthetics," Sayer said. He was in known territory. His teeth were perfect. He folded his hands together and commenced the expository. "It brings order to their universe. Then when they talk about those feelings to other people, the sense of order resonates and they don't feel so alone."

"How can you feel alone when you're about to flog someone until they shoot their load across the floor?"

Sayer made a small notation in his diary and pulled on his beard. Somewhere here, there was an angle. "Were you jealous?"

A faint smell of lemon cleaner came off the doctor's desk. The window pane was stained teak. Far out the window, past the city, were the Rocky Mountains with snow fields and glaciers, lifeless and unfeeling. Perhaps there was a village in the mountains of sterile rock and cold water. Nonni imagined the inhabitants as stone monsters with igneous lips and cupric eyes that sat around iron tables and forged their Blitzkrieg against the living. In the vortex of night they would make their way down out of their cold moraine mortuaries into the suburbs. Then, disguised as mailboxes, bread boards, and lamp lights they would arise and snatch their sanguine victims into a mirthless vacuum.

"I don't get jealous of those kind of people," she said.

"But you felt left out?"

"I felt ripped off. We go there for kink. It only happens once a week so I don't waste time talking aesthetics. That's what art museums are for."

"People need to have different forms of communication, and realize them communally. Don't you feel that need?"

"No."

The doctor leaned back in his chair. The ceiling fan twisted slow enough so one could watch the blades pass. There was a prescription pad on his desk, but he was the type of man who didn't like to be refuted on any issue. "Not ever? Not in hiking or music. Creating a business venture. Playing ice hockey?"

"So long as it leads to kink." Nonni pulled a menthol cigarette from her purse and weaved it between her fingers. She stared back out the window over the cold glass landscape that towered into the sky and wondered what life would be like if such gorgeous stone creatures came to life. If they came into her city, her home, her body, and crushed meaning into the listless vein. "I mean would you want to stand around all day and talk about the weather if that's all it led to, standing around all day, talking about the weather?"

"I'd want to do it once in a while to find out what people thought about their environment."

Nonni put the cigarette in her mouth and flicked her lighter. "Don't worry. I won't light it up."

Sayer smiled. She never had lit up a cigarette in his office.

The doctor slid the diary off the desk to the keyboard pedestal and drew a line. "Have you ever tried some organized social engagement?"

"Like what?"

"Charity work, for example. Perhaps with the poor, or working with animals."

"You're kidding me, right?"

"With children then."

"I hate children."

"That's a visceral reaction." Sayer put down his pen. He twisted a strand of scotch tape off the desk. "What is it about children that you don't like?"

"They are inhuman."

"Inhuman?"

"They are ignorant of human ways. How's that?"

"Of course they're ignorant. They're children."

She examined the tip of the unlit menthol. It was half worth the effort coming up with an explanation that made sense. "They are lonely."

"Some children are brought up in lonely environments. But loneliness is not is prerequisite for childhood life."

"Of course it is."

"Have you never met a happy child, Nonni?"

"They may think they are. But really, they're not. And I don't like movies with children or books about children or commercials with children in them. You see, in the end, Dr. Sayer, children are not sexual beings. Not erotic. Therefore, they cannot communicate on the primary wavelength that humans use in our cosmos to evolve. Therefore they are inhuman. If you follow my logic."

"Sort of," he said.

"Can I get a Canada Council grant for this?"

"When you have people over for dinner," he said and appeared to be consumed with ink the ballpoint was leaving on his finger. "And they ask if they can bring their children? What do you say?"

"I say no."

"That must limit your social circle."

"Kindergarten Christmas pageants don't fill up my social calendar."

Nonni imagined what her stone creatures might do when they reached the gates of the city. She thought of what they might do to the dead and what they could have done to Daniel had they gotten hold of him the other night at the club. Cloistured with knotted fingers, jade throats, and impervious will they might not stop with Daniel, but instead cascade through every human heart and plunder without pity. From the alleys in the concrete canyon beneath Sayer's very office they could strangle the weak and crush the timid into trilobites that knew no limits for pain or pleasure. And then she thought of what rapture she might inflict on everything had she the courage they possessed.

"Nonni?" the doctor said. "Are you there?"

"Pardon?"

"Did you hear what I asked about your holidays?"

"No."

"Your purse has fallen open."

The cigarettes, lipstick, a dozen credit cards, and a vibrator had fallen onto the floor. A coin rolled under the desk.

"I've made a mess," she said.

"Where were you, just then?"

"Nowhere."

Sayer leaned back and examined his tie. There was a small dot of ink on the fabric he did not approve of. "Remember once, when we started, we talked about the BS lever?"

Nonni remembered. Apart from the obvious, BS meant Banking Service, which was to say there was no point in paying three hundred dollars a session if you were just going to sit around and lie. You may as well just have cashed your chips, paid the bank the service fee, and walked out.

"I'm about to pull it," he said.

"The other night, when we were at the club, I had what people would call a hallucination. Although it didn't feel psychedelic."

"Hallucinations don't have to be psychedelic."

"What are they?"

"They are a perception without a stimulus."

"This was real. This was terrible. Not terrible as in bad, but terrible as in the classic sense. Like for example if you were standing beneath a huge concrete dam, five thousand feet high, and all of a sudden you heard the cement crack."

"Tell me what you saw."

"I was playing with this boy," she said. She touched a part of her cheek that felt cold. "His face became timber. I mean wood. I've had hallucinations before. When I was in college I did acid. But this was as real as you are right now. Of course, faces don't buckle out of the wall, do they Doctor?"

"What happened next?" Sayer said.

"Gerry wanted to go home, but I stayed up all night doing God knows what."

"What did you say you were doing when this started?"

"Flogging the boy. Sorry. Young man. He was in his twenties."

"So you were in a highly aroused state?"

"Understatement."

"And you have just come off some long-term medication."

"Yes."

"And you were not getting along with your husband?"

"Ditto."

"Do you see where I'm coming from on this one?" Sayer said.

Just change the water into wine Nonni, and float across the crevasse.

"You're the expert."

"I can't do it without your input. Give me an immediate response. Give me three ideas, up front and now. What was it?"

"An acid flashback."

"Ten years is too long for a flashback."

"Moral conservative revolutionaries attempting a coup."

"One last try."

Nonni nodded and bit down on her finger. A long time ago, when she was young, she had a book. A nineteenth-century, thick children's book that she kept under her bed. There were pictures, sketches, and puzzles, all in black and white Victorian Ink. The pages were heavy with soot, so when one turned them over the paper curled to the spine. There were stories too. One interested her. She couldn't remember the title. Beings came from another dimension. They were faceless wooden figures that drifted in and out of banks, parlours, and salons. They did not do anything evil, it was, after all, a children's book. But they lined up in inanimate rows. Waiting and silent they filed into stores, candy shops, and chartered banks to haunt the living and pass judgement on an oblivious human race. That was her best shot at a last try, and she was sticking to it.

"I recall waking up screaming in a state of terror," she said. "I've never been a nostalgic person so I don't know why I'd want to hang onto a memory that gave me nightmares. To this day I wouldn't be able to explain why such things left an impression on me."

"Did you tell Gerry about what you saw?"

"No."

"He is your husband."

Nonni snorted then shook her head. "It's not that kind of relationship."

"Who do you tell then?"

"I tell you, doctor."

3.

The cell phone vibrated across the kitchen counter. Nonni knew right away who it was going to be and what he wanted. All week long she had felt the warning signs of the call sift through her house. The plaster grew moist then sweated. The swirls of polished cedar tightened into coils as small as springs. Dozens of business calls had come and gone, and friends had been routed to voicemail. Finally, when the call came, she sat on the stool and smoked with her legs crossed. After a while, she answered.

"Can you remember me from the other night?" he said.

"How's vanilla life, Danny?"

"In and out."

"I'm sorry we couldn't finish."

"My friend got jealous."

"Bad trait to keep company with."

"She had the transportation."

"What was the outcome?"

"No resolution," he said.

“That’s too bad.”

No resolution. That was perfect. Nonni exhaled. She straightened her back against the wall, let a round smoke ring float out and up towards the alabaster light shade.

“I’d take an offer this time around.”

Promises were fine. Only trade mattered. She took the phone to the hallway and sat down at the desk. Gerry had left blueprints for a new kind of cabinetry sticking out of the drawer. Brass hinges. Inlaid ruts. She closed the drawer with the heel of her shoe.

“You’d have to prove that to me,” she said.

“Can we get together?”

The gardenias on the window flowered a deep yellow and the scent of patchouli floated through the dead heat of summer. She got her purse and sunglasses and found a tube of lip balm on the mantel.

“Where do you live?” she said.

“Mount Royal.”

Almost too close for comfort but comfort was done. “By yourself?”

“I live alone.”

“In a house, I hope.”

“My parents’ house.”

“Where are they now?”

“In a foreign country,” he said.

“On vacation?”

“They own a mineral mine. They are making way too much money to ever come back.”

“Do you have any brothers or sisters?”

“None.”

“Friends?”

“She doesn’t know where I live.”

There were laws in the universe, Nonni knew. They governed entropy and order, coincidence and chaos. Maybe even appointments in the Senate. But their consequences aside, it was foolish to simply ignore good luck.

"This is about me," she said. "Not about you. You'll do what I say. If you don't, I walk out and you never see me again. Do you get that?"

"I get that."

"When can you make it?"

"Tuesday?"

"It can't be Tuesday. It has to be today. Now. Otherwise not at all."

He did some kind of calculation. "Three o'clock?"

"Give me the address."

As soon as she hung up, the walls of the house grew dense in a torpor of stale air. The archway collected mass and gained weight. The cement foundations sagged. Nonni went to her closet and found her stilettos, latex pants, and corset. Then she found her bag and put in a length of half inch rope and three plastic bags, and they too, were heavy.

She stood in front of the mirror and stripped down. She was still young enough. If only there was some way to preserve the body while the libido lasted. Perhaps for centuries. The corset formed a skeleton over her torso and then the blush a second skin on her face. She could stay young a bit longer. So she put on her black rain coat although the sun was intense. Driving down the road no one would guess what she was wearing underneath. She would take the convertible. The plates were registered out of province. Not a soul would recognize who she was. She could take the top down and put on sunglasses. No one would know what she was about to do.

Mount Royal was the established part of town, south of the

city core, that people mentioned at parties. They either lived there, or did business there, or had friends there, or they wished they had all three. It wasn't as much a mountain as a hill. One of the few escarpments over the Bow River valley that wasn't part of the bald-headed prairie. The houses were two-storey mansions built between the wars, and the streets were lined with oak and it was the closest thing to old money the city had to offer.

Daniel's house was a large stone building with high hedges around the front and large picture windows in the living room. She drove past once and parked beside a tennis court at the end of the road. Then she walked up the back alley, pushed through an ivy-covered iron gate, and knocked on the door.

"I didn't think you'd come to the back," Daniel said. He had on university apparel. A polo shirt and baggy shorts.

"Take my bag." Nonni stepped inside. The house smelled of maple.

When he didn't move fast enough she dropped it on the floor. He picked the bag up and hesitated on her heels, and she knew events were pretty much preordained from there.

"Show me the living room," she said.

"Can we talk?"

"No."

The living room was done in hardwood with a thick Persian rug in the middle. Gloomy Victorian paintings hung on the walls and the room was filled with uncomfortable nineteenth-century furniture. On the far wall there was a stone fireplace and a large reproduction of *The Last Spike*. Nonni sat on the largest chair and studied the window. The glass allowed an aristocratic view, but the trees were high enough to keep eavesdroppers out. She pulled a cigarette from her purse. The boy made a brief motion with his hand, probably to tell her she couldn't smoke inside, but then his hand dropped and he said nothing at all.

"Take your clothes off," she said.

"What?"

"Don't say what, say pardon, and take them off."

His knees buckled in that perfect moment of helplessness. He was no longer human. He was an object, a subject, a subtext, and sublime. His jaw shook and then he reached up and undid. The manicured frame sunk onto the floor and there would be no getting up. She walked around him slowly. Her heels clicked on the wood. She flicked her ashes onto his head. Then the heels were on his spine. A trail of saliva smeared on the polished floor. In a moment, his wrists were bound and his throat was collared. She went back to the chair and sat down.

"You can whine and scream all you want and it won't matter," she said. "The neighbours won't hear you. Nobody cares what happens to you and nobody ever will. You're just a poor little rich bitch that is going to wish he had cut off his dick and swallowed exhaust fumes for breakfast and don't start in with me about class struggle."

A cumulus cloud drifted across the window.

"Are you listening?" she said. She knew he was. "Make a round circle with your mouth. Like the letter O."

That much he could do.

"Now crawl over here and suck on the heel of my shoe like you are sucking all that poisonous carbon monoxide, and then I want you to hold your breath until your face goes blue."

Daniel's mouth opened and his lips touched her heel.

"Use your tongue."

The room filled with sunlight. The poplar leaves moved back and forth in green ripples. The glory of the continental summer. Nonni sighed and the floors of the ancient house creaked.

Her head fell back into the puffed chair with the laced pillow and filigreed arms, and on the foyer wall hung a black and white print by Irving Claw.

"It's all so beautiful, don't you think?" She put the tip of a gloved finger to her chin. "It's so fucking incredibly beautiful."

Daniel looked up as if he didn't understand a word. His eyes were round, his face was empty, and when she let her legs fall open, the boy ran the tip of his tongue up her limb and then touched the shell of her leather-bound crotch.

Nonni ground her cigarette out in the potted plant then stood up.

"I can see this isn't working," she said.

"Why not?"

"You bore me."

"For what reason?"

"You're still breathing."

"What should I do?"

"Where is your room?"

The room was like many rooms of many young men she had seen before. A brass bed, a mahogany desk, a walk-in closet, and a walnut bookcase with unopened books. They were all the same and they hardly mattered.

She stood behind him and ran her fingers through his blond curls. There was not a strand out of place. He was a hologram of what was perfect so she let the plastic bag dance down over his head and ruffle around his ears and then she pulled it tight under his jaw. A tiny trace of condensation formed on the inside when he started to breathe.

In his male adolescence, the begging was not very good at first but when Nonni twisted him to the ground, he improved. He said, please don't. He said, please don't hurt me. And then he said something that was desperate and muffled. His eyes went white and Nonni saw the world was right.

“Please don’t what?” she said.

“Please don’t kill me Nonni.”

“Good boy. Now tell me why not?”

“Because I want you.”

“You’d want anybody.”

“I’ll do anything for you.”

“You’ll do that for me in just a minute, but now tell me that you’re afraid.”

“I’m afraid.”

She drew the coil of white rope out of her kit and wrapped it around his neck. In a second the air was sucked up and the bag turned damp. His beautiful cheeks and Roman nose were encased in a film of wet panic and how gorgeous it was to have him squirm in slutted fascination. She brushed her gloved fingers across his cheek and the plastic clung to every crevasse of his skin. His face bleached out. His eyelashes batted. Then she poked a tiny hole in the bag so he might breathe a little, and some of his sweat spattered onto the brass bedpost.

“Did you like that?” She cinched the rope one degree tighter and his tongue shot through the plastic seal. Outside a thunderhead moved across the summer sky and the trees scratched the window. The plumbing buckled.

Four more clove hitches and the knot was secured behind his ear. The young man swelled up in a pearl of rhetoric then Nonni leaned back and he kept saying God over and over again until a bead of her sweat splashed down on his spine and then it was done.

“*Quo vadis*?” she said, but no one answered. She had sprained her knuckles in the rope. There was sawdust over her palms and her fingers were bruised. She wiggled the knots loose from under his chin. “If you want to come on my shoes, go ahead, but hurry up. I don’t much like a slave’s company when I’m done.”

Daniel lay on his side, with his tanned body limp and beautiful and his hands still bound. She pushed a stiletto into his rib but he was inert on the carpet. His hair dripped with condensation. His eyelids were half shut. The rope had left fibers on his shoulder. She put an ear to his nose. Nothing. She opened his jaw and blew four stacks of air inside him. She had been taught that at swimming lessons. His chest rose and fell once, but not much else. She did it all again and the mountain ash branch scratched at the window again, its berries bulging with juice.

"You stupid bitch," she said. She took a cigarette from her leather pocket but didn't light it up because he had such a perfect atmosphere. Such a perfect life. This was such a perfect house. She opened his drawers. Beneath a layer of socks was a stack of cheap porn magazines with glossy photos. All young men had them. This one had plenty. A Swedish domme, a tall Negress in latex, a sub choked with a dress tie ready for misadventure.

She laced one end of the rope around the laundry bar so there was just a bit of slack and tossed the magazine at his feet. If he lived, he lived. Young men were tough, others were unlucky. There were a few dried stains on the carpet. She was no expert but she could guess. And if she guessed right then everything would fall into place perfectly for whoever had to clean these kinds of things up.

4.

Nonni's hand hurt. The rope burn had spread around her knuckles. The veins on her wrist darkened to purple braches and in a distantly classic overture, her fingernails shone as marble. The sessions with Dr. Sayer weren't helping. So instead she went to the pharmacist.

The drugstore was a small shop in the corner of an ancient strip mall, cluttered with bottles and adverts for herbal remedies. The windows were soaped and Nonni was not sure why she went there. The pharmacist was not likable. A small man of fifty with a bald head and thick accent, he wore the white smock that chemists of the last century used and stood on a raised platform, gazing down on his customers, judging their needs and their pains. She liked to imagine he was the kind of man who would have worked with the dead in ancient empires, an apothecary who spent years grinding up medicines for patients who were long past treatment, and somewhere down deep Nonni found that exciting.

"Can you fill this?" she said, putting the prescription up on the counter.

“Perhaps Madam.”

“Per-fucking-haps?”

“I must check if I have this in stock,” he said.

“It’s a Paxil substitute.”

The chemist examined the prescription then turned it over. It was impossible to gauge his true disposition, whether he believed all of his patients lied to him or if lying were part of the cure.

“Who signed this, Madam?”

“Dr. Sayer.”

“It does not look like one of his prescriptions.”

“Well, he wrote it.”

The chemist held the paper to his nose and smelled the ink.

“Does that help?” she said.

“This is not his.”

“I watched him sign.”

“How long ago?”

Nonni shrugged. “Thursday.”

“This is a very old piece of paper.”

“Maybe he had an old pad.”

“I shall have to call him.”

“His number is on the bottom, right below his name,” she said.

There was a faint smell of linseed oil on the counter. At the far end of the herbal row, a woman in a blue pinstripe suit examined a bottle of cough syrup. A woman who would shop in such a wretched outpost was weak. She had a satin scarf and a set of dowdy pumps. A figure out of the 1950s with sepia tones. A woman who dressed like an automaton in public could not be trusted. She was too close for comfort and the pharmacist was still not satisfied.

“What kind of symptoms do you have, Madam?”

"My flesh is changing composition."

"Pardon?"

"Permineralization."

The chemist raised his eyebrows and stepped forward to the wicket. Nonni unwrapped the tensor bandage and held her hand up.

"How did you do it, this wound?"

Nonni just smiled: "I can't recall."

"There must have been an instrument which inflicted such an injury."

"It's not inflicted, it's infected."

"Have you been in contact with industrial chemicals?"

"No," she said.

"Have you had exposure to fiberglass or construction material?"

"I don't go to those kinds of places."

"Fungi, algae, *vide veritas*?"

"I don't work in a zoo, either."

"One hour, madam."

"I'll wait in the mall."

"But the mall is under construction."

"I'll wear a hard hat." Nonni walked through the archway into the mall. A bargain basement with high ceilings and cement floors, and not really the kind of place she wanted to see or be seen in. The shelves were cluttered with second-hand wares no civilized person would buy. Packages of green underwear, toothpaste tubes, and vacuum cleaners stultified in the cold air as a jackhammer broke tarmac in a tangle of noise. Nonni wished she were at the club. Prescription checks took too long. She bumped against a table and the plastic castor scraped on the floor.

Far across the room, by the change room hallway, a tall

masculine figure leaned in the shadow. Ochre complexion, broad shoulders. Persian maybe, Mediterranean possibly. Of the Orient, for sure, but six foot at least, which was Occidental steadfastly. Nonni felt his eyes flit on her body and she knew that gaze. Men were like that. Didn't matter where they came from. Didn't matter what they wore. All she had to do was look back once and so she did.

Her fingers closed around a pair of clay-coloured slacks. Now she'd find out what kind of creature he really was. The boys would run. The men would stay. His features were old and square, like the writer, she thought, Hemingway. Or who was that one who was always doing dope and hanging himself?

He adjusted his tie, but his demeanor didn't flinch. Nonni tossed the slacks over her arm and wandered towards the women's change rooms. No need to hurry. Confidence was a stimulant.

On the pitiful display benches, there were sanders and lathes. Vice grips, spoke shavers, and drills. All on sale, none worth the savings. She picked up a package of screws and a tube of resin, some calipers and galvanized nails. As long as no one thought she was a shoplifter, this was going to work. At the saloon leading down to the dingy cubicles, she cast one glance back, and felt her suitor close in proximity.

The passageway was stacked with boxes. Another week and the store would be gone. She stepped over a barricade and pulled aside a line of red tape. Only a thin wall of broken plaster separated the tawdry closets. Nonni went into the second booth. He vanished into the first. The room had a brass lock, a stool, and a single hook on the door. Perfect. She shut the latch and flipped the lock. His black oxfords faced her from beneath the holed partition.

"Do what I tell you," she said.

Through a knothole, his eye flitted across her body.

"In English if you can," she said.

Nonni put the slacks on the stool and let her coat fall to the floor. His lungs emptied. Maybe it was the heels that got him going. She ran her finger over the cracks in the wood and wondered: how many people had changed here before, how many dozens had peered through the holes in derelict want? Perhaps this very booth had been a cult location for voyeurism. A pity they were tearing it down. How little the rest of the world knew. The buckle of her dress hit the carpet.

"Stick in what you've got," she said.

Buttons scraped. A zipper came down. The wall buckled out, so it appeared to be quite a bit. Nonni set the calipers onto her breast. The tissue ruptured yellow and she rejoiced. She was bleeding resin. The sap oozed out between her fingers and dribbled onto the floor. Her suitor moved through the hole. She marveled at how industrial and completely unfeeling his pink flesh stood and how at one they so quickly had become.

The wrecking blade of a tractor cut through the booth and a forest of splinters rose up. The tank treads split the door, crushed the wall, and shattered the mirror. Her dress shredded in the axle and the light panel above her head shorted out.

Nonni was pinned under a sheet of pressboard and drenched in sawdust. Her lungs hurt and her eyes stung with dirt. The driver of the tractor was screaming from the seat and punching numbers into his cell phone. An alarm bell in the corner of the store went off and then the world was covered with the spray of a chemical sprinkler.

After the coils of construction wire and plaster had been peeled away, Nonni sat in the back of the ambulance with a plainclothes police detective. Tall and vulture looking in a pinstripe suit, so Nonni thought trouble for sure.

“What were you doing in there?” she said. She had a notebook with her and she was intent on writing everything down.

“Changing.”

“I suppose that would explain the naked part.”

“It is a change room.”

“It’s been closed for a year.”

“They need better signage.”

A speck of plaster floated through the dirty air and settled on the detective’s knee. “It’s something of a miracle you weren’t killed.”

“I’ve now got places to go.”

“I’m sure.” She opened the coat of her striped blue jacket and stared down into the screen of her computer. “But we have to finish this first.”

“Why?”

“To keep you safe.” Her eyes had the defeated look of a woman who was only in her profession by accident.

“Isn’t that a uniform job?” Nonni asked.

“You can explain the details to a uniform if you like. In the back seat of the police car which is parked out on the street in plain view. Or you can talk to me in here, where no one knows what we’re saying.”

Cops pretended to give options, but they didn’t really mean it. The seat smelled of cleaner and the radio was static. A dull green light filled the inside of the cab and her eyes flitted across the green screen through the columns of useless numbers and names.

“Are you on any kind of medication?” the detective asked.

“A Paxil substitute.”

“Do you take it like you’re supposed to?”

“Does that matter?”

“I was expecting a homeless person on this call.” Her face

hardly moved when she spoke. Her eyes were fixed on a far-off winter omen. There was a note of disappointment in her voice as if a person with no mass attached to them might be easier to regulate. "Someone covered in shoe polish with Listerine in her hair. Instead we found a nude upper class woman with a Gucci purse and Gabbana shoes."

"I didn't see the barricades."

"They were painted bright orange."

"I was thinking about other things." Nonni put her purse against the window of the ambulance and let her head sag against the cool leather.

"What other things?"

"Meeting an acquaintance."

"A man?" The detective opened her book and drew a line across the middle of the page.

"Does their gender matter?"

"What I'm asking is should we be looking for someone else in there? A second party. An injured person. A body. Tell me if we should."

"He departed."

"Departed?"

"Ran away."

There was a peppered sigh that bureaucrats and plebes always gave when they were confused or couldn't follow the facts, and Nonni figured she was getting the result in full.

"So there's no one in the change rooms now?" the detective asked.

"No."

"How long before the tractor demolished the change room did this man run away?"

"Just before. Or just after. One of the two."

"What is his name?"

“No clue.”

“What did he look like?”

“Handsome,” Nonni said.

“White male?”

“White-ish.”

“How old was he?”

“I can’t recall.”

“Weren’t you in the room with him?”

“He was in the next room.”

The detective was working out the geometry. She was the type of woman who might resort to a slide rule and still not figure the world out.

“There was a hole,” Nonni said.

The detective clicked her pen. “Do you want to hurt yourself?”

“Pardon?”

“It’s a fairly straightforward question.”

“I don’t want to hurt myself.”

“There was a pair of pliers secured to your breast.”

“Why am I answering this?”

“Because we found you naked in a derelict change room, covered in fibreglass resin, with your breasts punctured with wood screws,” she said. “Because you can’t even slightly describe someone you said you were becoming intimate with when the change room you were in was run over by an industrial grader. Because right now a Form Ten is looking like our best option in this province. Prove to me that you are all right. Tell me you are planning a tomorrow. Prove to me that you are not going to get out of this car and walk under the next available bus. That would reflect badly on me, professionally speaking.”

The sun moved behind the drug store and the inside of the

cab fell into shade and became cool. Nonni closed her eyes. This was a disemboweled town that based itself on hard work and oil, she knew that. There was no time for spectre nuptials in public places. No time for sins in sewers. There were far too many hours, far too many days, until Friday night when the club doors opened again, and a few moral conventions weren't going to stand in her way.

"I'm going to go home and put up the Monet my husband and I bought," Nonni said. "I'm going to put it up right above the fire place."

"You like painting?"

"I am especially fond of the Impressionists. *The Garden at Giverny*, do you know it?"

"Not really."

"It's not an original, of course. The original is in the Louvre. But I like having that kind of artwork in the house. I'm taking a class on art history."

"When is it?"

"Tuesdays and Thursdays, nine a.m. in the Scarf Building at the University of Calgary."

"Then what will you do?"

"This afternoon I am writing a letter of support to my Member of Parliament about our military involvement in the Middle East."

"You're opposed to the war in Iraq?"

"We are not in Iraq. We are in Afghanistan. There is a difference. The United Nations has sanctioned our actions in Afghanistan. The elected government of Hamid Karzi has asked us to be there. It is in our nation's interests to be there. None of those things can be said about the illegal and imperial occupation of Iraq."

"You follow politics," she said.

"Detective, I have no intention of harming myself. My motivation for going into that ridiculous place was purely to consummate a tryst with a new-found friend."

"But your friend left."

Nonni stared at the floor of the car. There was a stain that could have been blood or tomato juice. The policewoman put down her notebook and closed the lid on the computer screen.

"I can drive you home," the detective said.

"You don't know where I live."

"You're already in our system, Nonni."

5.

Angiospores were a way fungi spread seeds. Neurosis was an unresolved conflict. String theory could transport matter between dimensions, and objectivity was relative. The electronic display screens at the museum tried to make a connection between them all but they weren't doing a very good job. Nonni didn't get it. She didn't care. She smoked menthols and pondered her new stilettos imported from a New York shop.

If Gwen hadn't insisted, she wouldn't have come along. It was too wet. Long streams of rainwater fell off the parapet and splashed on the sidewalk. There had to be a reason. Maybe Gwen had found a new playmate. She wasn't bad at finding good looking ones. Problem was, their idea of foreplay was usually agrarian revolutions in Latin America.

Nonni wandered inside. There was a history exhibit of a famous Canadian painter who lived in the wilderness and did oil canvasses of totem poles. Upstairs, the Chinese exhibits rusted away with fifth century dullness.

Sometimes, Nonni got pick-ups in the gallery because it was sheik. A lot of metro men got turned on by being someplace sophisticated. Nonni called them Sophists. They were in their forties, divorced, of the professional class, and wore expensive clothing. They owned prescription glasses that they'd stick between their teeth while they read the exhibit.

There were upsides to the Sophists. They were clean. They were horny and in good shape. The downsides were they were straight, had to be pandered with academic analysis, and lapsed into diatribes about urban angst or ex-spouses.

Then there were the noncoms. Too many of those in the museum, for sure. Not non-commissioned officers, but *non-comers*. People who weren't interested in coming or sex or getting picked up at all. They actually came to look at the exhibits. They'd spend hours gazing down into glass bowls or playing with the "touch me" pieces that had been recovered from ancient battles. They took notes. They nodded to invisible partners. They got old. It was the same bunch over and again. Who knew why they bothered or what they got. Nonni wondered. Probably they died here. Like elephants at a graveyard, they came back to the same old place, each time losing a little piece of their soul.

Nonni hoped there were beings, occult creatures, hiding in the museum's back rooms who feasted on the minds of these dullards. They'd creep out and rip the cardboard throats from their victims as they dozed. She imagined what it would be like to flog one of the pathetic noncoms as they screamed in a last, anguished death throe.

Gerry and Gwen stood at the far end of the gallery staring into a totem pole painting. They were in deep discussion over another sombre aesthetic issue.

"Do you think it's a neurosis?" Gwen said.

"No," Gerry said. "It's just a sterile existence broken by moments of intense euphoria."

"What neurosis?" Nonni said.

Gwen spun port-wise. "Nonni, I didn't see you there."

"What euphoria?"

Gerry turned around. He tucked a thumb into his belt loop, looked awkward and couldn't come up with anything to say.

"The Emily Carr," Gwen said. "She makes the forest euphoric by spinning towards the vanishing point. It makes everything three-dimensional."

"What did she do out there?" Nonni stared at the picture. It was a Haida longhouse in the middle of dense cedar forest at dawn and probably one of the three worst places in the world to be.

"She painted. She was there for years, when there wasn't anything but natives and lumber camps," Gwen said.

"That must have been thrilling."

"It was the frontier."

"Lumber camps, lumberjacks."

"Are you shivering, Nonni?"

"No."

"You look pale," Gwen said.

"I'm not."

"Sort of pasty."

"Pasty. Great," Nonni said.

"Why didn't you wait inside for us?" Gerry said.

"Gwen told me to wait outside yesterday."

"We didn't talk yesterday," Gwen said. "You were out all day with your phone on message."

They took a seat at the white filigreed tables outside the museum. The chairs squealed when they moved across the tile floor. The restaurant was partitioned off from the walkway with a row of potted plants. The waiters all wore white shirts and black ties.

"Are you and Don still going to the party in Vegas?" Nonni said.

"Don is putting a greenhouse in the backyard. We're going to have to settle for the kink party in Jasper."

"The Las Vegas show includes this scene where victim gets cut in half with a band saw. We're still going aren't we Gerry?"

"I guess," Gerry said.

The waitress came by with three glasses of water and she was fabulous. A petite blond with lipstick that was moist and pink. The silverware clattered between her fingers as she set it down in the wrong order. Awkward and fabulous. She smiled once then walked away.

"Hot," Nonni said.

"Bitchly," Gwen said.

"Bitchly?"

"Snotty. Elitist. Fascist. All the college girls are right wing these days."

The waitress leaned against the bar and stared into a silent cell phone. Awkward, fabulous, and lonely. Even better. Nonni wondered what the chances were of randomly dialing a number and having the desperate girl's phone ring. The chances were higher that the waitress would make a mistake and she could move in without having to dial at all.

"What happened to you and that blond sub?" Gwen asked.

"Which one?"

"What's his name, Daniel?"

"Who knows?"

"You two looked like you were having such a good time."

"Until he went unconscious," Gerry said.

"He wasn't unconscious," Nonni said.

"Right," Gwen said. "Girlfriend showed up."

"What a witch."

"She played the victim card," Gwen said. "I banned her."

"Did she sound like she's was going to make trouble?" Gerry asked. He sounded like he was getting worried about things political, social, anthropological, or evangelical, and none of the possibilities appealed to Nonni one bit. Outside, the sun broke through and the drenched concrete canyon shimmered into summer steam.

"Basically she was pissed that she wasn't the centre of attention," Gwen said. "I think we'll be all right."

Gerry shrugged. He folded his napkin into a knot. Then stuffed the knot up his sleeve. "Faith hath no fury."

"If she had quoted Shakespeare, I'd be worried," Gwen said. "But I don't think she gets past *People* magazine at the plastic surgeon's office."

"This stuff makes me nervous," Gerry said.

"Why?" Nonni said.

"We have moral conservatives winning by-elections."

"The vice laws are federal."

"If some detective wants a promotion, we'll have another Goliath's raid."

Gwen gazed down into her menu and seemed to be thinking of something very far away. Nonni knew that look too. Something was bothering her. Three or four moves down the chessboard. Something that she didn't want to be obvious about. That meant it was probably bad. And to do with the club. "Do you think Daniel will even show up again?"

"No," Nonni said.

The waitress leaned over the table. The shirt tucked out from her skirt. A tattoo flashed red at the base of her spine. A farcical attempt at an Aboriginal design gone cubist-psychedelic.

“Who ordered the sherry?” Gerry said.

“Not me,” Gwen said.

“Nonni?”

“I didn’t order any sherry.”

Nonni held out her glass and let the woman pour anyway. Her hands shook and a drop of the red fluid splashed on the tablecloth, but Nonni just kept smiling and the waitress kept pouring. Nonni watched her wade back through the tables to her till. “I know her type.”

“Who?”

Gerry tried a mouthful. Too sweet for him.

“The waitress.”

“What’s her name?”

“Don’t know her that well.”

“You mean you just slept with her,” Gerry said.

“Not yet.”

“Is that synchronicity or collective unconscious?” Gwen asked. She rolled the wine glass around in her hand. She had a talent for diverting conversations that were going south into a more palatable direction. “When you’re sure you know someone, but can’t place the context and so that changes what happens next?”

The waitress split a roll of coins on the till and they ran over the counter then clattered to the floor. Gerry turned to watch the nickels spin and saw there was wine on his cuff.

“I’m going to hit on her,” Nonni said.

“Christ,” Gerry said.

Nonni got up and went to the counter. The waitress stood at the soda machine and stacked the coins. Not quite enough blood to fill her face. Maybe she’d lived at the South Pole for a year on a celibate student project with penguins, or did rehabilitation work at a nunnery.

"Hey, hun," Nonni said. She leaned over the bar. Hun was good. Hun was loaded. Sort of on Old South, harmless type of greeting. The first moment mattered the most. That would load the lever. Then if the dice got thrown her way, she could come back and collect the jackpot anytime. "We didn't order the sherry."

The girl glanced up with the terror of a nervous introvert. "This is my first week."

"Don't sweat it."

"I keep screwing up the orders."

"Do you have any matches?"

"I'm not sure."

"Be a doll and check."

Doll was great. Doll was inclusive. Nonni left her mouth open a centimetre and her lip got dry. The girl thought for a horridly long time, then turned around, bent over, showed a fault line, and retrieved five packages from the bottom shelf.

"Nice tattoo," Nonni said.

"It's not supposed to show."

"Why ever not?"

"Management."

"Moral conservatives," Nonni said. "They'll destroy the earth, you know."

"They're destroying me."

"Did you have it done at the Smiling Buddha?"

"Do you know it?"

"Vancouver. Hastings Street. I've had piercings there."

The girl couldn't quite finish the calculation, pulled her earlobe, and gave Nonni the quick up and down.

"You can't see mine," Nonni said.

The girl's fingers still shook a little. Parkinson's maybe. Lust probably. "I had mine done at the Buddha, too. I wait tables in

Cow Town for the summer then I go back to UBC in the autumn."

"What do you take?"

"Archeology," she said.

Nonni leaned back on the counter. Civilization was more obsessed with beauty than truth. "I was on a Salish dig doing middens."

"Middens?"

"Graduate work. Seven months. No one realized what an immense Neolithic site it was."

The girl laid the matches on the table. Nonni's hand spread on her knuckles and an orange stream of sun crept across the granite.

"That must have been exciting."

"I collected, weighed, and calibrated over three hundred cubic metres of anthropologically insignificant dirt. That tells you what kind of social life I had."

"I've been trying for a year to get on a decent project."

"You have to know the right people," Nonni said.

"I'd love to hear your stories."

Open door. Snare snagged. Down to a sunless sea, and Nonni imagined a luminous Saint Andrew's Cross at the club, with her new victim garrulously extolling the virtue of suffering while all of her archeological peers jealously applauded.

"What is your name?" Nonni said.

"Dietrich."

Dietrich? Jesus silly Christ. Dietrich. Nonni held out her hand, and when the student took it her lip trembled in a car crash sort of way and her palm got clammy.

"Next time I'm in, I'll look you up. We'll shoptalk."

"I work Saturdays."

Nonni pushed the matches into her pocket and went back

to the table. Gwen sat alone and twisted a knotted napkin between her fingers.

"Where's Gerry?"

"Gone to wash the sherry off his shirt."

"He'll just buy a new one."

"I need a word with you," Gwen said. "There's no point in him hearing this."

"Why not?"

"He worries too much. It turns out there was a bit of an issue with your tart's girlfriend. I need a favour. Or really, the club needs a favour."

"You said she was banned."

"Banned with a legacy. Turns out that's not her phone number. Not her real address. All of those new people who came with her don't seem to exist."

"What do you want me to do?"

"What you always do best."

"David?" Nonni said. She flipped through the mental Rolodex. David. Hot body. Old CSIS employee. Repressed prig. Liked to talk. Mostly about himself.

"Could you?"

"He's a bit of an ass."

"Gerry has a point when he talked about the police. That's bad for business. I followed her to a car. A white Mercedes. I've got the plate."

Gwen held out the paper. It was folded over and wrinkled as if it had been stuffed in a nervous pocket all night. Nonni took the pledge and slipped it into her vest. David was a pushover, and she probably wouldn't have to do anything but talk dirty to him.

"You'll owe me."

"This is for a good cause."

"I don't give a shit about causes," Nonni said and got up.

Outside, the steam rose off the concrete in sheets of glorious white. There was white in the sky and cream in the windows and bliss around the sun because that's the way it was when people owed you. Nonni hit her electronic key chain. Her headlights rolled up. The convertible top came down. Indenture, augury, antagonist, catechism. A string of words ran through her head; she couldn't figure out where they were coming from because she didn't use those kinds of words, in fact she didn't even care what they meant. At the corner of Ninth Avenue and First Street, she sat in her convertible and waited for the light to turn. The traffic was blocked. A cement truck poured concrete into an excavation pit.

There was the sound of the wrecking machines and the asexual stench of mortar. This was the worst place in the world to wait and if she was late for the tanning studio, they wouldn't keep a bed for her.

Everybody wanted to be tanned in the summer. No one wanted to be white. Everybody wanted to be some other colour than they really were. She hit redial on her phone. The salon was still busy. Or worse, the line was entangled because of all the roadwork. Reams of static darted out of the cyberdark and fouled her connection. Pay the extra money and get the digital encryption, Nonni.

"Hey," the voice finally said.

"David," she said back.

"Nonni? Is that you?"

"I am on the way to the studio to tan my legs," she said. This conversation made sense to her.

"I'm working."

"What a shame."

"It's one-thirty on a Wednesday, aren't you working?"

"I don't work. I tan."

"There's some kind of conversation going on in the background. What language are they speaking?"

"They don't speak a language," she said. "They are construction workers."

The bumper of the Mazda struck a stack of tiles and the worker with the stop sign threw his lunch kit at her. Nonni called him a plebe, then cut across three lanes of traffic. She dropped down an exit ramp into an underground parking lot. In the catacomb of concrete, the noise from the street vanished. The floors were polished smooth. The air was damp and huge Roman columns of chiselled cement rose to a din of emptiness.

"Is that better?" she said.

"The reception is lousy, but at least I only hear one voice now."

"I'm the only voice that counts." She pulled off her scarf and tossed it onto the passenger seat. If it were going to be a humid summer, she would have to get one that was more porous. "And this voice is telling you I only go to stand-up salons now. The tan is more even that way. It browns the inside of your thighs and your ass so there are no lines. I hate lines. Really Dave, you should see my ass."

"I'm thinking about it right now."

"They're like two brass globes. I just put some oil on and I'd let you bite them, but they're so hard you'd probably hurt your teeth."

"Ouch."

"Dave, pull your cock out and stroke it for me."

The row of cement pillars faded away from Nonni to a vanishing point of grey exhaust haze and vexed yellow arrows. There was a thicket of plumbing tubes as well. Mortar could be arousing. The silicates, flying from ash powder, far away from reason. All that calcite at least having a quiver. She recalled once tying up a German industrialist named Heinz to a set of galvanized pipes in an underground just like this. Same smell. Same subterranean vibrations. She had covered him with 10-30 weight oil then just walked away.

"I can't actually do that, Nonni," David said. "My office door is open."

"So what?"

"The regional director is standing twenty feet away."

"Get her to blow you."

"It's a him."

"Even better."

"I don't think he's inclined that way."

"You're no fun anymore," she said.

"I went to Brazil."

"What's in Brazil?"

"Gems," he said.

"Sounds scintillating."

Nonni let her hand fall over the convertible's door. Her finger touched the argillite column. She felt the minute tremble of the skyscraper's being shimmer down its skeletal core and disperse into the earth. Differential heating. Seismic shift. Solar winds. Nobody knew what had happened to Heinz and nobody cared. The mirror vibrated a little. So did her steering wheel. If one used an ounce of imagination, the tremors sounded like his voice, or a voice anyway. In fact, if she looked hard enough, the faintest features of another old playmate became discernible in the concrete. A nose, perhaps; a set of lips, likely, and then Nonni felt another structural quiver move between her legs and perhaps an earthquake was possible even here.

"My partner and I are starting an import business when I

leave the civil service," David said. "We both like stones and there's a chance to make money."

"There's not money in being a civil servant?"

"Not enough to keep girls like you happy."

"I had a gem piercing in my clit once," she said.

"Maybe you can be my first customer."

"What are you up to this weekend?"

David laughed a noncommittal maybe. Still worth milking. The odds were good even if he had been prudish on the regional director.

"Come out to the club with us," she said.

"The fiancée might object."

"We'll tie her to a chair and she can watch."

"She's not too much into that stuff."

"You are."

"Times change," he said.

Nonni's eyes drifted out to the bumper. She couldn't recall parking this close to the pillar. The rubber touched the cement, so any minute cosmic sway might force a squeal through the underground garage. She undid a button on her blouse just to tease the world a little.

"You don't, David. If you like, we could just get together for a massage. A covert massage since that's your line of work. I'll bring the oil."

"I know, baby. You're beautiful. What do you want?"

"What makes you think I want something?"

"Because I know the two things we have in common is that we're both horny, and both devious, and when we call each other it means we want something."

There was a way she could squeeze her legs together so that devious sounded good. A way she could spin the tires on the floor so the squawk was celestial. And then what she wanted was to be heard in this great structure, so Nonni rubbed her front teeth and they squealed too, but there was work to be done and so she got around to it. "Gwen thinks we're having trouble."

"What, again?"

"I try to stay out of politics."

"So stay out of them," he said.

"The geography of this one is different. The bottom line is if the club runs into problems there's nowhere to go. This is a conservative town, David. If I don't get what I need then I get frustrated and have to call people at two in the morning."

Either the parkade settled or her conscience shifted. The car rolled forward. There was a mechanical convulsion in the gearbox and a figure moved across the passenger mirror.

"What does she need?" David said.

"A scan on new members who might be sticky."

"Criminals or journalists?"

"Nothing like that."

"They're not cops are they?"

"No, they're definitely not cops."

"Because if they are, I can't get involved."

Nonni shut off the ignition and popped the clutch, but the car kept rolling. A spigot struck the grill. She hit the brake then pounded the dash with her fist.

"Nonni?" David said. "Are you listening to me?"

The inside of her thigh went from damp to cold. Stay focused, Non. Get horny, think quick.

"No, Dave. Cops can't do that anymore. Don't you read the papers? These two are just a bent couple who have a lot of money to invest in a filthy little screw-hole like ours. Maybe they're Mormon terrorists. Maybe they're Ottawa separatists. We're just members of the *petite bent bourgeoisie* and can't afford private dicks. So, we have to rely on our cadre of cunning capitalists. Of which you are a faithful member."

"Who taught you those words?"

"I read them in *The Daily Worker.*"

"When did you read *The Daily Worker*?"

"I wrapped my dildo in one this morning."

"Can you do Chomsky too?"

The hexagonal pillar not only had a spigot, but a spigot with a brass hook that had latched under her hood ornament. When she dropped the car into reverse the barb caught the chrome and hit a High C.

"Who?"

"Never mind, sweetie. I'll fix you up. You give me the particulars. I'll get the facts."

"You are filthy, Dave."

"I'm going to collect on this one."

"I'll slut myself for your data bank."

"Not for me exactly," he said.

Nonni knew it. One of Dave's loser friends. This was the worst. They're always ugly and obsessed with process paradigms. Or penguins. A session with a wood lathe would be more erotic.

"Not that," she said.

"He's my cousin."

"Now he'll be ugly and dirty."

"Nonni, darling, I'm really enjoying this. It's making me hot."

Nonni bit the bullet and hit the gas. The car backed up. A cement bulkhead loomed in the rear-view mirror. Her head struck the windshield. The bulkhead buckled her headrest. There was lye on her shoulder. This was how people got decapitated, Nonni. Left intestate. Found with plumbing fixtures through their skulls and 1-900 numbers in their ears.

"Are you still there, Nonni?"

"I hate the physical world."

"Are you in?"

"How big is his dick?" she said.

"He's a relative. I haven't checked."

"What does he want?"

"He's lonely. He wants someone to talk to."

"Nobody wants to talk," she said. "That went out with Charlotte Brontë."

"He does."

"What's wrong with him?"

She reached up and touched a film of grease that covered the pipe attached to the bulkhead. She had driven so close that the fluid was in her hair. A luscious copper scent rolled off her neck. She rubbed the oil over her palm.

"There isn't anything wrong with him," Dave said. "He just wants an intellectual exchange. Why does something have to be wrong with him?"

"He's got Parkinson's disease, hasn't he? No wait, he's got Irritable Bowel Syndrome. Is he an amputee? He's an amputee. That's it. He's got no legs, has he Dave?"

"He's got legs," Dave said. "All right. He's a little eccentric. In fact, he's crazy. But he's brilliant and I owe my family a favour. He follows paranormal-political stuff. You two will have plenty to chat about. You can talk class struggle."

"I hate the poor."

"Who doesn't?"

"What does he want to talk about?"

"Aliens."

"Not ones from other planets I hope."

Nonni wasn't sure why but she rubbed the fluid under her

nose. Then along her lips and finally on her tongue. It wasn't like she thought, cupric and metal plated, but filled with musk and pulsating. Everything had a pulse. The grill. The pipes. The stone pillars. Everything that had wedged her into this dead-end corner of a buried underground, opaque and white. For a moment, she thought the pillars might be praying. Except of course, pillars did not pray. For a second, she contemplated the concrete settling, the wind tunnels forming, and peptides multiplying. But they had no place in the conspiracy of the living, so Nonni accepted the loss, punched the car into drive, and hit the gas again. Paint ground off her wheel well. The hood ornament flew off the exit ramp and rattled on a cleated grate.

When the underground door peeled back, a stream of sunlight erupted across her windshield. On Sixth Avenue there were gardenias, mirrors, and women with white smiles and short skirts. Nonni accelerated over a speed bump against a red then she was in the blur of rich pedestrians, successful blue skies, and Friday night closing in starboard side.

"Nonni, are you there?" David said. "Work with me on this one, all right?"

"*Quid pro quo*, sweetie."

"Just don't call my place at two in the morning, all right, Nonni? Certain parties might object."

6.

Nonni drove down to the row of slum houses just off Chinatown. The view was the back end of burnt restaurants, and iron fire escapes on orange brick. Bungalows were left over from the First World War with sagging porches and lawns that smelled of river water.

She put the top up on her convertible and locked the trunk. She had on her black pumps, red suit, and black dress gloves. Not enough skin showing to look like she wanted anything, but classy enough to let him know that she was in charge and the meter was ticking. Get in, score the points, get out. She tossed the cigarette into the gutter and made her way across the lawn.

Number 80 was the house without an address and a porcelain garden gnome on the lawn. The porch had been painted crimson to mock a Buddhist temple and there was a row of dead petunias on the rail.

David's cousin answered. Nonni closed her eyes. He was forty, overweight, with a soup stain on his shirt.

"You must be Nonni," he said.

"You must be David's cousin."

Inside the foyer, the floorboards creaked. The house was old. The living room was cluttered with stacks of books. Jung, Masoch, Ballard. The air smelled of stale tobacco and cats. There was a television, a small grey table that was covered with magazines, and a threadbare Persian carpet.

"My name is Edward, but you can call me Teddy," he said. "My friends call me Teddy. Do you want something to drink?"

"What have you got?"

"Coconut rum and cider."

"I'll pass."

He made his way around the cat dish and past an open fridge. She was probably supposed to follow and so she did. The hall was domed and stippled like a small mosque.

"I'm glad you could come," he said. "I don't get many visitors."

"I can't imagine why." She stepped over a plastic model of a reptile. The creature's eyes lit up.

"Don't mind him. He's on a sensor. He jumps whenever something gets too close."

"Bed bugs?"

"It doesn't eat those," Teddy smiled. "We can talk in my office."

Teddy led her through an archway that had been painted urine yellow. There were trade manuals on both walls and the smell of dried pulp filled the air. An entire section was dedicated to the art of embalming.

"You like to read," Nonni said.

"I've read over twenty-two hundred books in my life. But I also have the Internet. I spend a lot of time on the Internet. That's where the action is. That's where the real human drama unfolds. I don't watch television."

"Why not?"

“It’s all propaganda.”

The office was, at one time, a bedroom. There was a desk and a couch stacked with pornographic magazines. A soaped window let translucent sunlight in and a crab apple tree hovered outside.

“Where do you sleep?” she asked.

“I don’t. Sit down.” He pointed at a single puffed stool.

“I’ll try.”

Teddy pushed a pile of blueprints out of the way. The chair settled under her weight.

“Do you mind if I smoke?” she said.

Two ashtrays on the desk, three on the floor, and a mason jar filled with cigarette butts served as a door stop. The ash had settled into layers, with the dark fine particles on bottom and the lighter large chunks on top. A row of chewing gum hung over the rim.

“You smoke menthols, don’t you?”

“How did you know?”

Teddy sat back in his swivel chair behind the computer and steepled his fingers. “I know a lot about you.”

She crossed her legs and leaned forward. This was business now. Her knees were shiny because she had oiled them down with a lube called Gossamer that she had imported from Paris. The new coat of lipstick she had applied made her feel cold, hard, and that everything could be done quickly. “Did David tell you what the deal was?”

“Deal?”

“Why I’m here. What the arrangement was. I hope you don’t have any objection to me being up front.”

“I think being up front is always the best way,” Teddy said. “You are here because you need help.”

“I need help?”

"You want advice on certain issues that are troubling you. Issues that you can't speak with anyone else about because of their existential sensitivity."

That answer explained the peach fuzz growing on his jaw and the reek of Bengay that came off his skin. She picked up one of the magazines that lay on top of the stack near her chair. The cover was shiny and smelled of ozone. "You like transsexuals?" She flipped through the glossy pages.

"Oh yes."

She read off the caption. "Or hot young transsexuals with huge cocks for your sucking pleasure, anyway."

Teddy pursed his lips and rubbed his chin as if he found the proposition slightly troubling. "Not transsexuals exclusively. I wouldn't want you to get the idea I'm closed-minded. I'm open to all kinds of erotic interactions, on numerous wavelengths, with a variety of entities."

"Entities?"

"Like I said, I like a lot of things."

"Okay," she said. "I'm game. Tell me what kinds of things."

"I'm fond of the arcane and the sublime."

"Those are just adverbs."

"Adjectives, actually. But tell me about yourself."

Nonni sighed. Here we go, she thought. Confession, copulation, come shot. She glanced up at the ceiling. There was a contorted pattern of dirt embedded into the plaster. The lines formed the silhouette of an entombed figure with latticed features sandblasted into the face. A nick, a gneiss, an undone field. "I like girls mostly. Not much into guys. In fact, I'm not really into sex at all. Not penetration, anyway. SM is mostly what I do."

"Excellent," Teddy said.

Shit, Nonni thought.

"But I know all the trivial stuff about you. Tell me about the important things."

"What kind of important things?"

"Dimensional commerce things that are steeped in memory and transpose the space-time continuum."

"You obviously know nothing about me," she said.

On the edge of Teddy's desk sat a device that looked like a nineteenth-century chronometer. His lip pouted a little when he settled on it. Silver orbs flexed over a brass clock face, and an arc of glass ran around its equator. Nonni couldn't help but notice that every time she touched the photos in the magazine the current in the tube changed colour.

"I know you smoke menthol cigarettes." He reached over and took one. Nonni watched his hand. His fingers were puffy. "I know you smoke them because it turns you on. Anything that deprives your brain of oxygen or scares you turns you on. The first is called an asphyxia obsession, the second is a *paresthesia timori*. These afflictions may be caused by childhood phobias such as sleeping under the covers due to nightmares, or they may have a more occult cause. In either case, put the two of them together and you have a socially precarious libido. This probably accounts for your inability to express yourself on a day-to-day basis with other people. For example, when is the last time you talked about the weather? Or Emily Carr? Or starving children in Manitoba?"

She held the cigarette between two gloved fingers. With some effort, he leaned across the desk and lit her up. Out the window, in the backyard, a chokecherry with ripening fruit sagged against the glass. "Never been to Manitoba. And don't intend to go."

"I know also that you put those gloves on so you wouldn't have to touch me in case it came to a handjob. Don't worry. That's not what I want."

"Reassuring."

"I know that your husband and you aren't getting along. I know that you get too many speeding tickets and I know that you are never satisfied."

Nonni bit down on the words of this horny, devious bastard, because giving him a bone wasn't worth the price. A surge of deep purple sailed through the tube. Teddy had a cheap gold medallion that hung around his neck, but she'd have to forgive that, too. "Are you talking about me? Or half the population of this province?"

Teddy blinked. He rearranged the magazines by the computer so the edges lined up. "I know, too, that you've just done something that you regret and you're not going to tell anyone. Something violent. Something perverse and hidden."

A trickle of smoke crept out of Nonni's mouth. She gazed upwards. The ceiling stain could have been a plumbing mistake. Or an Oriental wall tapestry left to rot for half a century.

"What have you done to your ceiling?" she asked.

"I think its vagueness is pitched at the perfect level."

"It's vague all right. What is it?"

"What does it look like?"

"Cobwebs with coffee stains around the edges."

The lighter spots were probably some other kind of fluid. She'd need an ultraviolet light to be sure, but if right, Teddy had impressed her on at least one front. She did a quick calculation of what he might look like should he lose eighty pounds and get an ounce of sun.

"It's my rendition of the *Shroud of Turin*."

"The shroud was faked."

"You don't like art anyway," Teddy said. "That's another thing I know about you. You hate art and despise galleries. One should not ask bakers to judge beans."

Nonni checked her watch. "If you don't mind, maybe we can move on. What about you, Teddy? Tell me about you."

"My parents were foreign. I was born here. I like Pilsner beer."

"It ought to be pertinent," she said. "What I'm saying is, do you like to be flogged or have your nipples pierced? Verbal humiliation or direct physical degradation? Somehow you really strike me as a back-door receiver type. I'd sort of like to get to the point, no offence. David said you wanted me to talk, so I'm talking."

"I'm not into the base stuff."

"Base stuff?"

"Common. Banal. Fucking, sucking."

"You're a little more complex are you?"

"I'm selective," he said.

"Must be a lonely road."

"It is."

"You might find it easier if you lost a bit of weight."

Teddy sat up in his chair. There was a small glimmer of green light in his iris as if the insult had aroused his interest. He reached over and reset a dial on the chronometer. "Thank you for being honest. I admire frankness in a woman. And you're right. I don't get enough exercise and I'm a sloppy eater. I need a new wardrobe. For that matter, I could do with a bath. But so what? What I get satisfaction out of is the eroticism that goes beyond the body, beyond the human experience."

Nonni picked up a copy of *Bizarre Monthly*. The pages were pristine and cold, as if they had been kept in a freezer for decades, and the edges slipped over each other in a way that reminded her of beads in a carafe.

"You like aliens," she said. "That's what David told me. You want to give head to ET? Okay. I'm fine with that. I'm not much into science fiction, but I can improvise. Is it the blue-skinned girls with high eyebrows that gets you going or the big-titted aliens at the hatch you want? If you don't mind, I'd like to get the confessional part of the show done with."

Nonni flipped through the pages to a chapter titled Hedonistic Human Sacrifice. Two Amazons impaled a naked man with a spear. A tiny branch of crimson moved through one of the chronometer's tubes like blood spreading through empty arteries.

"All right." Teddy folded his hands and stared down at his stubby fingers. He appeared nostalgic. "I'll give you the set up. You give me one good story and we'll call it square, okay?"

"I'm in."

"There was a time when I wasn't fat. There was a time when I was sane and smart and told jokes and worked out at the gym. There's a photo of me."

He pointed to a brass photo inside a tarnished frame above a turntable. A tanned young man of eighteen lighted a barbell above his head on a white sandy beach and his chest was rippled with muscle.

"That's you?" she said.

"Yes."

"What happened?"

"I had girlfriends. And I've got to tell you, boyfriends too. I kept to myself, lifted weights, and went cross-country running. I was aroused always. Savagely, relentlessly horny. I woke up nightly. Soaked sheets. I'd see a girl in the hallway between English and Algebra class. Soaked underwear. I got aroused when the principal's voice lilted on the PA system. Soaked notebook. Needless to say, I was successful with none."

The chrome chronometer ticked over every other second. Whatever else its veins did, the hands also kept time and they told Nonni she had only been in the room nine minutes. So this, like every visit to the dentist, or the parking lot episode, had to violate every law of physics. Her mind drifted off — to a club in Hamburg, an Egyptian man in Cairo, a desperate business intern in Montreal — and then Teddy appeared, disappointed in the reading of his instrument, so he adjusted a dial and changed the tenor of his voice.

"I was at a weight-lifting competition," he said. "There was a women's class. This was rural Alberta, 1970. We didn't do a lot of that here. There was a girl named Denise. She was in the heavy category. She looked like a farm animal, but could clean and jerk her own body weight. She grunted when she snatched. People laughed at her. They called her Dumpy because it sounded like she was having a bowel movement when she lifted. No one wanted to talk to her. No one wanted to be near her. But I admired her desperation, and in a moment of insanity, I went up and said that suffering was good for the soul. She smiled and replied that the soul needed a body. We went back to her place and drank her parents' crème de menthe. She kept telling me how she found the male form inert and ugly. An article to be trespassed upon. She was besotted with her drama teacher, Mrs. Harris, and went on at length about her aesthetic achievements. But she evidently wanted something else from me. The conversation always got back to Nazi aquatic training, or Greek wrestling, and finally Aztec sacrifices. She leaned back against her parent's paisley sofa, played with the buttons of her blouse, and muttered about how even the most beautiful body had to be sacrificed in its moment of glory. Finally, she made the pitch: would I like to perform the last act of Agamemnon and Clytemnestra, a Greek tragedy involving athletes and betrayal? I'd never even heard of a Greek tragedy, but it would, apparently, involve us getting naked. And so, with the hormones at the helm, I blurted out that I consented and had wanted to be an actor anyway."

Teddy paused for dramatic effect. Nonni ignored the chair spring digging into her hip. She gazed into his lunar surface of a face and felt repulsed by how large yet how utterly shiny his acne craters were. Perhaps he truly thought he was Olivier playing Hamlet or Burton doing Lear. She imagined a sparrow landing in one of his blemishes, then a freight train, and finally a space shuttle — and when she knew it was she who would have to be the better actor in the end, she hated herself for that, too.

"Denise smirked at me in a condescending fashion," Teddy said. "And told me to take my clothes off. Then she took me into the bathroom and filled up the tub with warm water. Agamemnon had been a sailor, too. The little fox tied my hands up with her bra strap and prodded me in the genitals with a toilet brush. Then she grabbed me by the hair, bashed my head against the tub, and forced my face under the water."

Nonni thought of water, and bubbles, and a game she had played in an aquarium with a gorgeous blond lawyer in North Vancouver. The bubbles had flowed out between his pearl-white teeth and up over his stunned white eyes, but then the glass had broken and the tort was done. Nonni noticed at that moment that the beads in Teddy's instrument had rolled over and the equator had pitched a deep purple.

"*The Gong Show*," he said, "was a popular daytime program in those days where contestants with moronic acts performed before washed-up celebrities, and if their act was bad enough, they got gonged. Inside my concussed mind all I could think about was that show, either because my skull was making a sound like the gong or I was then a contestant. With my head completely submerged, Denise the weightlifter got behind me, rammed her crotch against my ass, and pushed my nose down the drain. The blue strobes of light moved in the soapy water and I was running out of air. The she-bitch was going to hold me under until she came or I drowned, and she was probably one of those girls who took forever to come. Water flooded up my nose. My first shot at human contact and I was going to die.

"She was a strong girl. And she possessed incredible determination. She kept pounding away, making the same ghastly noises that she made when lifting weights, and forcing my face against those flower shaped stickies that stopped people from slipping on the bottom of the tub. I knew it: she was crazy. I was finished. But I also knew there was something else in the room besides the two of us. A guest of great mass moved across the floor, crushing the bathroom tiles. A scrub brush snapped. A bar of soaped exploded. There was a tickertape, an algebraic computation. There were instructions. Erotic instructions from an outside agency. The instructions were clear. The only way to get out of this alive was to satisfy her earthly desires. Otherwise she'd just keep going in her sadistic frenzy, and I'd be under there until mom and dad came home, which might not have been until Monday morning. I pushed my ass into her crotch. Somehow the message got home and she screamed. Her larynx ruptured. Then her shirt ripped. Her weight was lifted straight up off my back. The ballast went from 150 pounds to zero in a nanosecond, and the mirror on the other side of the room shattered. Denise had been pitched onto the sink counter, smashed the vanity, then fractured the water closet. I think the plumbing bill came to about two hundred dollars. There was blood in her mouth and she couldn't speak. Most of her hair was shredded out. She pointed to the glazed window that was broken, as if the culprit had fled the scene.

"Then she just got up and walked out. No pillow talk. No thanks for the party. Nothing. She went truant and vanished from our school. Our gym teacher was transferred too, after an improper relation with a student on the field hockey team, and Mrs. Harris committed suicide. But I wasn't alone. The figure that was in that bathroom that afternoon was still with me, just out of sight, standing obsequiously with his kind — their huge hulking figures waiting, watching, and judging. They weren't going to leave me."

Teddy smiled. He leaned back in his chair, and riffled through a stack of bondage magazines with his thumb. His eyes grew large behind his set of thick glasses and the lenses fogged up. The arcs of the chronometer were a brilliant blue and Nonni was sure there was a preponderance of heavy gas in the room: argon, or fluorine, or a garish Latin halogen name that made all of life exciting and short.

"What does that thing do?"

"It measures things."

"I doubt it."

"Look, you don't have to screw me, blow me, or even tell me that you love me, Nonni. I just want you to give me your story about what happened the first time you met your creatures. Your beings. I know you have. Then you can go. David and the mortal world will be appeased. Make my machine light up."

There was a package of Winstons on the floor. Not her brand. Not Teddy's brand either. Nonni felt her ribs tighten, but she stood and plucked up the package anyway. She knew there was a pose any woman could strike with a stray cigarette to infer disdain, and so she blew a bilge of smoke across Teddy's face. In the cracked mirror on the back of the door, the reflection of a statuesque blond figure with high marble cheekbones and jade eyes stared back at her with such arrogance that only she was smart enough to catch the irony.

"Teddy, I've been in a lot of strange places looking for kink," she said. "Kink isn't a hobby for me. It's a way of life. I suppose you're right, I'm never satisfied. Probably that's because when it comes right down to facts, the human body can never provide enough satisfaction for either of us. We're alike in that one respect, you and I. We are scorpions. We need to molt. To shed our earthly skin so we can get what we really need. If I were talking to someone else, I'd use the cocoon and butterfly metaphor. That's more poetic. But poetry is coy and I'm not. Scorpions are dangerous and so are we. They sting during the process because that's their way."

Aliens and molting. Marvel and a gorgeous kind of mistrust that exists between all strangers, and so Nonni ground her molars together and let the fulcrum of her elbow drive the cigarette down into the ashen pit. She liked the way the length of the butt buckled into the shallow glass tray like a quibbling sub. There were probably a lot of things she should have said to Teddy, because that's all he really was: an ugly quibbling sub who never stood a chance with anyone. But fiction was just more endearing than fact, and so she pushed the ashtray across the table, towards the ripple in his gut, and got on with the game.

"We go through those clumsy stages at first. Before we've met those friends you mentioned. We try nail files and razor blades, scissors and pliers for pleasure. Augers and soldering irons. Bet you've tried your fair share of household appliances, haven't you skipper? You've tried with other people, too. Floggers and corkscrews, waterboarding and Spanish garroting. Personally, I was always partial to choking. It's the romantic in me. Watching their faces turns blue while they beg for mercy. For a while it's entertaining. But eventually the pleasure fades and you're left surrounded by a bunch of whining plebes, so what's a girl to do?"

The arc around the chronometer hummed and Nonni wasn't sure where she had experienced that sensation before. Near a hummingbird? At the onset of a tremor. Close to a didgeridoo. She felt it in her fingers first and watched a wave streak across the desk. Teddy doodled in the ashtray, then let his finger slip up his jaw and into his mouth, in a fashion that Nonni found both uncouth and accurate.

"Then one day, the opaque message came to me," she said. "Just like you. A clatter of coins, a series of bumps on your spine, some new form of venereal disease that spreads without any sexual contact. You know what has to be done. But you don't know how. And the next day, they're standing right beside you. In the same room.

"He was a newbie. A gorgeous boy. He had that malleable kind of face that you don't see that often. One that is feminine and pastoral. The kind that can't go unplumbed or undamaged.

"It was in the middle of the scene. Pretty standard scenario, really. The game was I would choke him out then just abandon him there, leave him tied up in his room and waiting, like an abduction from South America. That's where all the good snuff stuff comes from, Colombia. Has something to do with tax laws. Someone else would find him naked and tied up. The letter carrier or the furnace repair man. It would work out."

The text was pre-written, prescribed, preordained. She didn't have to make anything up. She didn't even have to think. Didn't even have to lie. Certainly not pay. She only had to open her mouth and the vestibule was commanded. The only thing between them was Teddy's stale breath.

"Then the whole thing got old for me," she said. "Dull. I didn't even think I'd be able to come. And there they were, those creatures, those wooden posts. As plain as mailboxes. Right there in the room. They explained how the ballast could be extracted. The poor waif explained. The human condition redeemed. There would be consequences. Of course there always is. But you can't say no to them Teddy. You know that.

"So I agreed. And my Machiavellian guests reached out and touched this victim so his skin became as hard as granite. And then they looked into my eyes and I became so aroused that my body was a monsoon pounding on a tin roof. The flesh speaks in those moments, Teddy. It cackles. It sings. It floats away."

A tinge of industrial solder drifted through the room. Nonni's cigarette had almost burnt down, but she didn't bother to flick. In the end, the ash just fell away. And she thought of a dirty snowflake, a sonnet's bad measure, and all the world came crashing down.

"They are the Cambrian consciousness of existence," she said. "Those things. When you're with them anything can happen. You can be taken anywhere, do anything. A crusade, a surgery, a sacrifice. You could be persuaded to go searching for the source of the Nile River or attempt a landing on the sun, and as long as they were speaking to you at night it would seem possible.

"They live in catacombs of pleasure. They are continents drifting. Other people don't hear them. Don't even know they exist. But we let them take us, we can go anywhere. Do whatever we want, no matter how bestial. We don't answer to anybody but them. Nothing is forbidden. Sometimes other people don't want to be taken as fodder, but that's too bad. I know this might sound cruel, but once these creatures have given us the instructions, then all collateral damage is permissible. Piercings, strangulations, incarcerations, and incinerations. All valid. You can build any kind of contraption to assist you, as long as they have drawn the designs. Gallows, garrotes, geostationary satellites, just stand back and let them suck up the pleasure from their victims as they —"

The chronometer squealed. Teddy pushed himself backwards. The castors on the chair skidded against the floor. A blur of fingers wrestled with his zipper and then there was a welt of flesh. Nonni leaned forward to finish the sentence. A white arc spattered across her blouse. A sycamore leaf bounced off the window pane and twisted to earth.

She stood up and looked around for something to wipe up the cataclysm, but there was none, and when she used the back of her hands the beads pearled off as calcified stone onto the dirty floor. Teddy dabbed the sweat from his brow with a yellow terry towel.

"Do you want a coffee?" he asked.

"I've got an appointment at four."

"I wish you could stay for a bit."

"I can't."

The sun had moved and sent a long shadow of a branch over the desk. Nonni felt a numbness in her throat. The surface was coarse and reminded her of oak bark.

"You fear them, don't you?" he said.

"Whom?" She lit a cigarette and held the ember next to a strand of lint that dangled from the door.

"Them."

"I don't fear anything. I was trying to keep you entertained as per a rather unfortunate contract I drew up with your cousin."

"You can't discard them, Nonni."

"Edward, I was doing 1-800 talk." She slung the purse over her shoulder and tossed the cigarette into a trash bin. "Don't take it to heart. And turn that stupid machine of yours off."

"You'll be back."

"You seem quite sure of yourself for a chubby young lad who spends his time jerking off in front of a computer. I don't want to cast aspersions on your intellectual pursuits, but is this what you do, all day long? Wait around for people to come so you can dump your stories on them? Because if so, you're deluded. It'll never get you anywhere."

"It got me somewhere with you, didn't it?"

7.

Ogden was an ugly part of town. Bureaucrats called it a multi-use area, an industrial transition zone, or a belt-line designation. But the truth was, the place was just ugly, and no one driving a new convertible with a three-hundred-dollar laser appointment in twenty minutes deserved to be there. Nonni tossed the paper with the non-existent address into the ashtray. The ashes blew around in a grey pattern that reminded her think of long dead novelists. Maybe David's intelligence was wrong, maybe it wasn't. On one side of the car towered a rock bluff with a few straggly spruce. On the other side, there was a warehouse that stored drilling parts. The air reeked of diesel fuel. The sun was bleak with betrayal. Nonni picked up her cell phone.

"Hello," the voice on the other end said. It sounded distracted.

"David, darling. How are you?"

"I'm actually very busy, Nonni."

"You work too much."

“I don’t work enough. That’s the problem.”

A caboose flew past the rail crossing. Beyond the tracks there were only thistles, a few grain silos, and coils of barbed wire. She imagined the way that novelists had lived and died in lonely places like this. She liked to think of their dying especially.

“I saw your cousin,” Nonni said.

“He mentioned that.”

“He’s an odd duck.”

“He said the same about you.”

“Did he enjoy himself?”

“He said you were one of a kind.”

“I’m flattered,” she said.

“He doesn’t get many visitors so I’m grateful for that. My mother is always calling just to make sure he hasn’t been committed. I suppose he went over that with you?”

“Extensively.”

“You don’t have to go back.”

“That’s rather what I wanted to talk to you about. You see I’m down in the industrial district now with those addresses you gave me.” Nonni flipped open the paper and let the page flutter in the wind that came in through the convertible. She liked to think that novelists killed themselves soberly and with poise, like Plath. In the end though, it was more exciting to think of other people killing them passionately, and so she saw Tolstoy go under the blade of the thresher, and Austin strangling slowly in the parlour.

“Can we talk about this some other time, Non?”

“Afraid not, Dave. You see, I’m not so happy. I’m on scene, as the tacticians would say, and the numbers don’t make any sense.”

“I don’t have the data in front of me.”

"Then I could come up and see you in person. I know you're busy, but I don't really want to waste my time driving around in Slumsville. I'm sure we can resolve this quickly. You see, there's not anything there except for a rail yard and an empty cement factory."

"That's possible," he said. "People register vehicles to corporate addresses."

"It's a field, Dave. There has never been anything here."

"They register them to non-existent places."

Nonni gazed down the thistle driveway towards the concrete storage shed. The windows were broken and the roof was tin. Rickets, wrecked, recluse. There wasn't anything of value here and there never had been. Not a writer, nor a reader, not a brothel, or even a Bohemian poet drinking himself to death on absinthe, and she wondered why she bothered being so coy.

"Dave you are sitting in front of your computer now," she said. "And you are watching gay porn. You were just at the part where the eighteen-year-old is wearing nothing but white gym socks. Now use your password and go onto your site and check again. Let me give it to you one more time. Or I can ask your regional director. How is it designated? I know you have that right in front of you on the screen as well, and I can always tell when you are lying, even if your fiancée can't."

"Industrial."

"Who owns it?

"It's a numbered company."

"Which number?" she said.

"Leave this one alone, Nonni."

"Why?"

"Because this is something more complex than you think."

"More complex than what? The Mossad? The Pope? Freemasonry?"

"I'm just saying leave it alone."

"This is my sex life, Dave."

"Most everything is."

Whatever type of hedge fund David was running, the credit was running out. Nonni remembered him gagged in the club's medieval room while the fiancée thought he was with the Solicitor General. And then there was the time when he was getting violated with an electric corkscrew when the poor woman thought he was in Ottawa. Nonni imagined Dave trying to explain that video as national security to the home front.

"This is the interests of civic society," she said. "Our nation. The enemy of tyranny. The constitution, John Stuart Mills, perversion, and all that."

"Are you reading books, or what?" he said. His voice was approaching some kind of denouement. "Look, Nonni, find another club. Maybe find another city. Even better find another avenue of interest. Great Danes or something. Probably forget we've ever talked and forget about this person you are looking for."

"What has this person got that I don't?"

"A philosophy, Non."

"How are we going to go out and party if we're not philosophizing with each other?"

"There's another club opening up. Starlight Swingers, or something. I'll go there. Private parties, maybe. Private parties are a lot safer, constitutionally speaking. Don't take anything my cousin says too seriously. Forget about him, in fact. He's a loser. I've really gone out on a limb for you on this one, so you owe me, hun. I'll be out of town until the end of the month."

The phone went dead, and so she threw the paper into the passenger seat.

"Plebe," she said.

Nonni drove her car up to a tailings pond, then walked to the shed through a row of brown sage. The corrugated doors sweltered in the heat. A pile of copper wire sat by a chemical silo. No one had done business here in twenty years. Even the dust was bored. In the garage, a vehicle had been covered with a stained tarp. Nonni pulled the cover aside. A white Mercedes stood there completely clean and utterly out of place.

Inside the office there was a desk, a computer, and a fax machine. A plumbing closet with makeshift bookcases. Carl Jung, Joseph Campbell. Criminal deviation and sexual aberration. A mask had been mounted on the ribbed wall. Bronzed cedar. The face was elongated, stretched with the heat of an ancient crucible.

The gravel on the driveway crunched. A woman stood outside the window smoking a cigarette. Nonni knew the smell at once. She was smoking menthols. She wore a blue pinstripe suit and low pumps. A typical reach for the top industrial wench who ended up doing clerical in the place of dead roads. She flicked her cigarette into a sludge pool, and then turned towards the building.

Nonni sunk into the closet and closed the door. The inside smelled of rust. There were rows of ancient pipes above her head. The bureaucrat came into the room, and tossed a keychain and notebook on the desk. She was preoccupied. This was the kind of woman who took notes in mausoleums. She had hard, unfeminine features, and some pasty white makeup that tried to cover an outbreak of middle age. Nonni half-recognized the face from some unpleasant encounter, but the latticed door hid her details. She pulled out a cell phone, stood before the masks, and her eyes monitored an element of disgust.

"That's the way we need them," she said into the phone. She fondled the chin of the bronze face. "The only reliable motivating factor in the human character is fear."

The woman listened to the phone with ambivalence and became fascinated with a paper clip on the desk. She ran the clip over a manual iron typewriter. Then down deep into its rib cage. The sound reminded Nonni of baseball cards on bicycle spokes, but that was so long ago, and then one of the black and red reels popped out of the machine and rolled across the floor. When it ran out of ribbon, the reel ran towards the cupboard door, and Nonni put her hand to her mouth.

"We're going next week," the woman said. "The regular channels are not an option. If we left this kind of responsibility to regular channels, we would be living in a cesspool."

She hung up and gazed at the trajectory of the ribbon. Then she stared at the reel by the closet door as if examining a far-away insect. Nonni pushed back into the rear wall, where the paint was moist and warm. A trickle of latex rolled over her shoulder blade and down her spine, and she wondered if closets believed in monogamy at all.

Being utterly motionless was the only thing that would keep her safe. She breathed from the top of her lungs. She thought of a ship sinking in a bed of sand, thousands of feet below the ocean surface. And for a moment, everything might have been all right. But in the next, a pipe contorted behind the drywall. A few random knocks at first. Then a syncopated calling. Finally, a seductive rapping on the chamber door. A spigot broke through the plaster. Nonni shoved three fingers down her throat. She dared not speak. Did not breathe. A ream of dust wafted past her shoulder and the metal serpent inched forward. She recited Poe and De Sade, but did not move. The metal wound up her calf, and in a moment of mock lascivity, imbedded a barb into her knee. There was jell. It only hurt a little. The creature curled around her neck and coiled next to her ear. It had known her for a long time. It could hurt more. It tinkered with her lobe then made its way inside. There was the sound of wet tongues and kissing, and Nonni thought of snails. Once as a girl she had awoken in a tent and found a snail in her ear. The animal had left a trail of damp sludge across her skin. She had screamed then. But that was her youth, and she could not scream now. Her ear calcified, her body hardened, and at that moment, the woman opened the cupboard door. She stared idly into the maze of copper valves, and seeing nothing, rearranged her focus off into space, through the furnace filter, and perhaps wondered where she would store her pension fund or spend her next vacation.

The fax machine started on the far side of the room and the canister of toner ruptured. A spray of black dust arced across the desk and drifted to the floor. The bureaucrat walked back to the machine and pulled some blackened paper out of the feeder, then walked out onto a patio to secure another call.

Nonni sidestepped from the cupboard. Her jacket was ripped. There was sawdust between her thighs and oil on her arms. Black lubricant between her breasts. She ran back to the car and picked up the phone that had been stuffed under the seat.

"Pardon?" Gerry said from the other end of the receiver.

"I was penetrated by a roll of copper wire."

"How?"

"Tied up and bound."

"By whom?"

"Not a person, Gerry. A plumbing manifestation."

"Where are you?" he said.

"In the car."

"A copper wire? Christ that stuff is poisonous."

"I was in a warehouse."

"Which warehouse?"

“I have no clue.”

“Who is with you, Nonni?”

“I’m alone.”

“Are you at a party?” Gerry said.

Pipe lubricant stuck to her hands. Flakes of plastic fell from her hair and lighted on the phone.

“Nonni we have rules about strangers and parties, remember?”

“I didn’t break any rules.”

Gerry took the breath of a man on a long voyage and spoke to someone on the other end of the line in a mumble. “Nonni, I understand you are hurt. You are by yourself and somehow you got tied up in a closet.”

“I’m turning into an industrial appliance.”

“Which new meds did you start?”

“I didn’t read the label,” she said. She turned the ignition over and the car started up.

“Don’t drive, Nonni. Don’t go anywhere.”

“If I don’t go somewhere, I am going to turn into a chunk of gneiss or a five-millimetre washer. Does that sound like fun, Gerry? I am being forced to act out things for other beings. Beings from another place. Another time. Another dimension.”

There was a silence on the phone. “Nonni, you’re going to get in to see Sayer today.”

“I’ve got an electrolysis session in an hour and then the party preview at the club this afternoon.”

Gerry muttered a complex set of directives to whomever the person beside him was. “Forget the club. Non, turn on the GPS and tell me where you are.”

“You’re with Gwen, aren’t you?”

“That doesn’t matter now”

Nonni had figured as much. Gwen was probably wearing the red dress. The Italian one. The one Gerry liked. The one they went to museums in. He said once it looked both academic and sexual, and it reminded him of the rise of fascism in Italy during the 1930s.

She tossed the phone down on the seat and put the car into gear. Bladder to basalt, liver to lava, and trachea to teak. It really was easier that way.

THE ONYX CLUB was full even though it was only three in the afternoon, on a Friday before a long weekend. The smell of locker rooms lilted in the air, as if two dirty combatants might take up copulation on the sallow floor at any moment. Nonni came out of the change room in a black latex suit and thigh-high boots. She had the outfit ordered from Brazil because the latex breathed out the heat. Two spikes protruded out from the breasts so that if anyone got too close they'd be impaled, and that gave Nonni a sense of comfort.

Two regulars in leather bikinis were tied up in the cage, and an X-rated version of the Nuremberg Trials rolled through its fourth act up on the screen.

Gwen came over with Don. She had on a black evening dress with a studded collar, and Don wore his chain mail kilt.

"Are you feeling any better?" Gwen said.

"I wasn't feeling bad, really."

"The Ativan helped," Gerry said.

"I like your suit," Gwen said.

"Got it from Rio."

"Must have been quite the fare for Gerry."

"Thirty-six hundred."

Gwen got distracted. "What's that on your ear?" She forgot the credit card tab and touched the top of Nonni's lobe that had been taped off. Metal filings and a few branches of blood still crept down her jaw.

"Lacquer."

"Very Mary Shelley."

"That's an incised cut," Don said.

"Like an open cut?" Gwen said. There were rules in the club about open cuts.

"To tell you the truth, I can't feel a thing."

"What did the doctor say?"

"Haven't been."

Gwen's jaw tightened. "It's not seeping, is it?"

There were rules at the club about seeping wounds too. "I've got your data on the way," Nonni said.

The seeping issue was done. Gwen folded her hands together and appeared appeased. "I don't think she'll be back."

"No?"

"Didn't you hear about our friend?"

"Which friend?"

"Your surfer-dude friend."

"What happened?"

"Strangled."

"How?"

"Auto-erotically, I guess," Gwen shrugged.

"To himself?" Nonni said.

"That's the auto part."

"Where?"

"Mount Royal."

A crash of Puritan stock posts shook the floor above their heads. Sediment, that was the joy of nights before, rained down with unknown social infections, and poplar dust with sharp edges got illuminated in the curved skylights.

"How did he manage that?" Nonni said.

"He had it all rigged up. Ropes, handcuffs. Dirty movies, play toys. You know, men. Apparently the parents were filthy rich. They own a mine in Guatemala and when they came back he was gagged, sagged, and bagged."

"Where did you hear all this?"

"*Stud-News Weekly.*"

Stud-News Weekly wasn't really news or weekly. It was more of a faded male gossip magazine that was published sporadically by the city's aged pervert sect, who were too old for computer dating. Nonni recalled vaguely being on the board of directors once.

"Police sources say it was a suicide," Gwen said. "Stud gets horny. Stud gets stoned. Watches kinky porn. Next thing you know he's got a rope around his neck and no balance, no oxygen, no future."

"Out, out, brief candle," Gerry shrugged.

"Did he come at least?" Nonni said.

"What?"

"Did he shoot his load?"

"It didn't mention that in the article."

Don finished his beer. He needed to lose some weight. His stomach was hairy. Nonni thought of mammoths screwing. "If it's sex and death you're into, you'll like the show. It's an electric demo by Mistress Patricia Electron Bovary. She's got an electric chair and she's going to fry one of her slaves."

Nonni straddled a stool, sucked her soda, and imagined green sparks flying off a terrified victim. Gwen counted out a roll of twenties in her hand. It was already a profitable afternoon. Upstairs, on the left-hand balcony, Mistress Patricia stood stoically beside a huge wooden chair that had straps on the arms and legs. She was a tall woman with jet black hair and a sour face that made her seem like she was unhappy about her taxes. Her cheeks were polished flat, and she looked as if she had been practicing her trade for a very long time. Nonni smiled at the performer, and when the woman smiled back, Nonni felt the lure of dust, of sandstorms, and sandpaper wearing away all things human. She ran her hand over the wood banister then started up the stairs. By the time Nonni got to the landing, Patricia had stepped into an alcove and leaned against a gloomy captain's window. Her lips had the permanence of knotted mahogany. Gwen called to Nonni that the show didn't start until four, but by then the good Madam was no longer beside the window, or even in the club, but out in the parking lot beside the stacks of sheet metal. Nonni marvelled at how perfect the woman's complexion was, as unblemished and uplifting as the aluminum itself, and then the ancient figure was at the far end of the factory. In a moment, down the street and finally Nonni found herself driving between the warehouses in search of the stone lips that lilted always towards the next intersection.

8.

At four o'clock Nonni stopped her convertible at a downtown traffic light and the smell of talcum wafted out of a perfume shop. During the day, the skyscrapers were chrome, the sun white, and the pavement lacked scent. But at four o'clock all the worries of the world evaporated. Dr. Sayer had said this was the brain producing serotonin. Camus claimed the Algerian sun. Nonni knew better. This was the moment when matter and soul traded places. Dimensions switched. Problems translated. Nothing was forbidden. All allowed. She turned up the radio and lit a menthol.

Nonni thought often of moving to a different, bigger city. Maybe Vancouver, or Montreal. Both bent. But in Vancouver it rained, and in Montreal they spoke French. New York was always being blown up, and Berlin was too far away and much too German.

Besides, the people in this city didn't look all bad. They were trim. They were fit. They had nice tans, nice cars, and nice houses. If one ignored that rash of conservatism that presided over the town like a dismal chapter from the Old Testament, then you might almost have a good time. You could find enough reasonably twisted people if you looked hard. You just had to look in the right places. Maybe that was her purpose for staying in the city. Perhaps that was her reason for being on the planet. She should have looked at it that way before. For each person that Nonni drove by, she tailored a sexual deviation especially for them. The six-foot cowboy standing on the corner with his hands in his pockets and his Stetson tipped down to a ridiculous angle. He would be stripped naked before Banker's Hall and tied to an import car. One that was embarrassingly fuel efficient. The bitchy secretary with pretentious high heels smoking at the train stop could be bound upside-down and given golden showers by street people.

For those who Nonni felt both scorn and attraction, more elaborate fantasies were developed. The spoiled call girl who stood on Third Street and hoped for an executive date out of the Palliser Hotel. She enjoyed a special fate. They would get a suite overlooking the river. Nonni would wear a uniform. A mean, vicious uniform. She would bind the girl naked inside a huge suitcase that had only a few air holes drilled in the top. Then she would order the girl to give a detailed report about the various acts they had performed with her customers. Nonni would write them all down. She would make a computation. Perhaps with a slide-rule. Perhaps an abacus. If the score was high enough the poor girl would live. If not, Nonni would seal the holes with olives from a martini as she sipped the gin.

Nonni thought of a fantasy involving Mussolini as she spun the convertible through a crosswalk. A woman in a pink top stepped onto the pavement. She screamed. Her eyes went white. There was a filling in her front tooth. Two textbooks struck the windshield. Nonni hit the brakes. An orange rolled into the gutter. A body was on her hood.

In the silence that followed, the pedestrian sign blinked from red to green. The woman's face came into focus. Who was she? What was her name? Francis, Felicity, fellatio, no that wasn't it. You can't almost run someone over and not know their name.

"Dietrich?" Nonni stood, and leaned over the top of the windshield.

Dietrich took her hand off the hood, and leaned against the light standard. Her papers fluttered across the road. Nonni pulled into a No Parking Zone. Her almost-victim came back to the door, and her eyes roamed over the polished hood, the chrome tires, and leather upholstery.

"I didn't think I'd ever see you again," Dietrich said.

"You walked against the light."

"I was thinking about you."

"Get in."

Nonni popped the lock. Dietrich forgot her books. She got in the passenger seat, ran her hands over the glove box, then her eyes flitted to the gear shift, and Nonni's neoprene knees.

"Where are you going?" she asked.

"I can accommodate you."

"That's an outfit."

"Just out from a party."

"At four in the afternoon?"

"I have another that starts at five. Come along."

"I'm off to an exhibit at the U of Calgary."

"I'll drive you," Nonni said.

"I couldn't let you."

"I can't cut you loose." Nonni put on her sunglasses. There was a gorgeous caragana on the boulevard that the city had just watered. She raced the motor and pulled into traffic. There were sparrows flying in the glass canyon and fescue scuttling under the feet of bronzed bison, and if there were a more gracious moment when the tachometer hit five thousand, she did not know one. "You might be injured. You could go into shock. You will probably do something foolish."

"Those are beautiful boots," Dietrich said.

"They're imported from Argentina."

"Can you drive with them on?"

"I can do anything with them on."

The sun and slipstream rushed through the open car. Dietrich's hair danced back and forth across her face, and bounced up to the visor that reflected a prosperous city. She smiled and let her hand dangle out the door. The air was warm. The dahlias bright red. This was the summer that had at last come true.

"What kind of business are you in?" Dietrich said.

"Appropriations."

"I bet you get what you want."

"I like pretty things."

"How long have you had the car for?"

"I trade them in every year." Nonni pulled out onto the highway by the river that was a thousand pieces of glass moving under the sun. There was wind in the willows and white water rushing over sharp rocks. "I had a Morgan last year, but they are hard to get parts for and the undercarriage scrapes on our roads. Have you never owned a convertible?"

"University students don't own convertibles."

"How is school?"

Dietrich shrugged. Nonni knew that shrug. It meant either summer school was poor and friends were all right, or school was all right and friends were bad. Either way it meant she was lonely, and that was good.

"That's the problem with summer session," Nonni said. "Not many people of interest on campus."

"None who I can find."

"The campus was always a monastery in summer session. I hated it. In the middle of the morning you'd walk around and the hibiscus would be out, the tennis courts would be empty, and everything reeked of pollen. But there would be no one to do anything with. You might as well have been on the moon."

Nonni pushed the car up to a hundred and touched her menthol with the red lighter coil.

"Did you ever meet anyone on campus?" Dietrich said.

"You should come out to one of my parties."

Dietrich's eyes darted across the metal studs on Nonni's hip, to her gloved hands, and then out across the sparkles in the Bow River. Her chest rose once and that sparkled too. When the slipstream curled under Dietrich's dress, a red cherub exposed himself on her thigh.

"I don't have what it takes for parties."

"I see you got another tattoo."

"Drinking with friends. Spur of the moment kind of thing."

A lie, of course. She hadn't gone with friends. She had none. And of course there was no spurred moment. She didn't do those, either. She had gone alone. She hadn't been drinking. She had found a tattoo parlour in the middle of the night when she was sober, lonely, and melancholy after watching a bland movie that an ancient boyfriend had left behind when he had moved out months before.

"Were you ever a model?" Nonni said.

"God. No."

"Why not?"

"I lack the equipment."

"The Monroe look is out. It's repressive. You're in such lithe shape. All the agencies want that these days. The ones that look pouty and capable of great mischief. You have that look. Do you spend a lot of time in the gym?"

"Some."

"Very svelte." She hoped that was the right word. She'd seen it in a diet commercial. There was a tiny piercing in Dietrich's ear that looked like it been passed on from a German grandmother, but Nonni touched it fleetingly, like Dior from Paris, or a cocktail bar in Madrid.

Nonni pulled the car over to the side of the road at the university entrance gate. On the green lawn, a student strolled without purpose towards the library tower. Dietrich toyed with her necklace. She stared straight ahead to a birch tree. The cheap gemstones rattled.

"Where is your display, Dietrich?"

"In the Nickle Arts Museum."

"I remember it."

A black crow landed on the grass. Far in the distance a few women in white dresses batted tennis balls across a net.

"Would you like to come?" Dietrich said.

Nonni gazed up over the stone bell tower. The edges were lined with solitary silver strips. There were some moments that were worth drawing out, even if it caused your date torment and fear, and this was one of those beautiful moments.

"Let me park the car."

The Nickle Arts Museum wasn't made of nickel and it didn't seem to have much to do with any kind of art. The inside was dark and smelled of stone. Random pieces of iron, that looked like droppings from a midair collision, dotted the rooms, but the clerk at the front desk was tall and had a beautiful Polynesian smile.

What's the display?" Nonni said.

"Neolithic masks."

The air in the gallery was sallow. The walls were lined with countless chunks of dead trees that dead people had carved into dead faces and water ran down into dead adobe drains. Down the far hall was a small red fire exit sign and a set of small soaped windows. There was a cleaning room in the corner. A door was held open with a wash bucket. Maybe that would work.

"Give me the shorthand on the heads," Nonni said.

"Masks probably served as hunting camouflage originally." Dietrich's words quickened. "Probably as far back as a thirty-thousand years ago. Later they were used not just in the hunting, but in the preparation before the hunt. When the preparation for the hunt became a ritual, then the masks became ritualized too. Soon they appeared in other ceremonies, in marriages and funerals, feasts and political gatherings."

Nonni ignored the DO NOT TOUCH sign and tinkered with a collection of copper shavings that were glued to an arbutus skull. She felt a nervous flinch come from her new friend's frame. Yes, she was breaking the rules. Perhaps alarms would go off. No, she did not care.

"Were they ever used in sacrifices?"

"I suppose."

"What is your interest in them, personally?"

"Masks?"

"Either."

"I had a collection when I was a girl," Dietrich said. They walked down the corridor together and stopped at a case. Inside hung a wooden face two feet across. The eyes were opened in surprise. Blue straw came out of the temples for hair. A single crass light bulb was hung above the forehead, making the nose shadow long and thin. "I still collect them today. Masks separate the conscious from the unconscious."

Not bad, Nonni thought. Play the right-hand side of the brain if the left won't go along. "So with a mask on," Nonni said. "You could do things your conscious mind wouldn't normally let you do?"

"Of course."

"I'll buy you one then."

"The masks in here cost tens of thousands of dollars."

"We'll find you one somehow."

Dietrich touched the display button and a blue light gave the mask a bucolic hue. Some of the blue light cast on Dietrich's cheek and she smiled, but this was not the way Nonni wanted the visit to be.

"I like the melancholy ones," Dietrich said.

"Melancholy is a primitive emotion."

"Pardon?" Dietrich said.

"It's an emotion for cultures that have no future."

"That's a rather neocolonial attitude, don't you think?"

"I'm a colonialist at heart." Nonni put a thumb to the glass and ran her nail down a crack. "Melancholy quells desire. Only cultures with desire have a future. They are violent. They are robust. The genius of a culture is defined by its sexual violence."

Nonni's spine hardened to an iron keel. She liked it when the words came out precisely as she intended them. She hadn't realized that as she spoke, her mouth had closed to Dietrich's ear. Her lips were touching the stray stands of her hair. A tiny fleck of crimson lingered on the strand, but then the girl turned away, staring at the flat features of a wooden mask locked in a glass cube.

"The man in the coffee shop," Dietrich said.

"My husband."

"You're married?"

"After a fashion."

Dietrich made a few puzzled steps to a bog man entombed in a sea of formaldehyde. His eyes gazed back in opaque ambivalence. The years of peat had blackened his corpse, and his body was ensnared with rope and twine. A thin layer of oak bark had been sealed over his torso.

"He knows what I'm doing."

"What are you doing?"

"Spending my time with a good-looking college woman."

"He doesn't mind?"

"He doesn't have a choice," Nonni put her hand on Dietrich's shoulder and lingered past the casual limit.

"He likes it?"

Nonni leaned against the brass rail that surrounded the transparent sarcophagus. The ropes around the bog man's neck had been cinched so tight his jaw collapsed. "I wonder why they didn't expose the genitals?" she said. She licked her finger and pushed it against the glass until the pane squealed. "It would have been nice to know what he was thinking when they killed him. There's no other way to find out what a man really likes than by looking between his legs, wouldn't you say?"

"You say the most eccentric things."

"I'm an eccentric woman."

"Why do you bother with me?"

Nonni slid a menthol between her lips, and let her eyes wander up to the No Smoking sign. Dietrich wrapped her arms around her shoulders. Perhaps she was chilled. "You're gorgeous. You're rich. You're smart. You have an exciting life. I'm not anything like that."

"You could be."

Dietrich gazed at the tiled floor. There were a million tiny patterns that one could take all day either memorizing or avoiding, but Nonni didn't have that long.

"Do you have a boyfriend?" Nonni said.

Her forehead vexed. Her brows furrowed. Those beautiful coy signals of surrender that the conscious mind cannot control, yet when they are done they are always followed by a single shake.

"A girlfriend, maybe?"

A wisp of hair fell down over her sad white eyes. Inside the glass case, a single bubble emerged from the skull and shimmered upwards.

"I had neither in college," Nonni said. "I went to movies by myself. I went to plays by myself. I had imaginary lovers by myself. I memorized Keats. I married Coleridge. Once I fantasized I was having an affair with Mary Shelley. Unfortunately, it was a fantasy that went on for seven years and, in the end, I had to conclude that she loved Frankenstein more than me. I don't have to tell you how a woman with a deviant mind scares off most men."

"How did you fix that?"

"I stopped trying to impress the people who didn't matter to me and went out and found those that did. It's quite easy, really. Every time an opportunity comes up, you engage. Win or lose, you engage. Opportunities always come up."

"Name a time."

"When you were getting pierced did you have sex with the tattooist?"

"Of course not."

"Do you go to clubs?"

"Once."

"What happened?"

"All those people milling around, laughing, shouting, screwing, turned me off. I felt like I was made of slate. I don't think anyone can help me in that department."

"My dear. I. Am. Trying," Nonni enunciated the words as slowly as she could. Then she pulled the girl back by the cuff into the cleaning alcove. She held Dietrich's jaw in one hand

and the girl gazed back in an act of supplication. The mop fell over. Water ran into a drain and Nonni felt a compunction of argillite creep into her lungs. "I have been trying for weeks now and you have been ignoring me, so I'll tell you what. I'm going to make you an offer and I'm only going to do it once. You can say yes or you can say no, but there's not going to be another chance."

Nonni tucked her lighter under the girl's belt. Dietrich breathed in once, and when Nonni knew her captive could not refuse she said: "Light my cigarette."

It took Dietrich three tries with the flint. Then there was the shaking of nervous palms and a plume of smoke between them. The fire alarm went off. Nonni imagined her fingers around the girl's neck. If I were an animal, Nonni thought, I'd rip her throat open with my bare teeth and suck up all that prettiness right here in the museum. But I am a civilized woman and so I'll wait until she's ready, or a more barbaric century rolls around. And so, Nonni leaned forward and said: "Now, you're going to do the important thing for me. Get up. Walk over to the display. Undo the latch. Take the wooden mask. Put it under your shirt and walk out. Walk out the fire entrance. No one will know the difference. The bells are ringing always. Keep it for us. I'll call you. But do it now. Don't think, just go."

Dietrich stood up. She walked directly towards the target, finding her way through the dark display posts with the wood faces pressing around her, threatening to crush the air out of her lungs. Her rail-thin figure glided down the corridor and cast a thin reflection on the painted tiles. Then she stood in front of the mask and reached up into sin.

9.

The convertible had to have its grill replaced. The hood ornament needed to come from Hamburg. And the mechanic with the baseball cap didn't want to know the difference. There were taxes, forms, affidavits, and even an amber residue on the signature card. A Chinook in summer, which was called something else in July. A marriage in ruins, which was called anything else in frailty. But worst of all there was public transit on a Tuesday night which was the nadir of self-redemption.

Nonni had tried to call a cab. But the wait was an hour. She should have called a limousine. But the limousines on football nights were booked. In the end, she got on the train and stood at the back of the car with the ticket crumpled in her pocket because she could not bring herself to sit on the seats. The vinyl was dirty, the aisle was dirty, the advertisements peeled off the ceiling, and perspiration permeated the air with a dank smell that was foreign and rife. She couldn't imagine what sort of people would cultivate such a stench. She didn't want to know. She kept her head down and almost wished she called Gerry, who might have been out with Gwen, who was probably screwing Steve. The train went through a tunnel. The rails rattled. A few stiff figures moved from bench to bench in near darkness. She couldn't recall the last time she had been on public transit and then was relieved when she concluded it was probably never at all. Her mind drifted to the list of boy toys that followed Gwen around like servants and she knew even being with them would have been better than this, too.

When the car emerged from the tunnel, the line of skyscrapers faded into industrial yards. Nonni pictured pyramids decaying into sand. Reason into rubble. Lust into love, and she tried to recall on which holiday she had found decay arousing. Perhaps Dresdin with her husband. Or maybe it was just a weekend in Drumheller with a paleontologist no one knew. The train made a stop at a charcoal station. People got on, but no one got off. No wondering why. Outside there was nothing but pawn shops, creosote lanes, and a tangle of electric wires that stretched between black poles.

The train started up and the dull faces of fellow passengers crammed around Nonni. Idle with the half-lives they might have lived and probably lied about, they kept packing the train past the level of sanity and kept looking away. That a custom grill should take two days to replace was obscene, that ugly people huddled so closely together was just wrong.

When the car hit a curve, an elbow caught her in the rib. It was a plebbish, angular bump, and so Nonni bumped him back. He was the kind of hulking submissive she liked to whip until they cried at the club. That highest of all art forms: taking a stupid sub on a long ride through yellow then dangling them on the edge of red. Spitting on their face when they broke. All bliss and crushed bones. But this rigid frame on the transit car didn't budge. Didn't flinch. So she stepped on his foot. The air smelled of chalk. There was a condition people got when their muscles went hard and their bones became elephantine. He probably had that. She knew the type. They exuded simian smells from their glands. They did poorly in grade school and worse at parties. She pulled a handkerchief over her nose.

Construction cranes stood black as outlines in the western sky. If only one of them could descend like a praying mantis into the train and delete the common people from life. There were a thousand ways to spend cash in this monied city, but being trapped on public transit wasn't one of them. This was night and nights were meant to be spent at parties, in clubs, with escargot and tit clamps, or even watching plays if someone had hashish and there was nothing else on the scene to do.

The windows steamed over. Pebbles rolled across rubber mats. Air that was going in and out of the public lung was incontrovertibly going into hers, then condensing on the glass as proof. If there was any way to hold her breath she would have done that, but instead, she could only crush a menthol cigarette into the handkerchief, cough, gag, and relent.

Depression-era brickwork flew past the window. Curls of barb wire and a bolt supply store. Gauging what continent one was on became impossible. There were no maps. No charts. Overcoats blocked the exits. Alien language filled the car. She couldn't place the accent. There were no inflections in their voices, no hue, just an endless drone that might as well have been ball bearings rolling in a tin kettle, and Nonni realized she was lost. The train was lost. The nation as she knew it had gone astray. She shuffled towards the door. Four damp overcoats obstinately refused to move.

Screw the ingrates. Death to the Goths. If she got groped,

she'd grope back. She was brave. The thought of a handful of bloodied organs amused her. She recalled a scene from a horror film. Female cannibals held severed testes above their heads and that excited her.

The train curved once more. A hip bent. There was the chatter of tracks. He might have sighed. His gloved hand tightened around the ceiling rail. This was probably the only human contact he got.

There were many hands on the rail then. People holding on for balance and posterity, and they all wore gloves too. Nonni wished she had brought hers. Everything about the train was unclean. Her gloves were from Florence. Smelted in the same ancient villa for six hundred years, they had cost more than all of the fares in the cab put together, and she had once worn them to a fetish club in Berlin. Yet here she was. Aerosol. Mercury. Poison elements of passion that made hatters in Montreal go mad four centuries ago.

Her eyes fluttered to his overcoat belt. Unhitched. Grey. Everyone was wearing the same kind of drab belt. The same buckles too, and then she saw that they were all wearing the same hats. Badly out of date wide brimmed fedoras that might have been in a second-string charity walk during the Korean War.

A pair of feet shuffled closer. Oxford shoes, thick black shoelaces. Blakeys. Everyone on the train was wearing exactly the same kind of laces. The same ties, sweaters, collars, and cuffs. The same faces turned away in deference, and when an asymmetric groin pressed into her hip the passengers muttered and mused. They were contextualizing. Confiding. Not talking really. But humming. The sound of an electric drill going through bedrock. A gloved finger moving through her hair. She saw the emergency handle. There was a fine for frivolous use. At the far end of the car, one of the figures looked up through the sea of hats to reveal his smooth cheeks, sandblasted into perfection by a thousand years of wind, and Nonni broke the glass and pulled the lever.

The train squealed to a stop just as the car hit the station. Couplings crashed. Nonni pushed open the door and jumped onto a platform of silence. There was not a soul in sight. Not an automobile in the parking lot. Not even a dog in the night. Just saliva on her collar and a few wood chips on her chin. When she went to wipe them off her necklace broke, and a string of pearls danced on the concrete. Inside the train, a hundred hats turned slightly in her direction as the car moved away.

The street lights did not work, her phone had no reception, and the traffic appeared as a distant stream of red on the far side of the Bow River. She did not want to go home. She had no clue how to find a club. No method of finding an escort. To be lost in the city of the dead was bad enough, but to have no date to go there with was quite another.

Down the alley, a corrugated fence surrounded a scrap yard. There must have been a night shift because the light in the office was on and the sound of worn tappets echoed off a warehouse. Nonni went past the sign that warned of a guard dog, and stepped over an engine block. There were pumps and train hitches, turbines and fans. The moon made the metal white. Inside, there was possibly a clerk, probably a landline. The Onyx wasn't open, but there was always Starlight or Swingers.

Inside there was only a bell, and she rang it and no one came. The door to the machine shop was open and she called, but of course no one answered. On the far side of the warehouse sat an intercom with a blue flashing light on its dial, which was worth a try.

The ceiling of the factory was open and stars speckled the black night. Three storeys of cranes and conveyor belts chewed and digested metal without sleep or pity. There were muffled rhythms and noises that might have been muted screams.

On the southern wall of the warehouse, stacked columns of wire cages reached up to rows of mesh boxing. Hundreds of interlocking metal threads formed thousands of metal knots. Nonni tried to calculate the number, but gave up when a green glow in a corner alcove caught her attention. The vestibule had been set up like a shrine with ornate wood carvings that framed a glass terrarium. Behind the glass there was a bare arbutus trunk. Its orange bark was toned with an infrared heating lamp, and hanging from one of the branches was a sleeping three-toed sloth. A small brass plaque attached to the bass of the trunk read: *Gloria In Nocte*. Nonni put her finger to the glass, but the animal did not move.

In the centre of the room, a truck-sized compressor spat out heaps of slag resembling crumpled television antennae. The machine rested for a few minutes, then convulsed back into life and consumed everything that was fed into its gaping jaws. A chunk of solder fell at Nonni's foot and she pondered the perversity of polymerization. The gills of the processor seeped yellow grease, so she contemplated the erotic beauty of crystals. And when the intestinal track sublimated the next load of iron into ferrous gas, there was no stopping the blissful images the machine evoked: a hundred luxurious deaths. Boiling in hydrocarbons, strut suffocation to silence, auto collisions in slow motion, and then even slower, the twisting of blue glass mannequin victims at the end of long fibrous ropes. The tension grew. Nonni undid her collar. If anyone came in, she would tell them that she was lost. That she had hurt her head. That she only needed help finding a cab.

In a crevasse between the belts, a control panel with levers and lighted dials exuded the smell of citronella. Inside the cockpit there was a row of sensor bars that she longed to touch. She stroked the handles and turned the dials until her breath shortened, dams broke, and buildings collapsed in pleasure so the only sensible thing to do was let her coat fall from her shoulders and of course her blouse had to go, too.

A bristle on the control lever punctured her palm and a pulpit of blood trickled down her wrist. From deep within the machine, a note of half interest sounded. When she bent down to listen closer, a metal burr caught her rib and the note became a soprano voice. Then a heating coil snapped out to singe her thigh, and the voice became a chorus, a choir, and finally a train rumbling down the tracks.

Drops of her blood splashed onto a sieve. The blood was crimson. The dots accurately round. So beautiful, because it had, in fact, come from her. But then the puddles shrank. Either the conveyor sucked them in or the motor oxidized it out, so the red turned blue and then the blue was gone. This was going to mean another long evening of explanations to Gerry and probably to Sayer as well.

Sheets of wax flowed in wafers from a slot above her head. Perhaps that was all the machine did — produced endless layers of waffled cloth. Maybe they were used to produce papyrus or entomb the dead, but probably only to seal cat litter or wrap wire cages. She used one of the wafers to bind her wound. The fabric flooded into the incision. The relief was instant so she kept wrapping. She wrapped one arm and felt secure. She sealed herself from nipple to pelvis and saw beauty. She used bailing wires to keep everything in place until her torso and hips were covered and understood what the unified theory was.

Her reflection was stark in the polished metal of the machine. An affluent woman, injured slightly, with perfect hair and perfect thighs, and more than perfect diction, was coiled up in strands of an element that might have been shaved off an asteroid. She thought of asteroids then. Of supernovas and quasars and canyons and Parthenons, and she decided that the look suited her, so she undid her belt and let her pants drop to the floor. She wrapped silver cable around her legs and clove hitched aluminum through her crotch. The wires took on a fluvial quality that made her wet when they quivered. And she thought of water, of nymphs and drowning reefs and sailors begging. She had read a pastoral story in school about either sheep or sailors being saved. But she had liked the tragedies more, had empathized with Macbeth, and flirted with Richard III. And so she discarded whatever modesty she had left and allowed the machine to take her bra the same way it had her blood. For insurance, she wrapped three layers of zinc around her temple, in case she were to get wounded there, also.

From the far side of the room, a breath moved over kilns of copper. Creeping like a respiratory ailment. The indenture of owned land. A free vote in parliament. They stood by the door. Sage and insomniac. Same overcoats. Same hats. Same grey trousers. One of them had his hands together as if he had been clapping when time stopped.

Nonni backed up against the machine. She felt her lip quiver and remembered a time in grade school when her lip had crumbled. She had been called to recite a poem and all of her classmates had looked down upon her in judgement.

The wires around her body vibrated. A breach gun ringing or perhaps just her teeth chattering, and they seemed to like that part. One of them held and ochre palm over olivine lips. Another had black basalt eyes. And that was what worried her. They were still, but they were not weak. If they had been rheumatoid or arthritic it would have been comforting, hunchbacked or lame palatable. But she knew their mere presence was causing every inanimate object in the room to tell the truth, and with the truth they trembled, and then the trembling turned into an oboe note that kept rising, and Nonni wondered what their skin tasted like. If their tongues were wet or if their massive hips would crush her before the moment came. She thought of being split in two by their glacial affection — arrows through armour, axes into bone.

Wondering wasn't enough for them. Wishing didn't keep them happy. Nonni wasn't doing and they were not the type who appreciated second sober thought. So, in a semicircle, they closed around her. They could walk without moving their legs, and the rear wall of the warehouse rolled apart. The moon was full. The scrap yard glittered. She might drink the best Beaujolais on the streets of occupied Paris with them, the wine, of course, running down the jowls of their petrified cheeks. The warehouse was in a forest of debris and she was in the middle. For foreplay one of them could plunge his corrosive hand through her sternum and pull out her beating heart. How much she admired the columns of collapsed rebar by the compressor. How little like a breathing being she felt. Disc brush hair. Tie rod fingers. They were waiting for her to speak. But when she tried to cry out, only dust fell down from a set of pulleys that ran on the ceiling tracks.

This was the strategy of an industrial city doing whatever it did at night. And that was too bad. At first she thought the wail in the sky might have been a jet landing or a meteorite striking the building. Perhaps a pterodactyl, but of course those didn't exist anymore. So there was only the common truth left to witness — the shadow moving towards her was that of a wrecking crane, swinging in to pick up its next load of debris from which she was indistinguishable.

She thought of krill in the ocean. Of mercury beads running together on a classroom floor. The iron jaw dropped down at terminal velocity and impacted the bundle of scrap. A stray incisor tooth caught a coil of wire trussed to her midriff and her feet left the ground. Two stilettoes, imported from Milan and autographed by the designer himself, spiraled into darkness. To fly. To sleep. The wire strands snapped. Nonni's stomach bottomed out and she felt herself falling into sod, gravel, and a dozen other industrial fillers that were most likely destined for a trash heap. A bone in her ribcage cracked. Her audience was gone. But what hurt her most was what she had been mistaken for and that was surely against the Charter, or at least unconstitutional.

10.

In a vacant lot, behind a Chinese restaurant, a cluster of wooden posts stood as tombstones. They had rotted and leaned over, huddled together in a drab urban conversation.

Nonni parked the Mazda outside Teddy's driveway. She had put on a leather skirt and a rubber top with a gold zipper, and she hurried past the sentinels, averting their stare, and went straight through the door without bothering to knock. The living room reeked of Arabic tobacco and there was cat hair on the couch. From down the hall came the sound of thick fingers striking a keyboard.

"Are you in?" she said.

"You know where."

Teddy sat behind the desk in his office. He wore a green jersey with an outdated hockey emblem and a thick pair of reading glasses.

"I thought eventually you'd make it back." He didn't bother to look up. "Your type always does."

She looked around for a clean space to sit. There wasn't one. "What's my type?"

"Just pull the papers off the blue chair." He pointed with his pencil.

She sat on the chair and crossed her legs. "Tell me what my type is, Teddy."

"Nervous, insecure, and over stimulated." He pushed the glasses up on the bridge of his nose where there were two red creases and leaned back. "Anxiety and sexual psychopathia go hand in hand."

"You are so full of shit."

"What's your issue with the fence posts outside?"

"Which ones?"

"The ones you sprinted past," he said.

"Were you spying on me?"

"It's a device called a window, Nonni. They're installed in most houses so you can see out onto the street without having to open the door."

There was an open jar of green olives on the desk. The water was murky and there was mould around the pimentos. She couldn't stand the sight of it so she thumbed through a copy of *Alien Orgy*. The pages were smeared with sawdust and the edges stuck together.

"Check out page sixty-seven," he said.

Nonni flipped through a dozen glossy pages of rubber aliens fondling blond women. A hard-skinned creature with a thick phallus forced a nude unfortunate to the controls of a space vehicle. One of the photos was subtitled: The Cerebrion forces its victim to commit senseless acts of wanton vice before occluding them into a vacuum of space-time.

"What is a Cerebrion?" she said.

"It's just a name, really."

"Isn't this for ten-year-olds?"

"Not with cocks that size."

He had a point. Nonni turned the magazine sideways.

“I’m just curious,” he said. He examined a fingernail. The tip was green and he wasn’t about to do anything about it. “They’re only fence posts. I mean, I understand subliminal symbolism. But you stretch the paradigm. Something from your childhood?”

“My childhood has nothing to do with this.”

“They must remind you of something.”

“They remind me of those things on Easter Island.”

“The moai?”

“Them.”

“I think they’re a syllogism for your lack of erotic expression,” he said.

The back of Nonni’s elbow was badly bruised. So was her right temple. She had used Diorskin to cover up. The doctor at the emergency room had told her that she had a cracked rib and there wasn’t much to do. She knew a different doctor who would fix her for the pain. And a third who did massages for free. The corner of her left eye was swollen and mascara could fix that, too. The discussion with Gerry had been unpleasant.

“They’re an ugly bunch of posts in a shitty neighbourhood,” she said. “Why doesn’t a city worker clean them up?”

“Nobody pays any city taxes here.”

“So why do you live here?”

“I don’t pay taxes either. And it lets me focus on my work.”

“What exactly is your work, Teddy?”

He flicked the computer monitor off and pushed the files to the corner of the desk. When he was certain they were properly stacked, he gave her a look over, starting at her zipper top, and then working his way down to her ankles.

“You look very charming today,” he said.

Nonni ran her heel up her shin just to piss him off.

“What did you put on your legs?”

"Aqua-Elite."

"Never heard of it."

"It's lubricant. You probably can't notice it on your computer screen if that's what you're used to watching."

"Very viscous."

"All the dommes use it," she said. It was amazing how even the smallest of compliments could make the most embarrassing injuries go away and even talking with a plebe might not be so bad if the purpose was served. "I picked some up on a New York vacation."

"Dommes?"

Teddy's nose screwed up a millimetre, but Nonni recognized it as the look of a pathetic soul who had no nuance of the world except from travel brochures. In club language, a short ride yellow.

"Dominatrixes," she said.

"I didn't know you were one."

"I'm not a Pro-Domme."

"What kind are you?"

"The kind who does it for pleasure. Or just to screw other people around if they have it coming."

Her jaw ached on the last word. In fact, all of her spine hurt. Her elbow, too. She recalled dredger size teeth bearing down on her and slipping on whatever kind of fluid covered the floor. There was a civil suit in this for sure.

"And if somebody slips you a trip to Rio in the process?"

"Have you never read Machiavelli? The world is a better place for self-interest."

She pulled the zipper down an inch. Teddy folded his hands together. They were yellowed from tobacco.

"Did David ask you to come over again?" he said.

"He doesn't know I'm here."

“Interesting.”

“That doesn’t mean we can’t talk.” Nonni pushed the zipper ring from left to right. Men might make one or two logical steps on their computations towards coitus, but don’t count on more than that. “I had such a good time talking with you last time.”

“Me too,” Teddy said.

Nonni put her palms together and smiled. “But this time we have to talk about what I want.”

“I’m open.” He leaned back. Pink paint crusted off the wall and fluttered to the floor. The furnace turned over. “What’s on your mind, Nonni?”

“What’s wrong with David?”

“I have no idea.”

“He’s acting like a flake.”

“He is a flake.”

“More than usual. Has he said anything to you?”

“Haven’t heard from him.”

“Nothing?” she said.

“He never calls. He never writes.”

“I thought you two were close.”

“Only if he wants me to stay away from a family dinner.” Teddy brushed a flake of paint off his knee. He stared down at a bronze protractor on the floor. His lip curled up the way Nonni knew it did when people were embarrassed and wanted consolation.

“Their family doesn’t like you?”

“I’m a porn merchant, Non.”

“You do each other favours don’t you?”

“Prid-quo-pro.”

There was a scrapbook filled with flattened insects on the desk beside him. The creatures all had the same metallic hue to their bodies. He touched one of the dead wings then secured the edge with a tube of glue.

"What are those?" she said.

"Petrified bugs."

"Petrified bugs. Listen, I called him up the other day. He wouldn't say squat to me. He was a completely different person, which was bad because I needed reliable information."

"He's a skitzo capitalist. What do you expect?"

"He's also a horny skitzo capitalist. That is what worries me. He wouldn't give up a cut in the action unless there was a reason."

"Maybe his fiancée found out," Teddy said. There was a bowl of pretzels on the desk. He picked one up, rolled it over his chin, then attached the pastry to his keyboard with another dob of glue.

"David wouldn't let a medieval arrangement like marriage get in the way of his primordial urges. He'd screw his mother's dog if he got the chance."

"Why is this so important so you?"

"Did David ever mention the Onyx Club to you?"

"Sounds exotic." Teddy sniffed the glue cap. "Can you take me there?"

"I don't think it's your crowd."

"Figures."

Nonni picked up a specimen brush from the table and used it to scratch her wrist. The scabbed skin from the Mount Royal accident had settled into the joint, so she'd have to ask Dr. Sayer for arthritic medication as well as antidepressants. Which was more depressing than actually being depressed itself. Then she used the bristle in her ear. The shock left over from the scrap bucket dump had damaged her hearing. Voices were far away and tinny, but she doubted Sayer knew anything about that kind of medication.

“David was doing some sourcing on new folks for us,” she said.

“From the secure data banks at his top secret federal job.”

“What else?”

“Our National Security Service at work.”

“He told me to back off. He got paranoid.”

“Well, he is. Nonni, this is a swinger’s club we’re talking about. A bunch of middle-class people screwing each other on Saturday nights. What’s the big deal?”

“The powers that be find that kind of thing offensive.”

“Let them.”

Nonni leaned over and tapped him on the wrist with the brush. She smiled. She hated stooping that low, but if the ends justified the means, pretending to smile wasn’t so bad. “I don’t like disturbances in my club, Teddy. It’s how I make acquaintances. We all need acquaintances.”

“You could make acquaintances anywhere,” he said. “You didn’t come halfway across town to fill me in on your social calendar. What’s going on Nonni? And what the hell happened to your hand? Or the side of your face for that matter?”

Nonni stared out the window to the crabapple tree. The more interested Teddy got in a subject, the stronger the smell of cordite became around his person, and Nonni found the words from a poem about hollow men repeating through her head.

“Industrial accident,” she said.

“What’s motivating you, Nonni?”

“Sex motivates me.”

“Not this time.”

“Sex motivates everything and everybody all the time, Teddy. You, me, Leonardo Da Vinci. Bertrand Russell. Everybody is in it for the Super Id.” Husbands, wives, club owners, friends, astronauts, Nonni could have made the list go on forever. Fuck buddies, slaves, tops, bottoms, transsexuals, Senate appointments, and even aliens. Don't bother denying it, world. She tried to stare through his Coke-bottle glasses, but the lenses were too thick. She wondered how many times he had been beaten up in the school playground and figured it wasn't enough. "Getting the girls in here under a ploy of scientific endeavor is cute, but you can't tell me it's not all about sex."

"Have a pretzel," he said. He held out the bowl.

"Thanks, no."

"You talk different when you get excited, did you know that, Non?"

He put down the bowl then arranged the insects in his catalogue. The creatures had been arranged by wing colour with the emerald green at top and the midnight black on bottom, but something about the order displeased him. An amber winged moth fluttered to the floor.

"Now I'm curious," she said. "Do you suck and swallow? Or do you just need to have your face pissed on then be locked in the closet. Maybe in the end you only want to be held and told that you're not fat. What motivates you, Teddy?"

Teddy gazed down at his belt line. A spider dropped off the ceiling in a spindle of silver. "I do it for them," he said.

"Them? Okay. Them who?"

"You talked about them last time you were here."

"I was talking you through a wank fest."

Nonni felt a sour taste in her mouth and couldn't decide if it was lime or copper filings. A vague sexual memory of an orthodontist filling her mouth with titanium flashed through her mind and then she pitched the brush into Teddy's waste basket.

"You were talking to them outside just now. And probably last time at the club. Was the best time when you went over to that innocent's house to play bad girl? Did they infect your hand first, Nonni, or was it your breast?"

"I'm not following."

"Couldn't help but noticing your *blessure de guerre* there. You have a tendency to wear see-through tops. Portside. Looks nasty."

"Changing accident."

"A woman like you doesn't have accidents, Nonni."

That much was true. She disliked his sweater. She despised the grease stain on his chin. There had been the club in Frankfurt where the tourniquet was too tight. The fire in Marseille with *charge de faire*. Gerry's crushed ego in Algiers, and so, accidents were unreliable options.

"It's the way they work," Teddy said. "They start with the extremities. The hands, fingers, but then they quickly progress to more uh, central areas. That's their modus operandi. Whenever you get desperately horny, as your nomenclature dictates, they move in. Then they make you do things. Things that you wouldn't have otherwise done. Things that will leave you in compromised situations, embarrassed, and alone.

"And when you feel that way, they make their pitch. They'll offer you another fix. Problem is, every time you do their bidding, they leave you changed, looking a little more like them. A voice less tonal. A tear with fewer salts. An empty house. Does that sound familiar? If I've got this wrong, fine. Walk out. I'll ply David for more information on your club, no hard feelings. But if any of this rings a bell, then please talk to me."

"Who told you about the time at the house?" she said.

Teddy took off his glasses. His eye sockets were sunken, but somewhere down at the bottom of that dark well a penny glimmered. "Nobody told me. They follow the same pattern with everyone."

"Everyone?"

Across the hall in the living room, the black Persian cat jumped off the couch and knocked an ashtray over. Teddy drummed his fingers on the table and reached over to the stack of papers that were held together with paper clips. He opened a file that was scrawled in black ink. There were diagrams of industrial revolution machines, medieval inquisition devices, and nude bodies bound with wire cables.

"I have over three hundred files of people who came to know these beings," he said. "Exceptional people. People just like you. People who burned as strips of magnesium and put out calling cards to places they didn't even know existed. Until one of those cards got answered. They got a visit. An inconsequential visit at first. An erotic encounter that produced resin. A pattern of leaves that was algebraic. Most people would ignore those things. But you noticed. And they noticed that you noticed.

"This is Sandra." He tossed a file on the desk. "She was an engineer. I saw her first about a year ago. As per usual, David sent her along. She was brilliant. Had a PhD in mechanical engineering. Not much into people. She drifted away from her husband. She drifted away from her family. From all human contact. She had a curious definition of what bent was. For her, all sexual activity was conducted through electromagnetic means. Amps. Ohms. Watts. Resistance ratios."

Nonni felt herself lean over the desk and peer at the photo that was attached to Teddy's yellowed folio with a single paper clip. The woman was young and blond. Bland, but healthy in a way that suggested she might have been good at basketball.

"Jesus, Nonni. You're dripping on my floor."

Beneath Nonni's stool, a pool of brine water had collected. When Teddy's air conditioner clicked on the puddle quivered. A drip splashed onto the seat from her elbow, then ran candy cane style down the leg. There were rules in the club about seeping wounds, but Nonni wasn't sure if Teddy's place came with them too. His breath shortened. He bit his upper lip and pressed his fingertips together, so she guessed not. He pushed a plastic first aid kit across the desk. Inside there was only a roll of telegraph wire and some zephrin wrapping. When she wound it around the wound the room smelled of photographic residue.

"What happened to Sandra?" she said.

"Unfortunately for Sandra, the human body was not as good a conductor of electronic transmissions as she'd hoped. She got piercings. Earrings. Naval piercings, clit piercings, nipple posts. She looked like a porcupine. Her hubby deserted her. Family tried to have her committed. Nothing satisfied her. She came to me one day, just like you. She told me erotic paradigms in alternating current were being sent to her. She wasn't able to decode them. Didn't know where they were coming from. She sat on that very same stool you are in now. I tried to explain who was really sending the messages. I'm not sure how much she really wanted to listen. She liked getting the signals. The erotic charge was unbelievable. Same story. She played harder and harder with the circuit boards. The piercings got bigger and bigger. Soon they were getting caught in car doors and she couldn't make it through airport screening devices. She had her esophagus pierced by an artisan of dubious skill. As a cover, she converted to Islam and wore a Burqa so her wounds wouldn't show. The police thought she was part of a terrorist cult. She wore gloves, just like you. Soon she was administering jolts of direct-current electricity for stimulation. Batteries. Car cells. Solar packs. I think she had a transformer hot-wired out of a socket in her bedroom. The utility company threatened to cut off her power. They found her at home in the bathtub wearing a pair of aluminum plated underwear. The entire block suffered a blackout."

Teddy closed the file and rested his palm on the title page. The foundations of the ancient bungalow settled. A great weight moved down the hall, warping gravity, rolling a cat's eye marble along the baseboards, and leaving its indictment at the door.

She wasn't about to turn around. She wasn't going to let on. Teddy watched her eyes for the slightest perturbation. But when he couldn't detect anything, he gave up and rummaged through a stack of files on the shelf. A piece of gum stuck two of the pages together. He peeled off the wad and stuck it in his mouth.

"Here is Tracey," he said. "Nineteen. She was going to be a swimsuit model. Puritanical. No drugs. No drinking. No saturated fats. Summa Cum Laude at university. No problems at home. One day, she started going to the clubs. She picked up mechanics, machinists, architects, welders. Anybody who had anything to do with the moving parts of machines. She was convinced that the essence of eroticism was the transformation of the human body into a functioning mechanical union. Any kind of machine, actually. Lawn mowers, locomotives, mix masters. Simple things like a Roman catapult. She became enthralled with the Industrial Revolution. They came to her then. In the form of pistons, that's how she described them. Of course, they wanted something in trade, but she ignored that part. Instead, she formed an acquaintance with a man who collected train parts. A large part of their erotic conversation revolved around the CP Railway. He went away for the weekend and left her in his hobby shop. The police said he should have known better, but really it wasn't his fault. She used all five hundred metres of track, and the medical examiner had to use industrial pliers to extract the mess."

"Were they all women?"

Teddy pretended. He gazed up at the ceiling, and then out at the window, and then finally down at the glossy patch of skin on Nonni's ankle.

"My last case was a young man. Very handsome. Surfer. Captain of Team Everything in his freshman year. He was obsessed with asphyxiation. He had a collection of over a hundred hanging movies. He believed that a woman who looked like a doll, or a piece of china, would liberate him from his earthly coil by choking the life out of him. He'd practice with a rope in the cupboard. No doubt shooting his load in the process. I kept saying to him, there's more than that, listen closely. He didn't. They found him with a bag over his face a couple of weeks ago."

Nonni picked up the package of Winstons and examined them. "Whose are these?"

"I threw her out," he said.

"An escort?"

"I don't pay for it, Nonni."

"What was the boy's name?"

"He wouldn't tell me."

"What did he look like?"

This amused him. "Never saw him without a lot of makeup. It was a neurosis. His face was always fifty percent plaster."

"Does everyone who comes in contact with these things end up killing themselves?"

"Some of them stay medicated," Teddy said. "Some of them move away. One or two of them close the door and end up being stenographers or working in coal mines. Ninety percent of the stories don't have happy endings."

Nonni pinched a strip of pine off the stool. Whatever deadweight had shuffled down the hall was standing behind her. A seed pod from one of Teddy's dried plants fell from the shelf and rattled beneath the desk.

"What happened to the other ten?"

"It's part of the research," Teddy said. He put a key into the lock on his desk drawer and pulled out a notebook.

"You must have some data."

"The successful ones evolve," he said. "The data on those ones is harder to find. The failures end up in an obituary or a medical examiner's report. But with the successes, the facts get skewed. Concrete evidence is subjective. Metaphorical even."

Metaphorical, subjective. What Nonni knew for sure was a film of sweat had collected on her calf and ran down her ankle. Her wound reeked of battery acid.

"Isn't there like an AA club for this?"

"You go out soliciting help on this kind of topic, and you're charting dangerous waters," Teddy said. "Walk into an AA meeting and tell them what has happened. They'll ask you if you've ever had a drink. When you say yes, they'll tell you you're an alcoholic and try to sign you up. There are doctors who will tell you all this is an alteration of the hippocampus. There are recluses who believe we are the subject of government experiments. There are churches, cults, and association guilds selling magic bracelets on the topic at two a.m. on Channel Nine."

"Aren't there qualified experts somewhere?"

She hated herself for asking that. She loathed the politic of asking him. The question was weak and pleading and desperate in a sort of way that revulsed her character. She tried to think of a cover-up line before Teddy had a chance to score a point. But he only examined his fingernail and gave the matter thought.

"There's not much of a standard for this area, Nonni. It's not exactly a university research topic. There are pretenders, of course. But they're not even private investigators. They're mostly just losers. Broke, wayward individuals who smash their cars, have no fixed addresses, and absolutely no sex drive. Is that the kind of person you want to get advice from?"

"They don't sound like my type."

"They're not." He rubbed his hands together as if they were cold.

"So who do I tell?"

"You tell me."

Nonni reached into the pocket of her blouse, pulled out a lighter, and flicked it open. The flint wouldn't catch. This was the time to stand up, walk out, and drop an unlit cigarette in his trash can on the way. Even without the flint, the smell of gunpowder was intense in the room. Nonni imagined great greased pistons striking the lid of a cylinder in a green flash of excitement and so she stared at Teddy, letting the end of the cigarette touch her perfect marble lips.

"You have to promise to do three things for me," he said.

"What things?"

"One: don't tell anybody else."

"I'm hardly going to be printing this in the *National Post*."

"Two: you must give these beings a name."

"What name?"

"Any name. They feast on ambiguity. You must defeat that."

"I'll call them the Woodenheads."

Teddy turned his notebook around on the desk and picked up a black plastic pen. He began to scrawl left-handed in the margin. "The Woodenheads. Fabulous. Very Victorian. Three: the infection. Tell me how it came to be and describe it to me. You don't mind if I write this down, do you?"

Nonni held up her hand and a roll of brown bandage curled

off her wrist. "They turned my hands into a dredger that could not feel. My lungs have been metastasized. I was on a museum date the other day and I lost the sensation in my tongue. They're interfering with my sex life, Teddy. What's going on?"

Teddy put down his notebook and cleared his throat. "Show me the other injuries."

Nonni stood up. She pulled off her blouse and it fell like burlap to the floor. Teddy's face went blank. His eyes darted back and forth across the room in desperation, and then he looked up and did something Nonni had not seen before, he smiled.

"You must show me everything," he said.

Nonni let her skirt drop off. Her legs hardened into a slab of tungsten, and Nonni thought of a gorgeous metal spiral standing tall and erect, thousands of feet off the surface of some lonely planet, like Mars.

11.

Red bricks were plebbish, parking lots were cheap, and Mindy's was closed. So Nonni couldn't even return the shoes she had bought only nine days before. They had to be discarded because the cottonwood shadows contaminated them. That was the problem with minimum wage clerks on Seventeenth Avenue: they were either on their cell phones and didn't bother to show up for work, or else couldn't figure out how to fill out the exchange receipts. Nonni picked up a roll of pink paper that had been stuffed between the bricks. It read: *Good News for Modern Man!* Her cell phone rang, so she answered.

"This is detective Pierceman," the voice said.

"Should that mean something?"

"The mall."

"Which mall?"

"The one that left you covered in dust and not much else."

"That mall."

"We need to talk."

Nonni checked her watch. Opal face, gold hands, and leather strap. "I'm tied up today."

"Untie yourself."

"Can we make it Saturday," Nonni said. "No wait, Sunday?"

"We can make it right now."

"I don't talk to police. If you want to come arrest me, I'll give you my address."

"If I was going to arrest you, I wouldn't phone first. I'd have a pair of uniforms drive into that parking lot beside the cottonwood tree and stuff you into the back seat of a unit car. It's about the club, Nonni."

Friendly type. Nonni toyed with the antennae on the hood of her convertible. She let her eyes roll to one side and saw nothing but a telephone pole, a green letter box, and a pile of coarse gravel slumping against a shoe store. She shot a curl of menthol over her shoulder, and that, too, was unanswered. The windows that looked back on her from small tenement shops were shuttered and soaped. No one had lived in them for years. Certainly no one was looking out of them now.

"All right," Nonni said. "I'll come down to the district office."

"Meet me at Mulberry's."

"At a bar?"

"In the back room."

"When?"

"Now," she said. "You're not far off."

The detective hung up. Nonni closed her cell against her jaw. A blowfly buzzed off her wrist. The police were a bitter bunch. Liquor laws, tax receipts, vehicle registrations, and inopportune interviews were just some of the things they used to make life difficult. Anything was fair game. The laws may have changed after the bathhouse raid, but the police had not.

Seventeenth was the kind of strip where twenty-somethings came to spend money before they turned into thirty-somethings. The shops were pastel with broad picture windows, and the mannequins sported twelve inch waists. The sex shops were gone. The tobacco stands had vanished. Now there were Jaguars, Audis, and Corvettes parked outside antique parlours with outdoor patios. Deco art for alabaster living rooms. The women wore low-cut tops and thought they were risqué. Nonni didn't spend much time on Seventeenth Avenue except to buy shoes.

Mulberry's was a bar in the middle of the strip. It was popular after hockey games. Occasionally there were riots. A wood patio baked in the sun and baskets of gladiolas hung from posts. The inside was done up in fake Mexican décor, and the girls wore short skirts and red lipstick.

After Nonni had sat down, a tall middle-aged woman came in the front door. She had on a blue pinstriped suit and flats. Her hair was blond going grey, and her face had an embalmed look that stopped aging at fifty-five. She put her black note folder on the table and took a seat.

"How have you been feeling?" she said.

"I feel fine."

"Can you recall my face now?"

The face. Rather not. Why were female civil servants so septic? But there was no point in arguing the past. That was for museums.

"Thank you for your help," Nonni said.

"How are things at home?"

"My dryer is broken. The convertible needs a new transmission and apparently FM waves kill gardenias. Are you still on mall patrol?"

"I'm in vice."

"Wouldn't vice do interviews in the district office?"

"This isn't an interview." She arranged her books side by side on the table. There was a particular order they had to be set in. "I just wanted to chat."

Whenever police said they just wanted to chat it meant they didn't. Pierceman thumbed through her book, found the right page and studied the text. She smelled vaguely of glycol. Her joints moved awkwardly beneath her suit as if she were a bird, and Nonni wondered if she was wearing underwear. "Do you know a Hans?" Pierceman said.

"Can't say that I do."

"You've never met him?"

"Not that I know of."

Pierceman breathed in quick once through her nose. "Perhaps you know him by a different name?"

"Try one."

"Lance, Dash, Dan."

"I definitely don't know any Dashes."

"I think he might go by the name Daniel in the underground world."

"What underground world?" Nonni said.

"The sexual underground world."

"Oh, that underground world."

The detective tapped a ballpoint pen on the table as if it were a cigarette. Ex-smoker, Nonni thought. An ex-smoker who can't get laid. All roads led to Rome. In the corner of the bar was one of the archaic wooden Indians that stood holding a package of cigars. Nonni thought that they were outlawed either because they were racist or tobacco was bad for you.

"Perhaps you would recognize a description if I gave you one."

"Try me."

"White male, twenty-five years old. Five foot eleven, one hundred seventy-five pounds. Blond hair, blue eyes. Has a tattoo on his right ankle. Something like a surfer, apparently."

"A surfer?" Nonni said.

"Tanned, athletic. Beach culture."

"You mean he's hot."

Pierceman cocked her head off an inch. She had a lifeless void around her, as if she was sucking the air away from the palm tree that was potted by the booth. The waitress stayed on the far side of the room and let nickels drop into her register one at a time.

"Hot?"

"Handsome. Sexually exciting."

"I wouldn't know about the adverbial part, but you've seen him at the Onyx Club?"

"I go to a lot of clubs."

"Which ones?"

"Starlight. Close-friends. Moonshine. I used to go to Doubles before it went queer, and before that I went to Lucky's, but it got closed down because of the asbestos."

"Asbestos?"

"In the couches. Apparently it's bad for your lungs."

"These are all swing clubs you mentioned?"

"Vanilla swing," Nonni shrugged. "No SM."

This must have been a complex equation. The policewoman nodded as if the definitions might take a very long time. "Have you seen him at one of those?"

"Doesn't ring a bell."

Pierceman's pale pink fingernail slid down the column of notes as she studied the page. Her handwriting was sharp and all the upside down t's had punctured the paper. "It says here he signed the Onyx registry on Friday, June eighth, and that you signed in as well."

"I'm always there on the second Friday and the last Saturday of the month whatever dates those were."

"What's the second Friday?"

"The Fetish Play Party."

"Fetish Party."

"You know, dress-up." Most people understood dress-up.

"Can you recall him from that night?"

"People are in costume, so recognizing someone you don't know can be difficult."

"I'd think a young man like that would catch your attention."

Explaining to the detective what actually caught her attention would be hard. Confessing what held it for more than three minutes probably dangerous. Nonni figured she'd have better luck explaining the laws of lust to the Mayan textile on the wall, or the Blackfoot tobacconist in the corner.

"There are a lot of people there," Nonni said. "Fifty or sixty, and they change every week. There's lots of handsome men there. Very handsome men, so one is not really more memorable than the next, if you get what I mean."

"Not really."

"Detective, I don't mean to be self-aggrandizing. I know you're a busy woman and don't have time to waste on coyness. I don't have any problems garnering attention from as many men as I want. I can get them to do whatever I like. So sometimes it's hard to recall them all. As individuals, I mean."

Pierceman touched her pen to her ear. She put a grainy high school photo on the table. Ten years old, one inch square and bent, this one had been stored in a musty archive for years and mildew had collected at the edge.

"Can you look at this," she said.

"This is a graduation photo."

"Can you look at it closely?"

Nonni held the photo to her face. A bland photo of a bland student that had no sexual existence wouldn't come into focus. "It really doesn't mean anything to me. Can you tell me what this is about?"

The detective gazed up at a pink, stuffed parrot that hung from a brass ring on the ceiling. Not many things in life deserved her attention. "There's been an accident."

"What kind of accident?"

"Someone was strangled."

"By accident?"

"This Daniel fellow, by whatever means."

"Okay."

"What I'm saying is that he's dead," Pierceman said. She brushed some lint off her jacket. Nonni lit up a menthol. The detective glanced up at the NO SMOKING sign on the wall, and the parrot rocked forth once in the breeze. "Can you tell me some more about the Onyx Club?"

"I'm sure you already know a great deal."

"Give me your take on it. I wouldn't want to make prejudgments."

"It's an SM club where adults go to have fun," Nonni said. The lime in the neck of her bottle got stuck, so she used a tooth pick to wedge it out. "Consenting adults. They don't serve liquor. There's no money exchanged, anyway. It's private. You can't just walk in. You have to buy a membership at another place, on another day, and go to one of their meet and greets first. So I guess it is what you would call a private place as defined by the latest Supreme Court ruling, and definitely not covered by the Gaming and Liquor Act regulations."

"I've read the rules. Tell me the kind of play that goes on there."

Chinese water torture had a particular rhythm to the drips, and the detective was doing a good job of imitating that with her pen on the table. Nonni tried to imagine her naked, then bound or doing the binding, or soaked in latex, and even dressed as a cruel prison guard with garish lipstick. But none of that worked, and Nonni knew at once that the woman lacked any erotic confluence, so a merger of their minds was an impossibility.

"How much detail do you want?"

"As much as you think is relevant."

"Flogging, spanking, role play, bondage, electric wands, fisting, domination, orgasm denial, erotic humiliation, submission, transsexual parades, probing, piercing, and punting."

A magpie lighted on the balcony rail. Outside on the sidewalk, a gorgeous twenty-year-old stopped and checked the heel of her red stilettoes for a wad of tar, which at that moment appeared to be the centre of the cosmos for her.

"None of that bothers you?"

"No," Nonni said.

"What else?"

"One of your agents must have given you a complete list."

"We don't put agents in there."

"Of course not."

The detective tapped the eraser of her pencil on the notebook. The utensil was obviously essential for her computations. In another solar system, this woman must have sat on the couch with her lover, read Anaïs Nin out loud, or hidden a vibrator beneath her pillow — but no matter how hard Nonni tried, she couldn't place that black hole of the universe.

"Is there ever any choking?" she said.

"How do you mean?"

"I think that's self-explanatory."

"Not really. There's bagging, masking, face sitting, manual breath play, fantasy breath play, tit suffocation, hand smothering, and latex mummification. There's also a kind that is done with a form of Japanese rubber that the victim has to chew his way out of to breathe, and a few months ago two of the girls were experimenting with enriched oxygen play. It has something to do with ions in the air. Which one did you mean?"

Nonni settled back in the chair. The leather felt soft. A pink geranium fluttered in a pot above the patio. The wooden Indian had blue, puffed lips and orange feathers sticking out of his headband. His smile was large. He'd made a sale.

"Does anyone ever pass out during these games?" Pierceman said.

"I have."

"What happened?"

"I came really hard."

Pierceman's notes were in shorthand. "Don't people get hurt?"

"Some of the fellows go home with pretty large welts if they've had it with the nine-tails. I don't think they sit down for a week."

"Has anyone ever been hanged with a rope?"

A rope, a rope, three kingdoms for a rope.

"In fact there has been a few. There was a fantasy execution last fall. For some reason our visitors from the United Kingdom are particularly fond of that one. They used a trap door and a harness under the shoulder pits. It took them weeks to set up. They were very fussy about the details. The kind of wood. The length of rope. The difference between an elected and appointed Senate seems to be an issue. They liked the Italian hemp."

"Has anyone ever done it for real?"

The wooden Indian was closer then. He was standing only a few booths away from Nonni. His face was shiny and his wooden mouth was round, like saying the letter O to an inside joke, and his cheeks made Nonni smile too.

"Not at the club. That's for the serious players."

"Are you a serious player, Nonni?"

"I'm an innately sexual person. It's what I do. It's who I am. Do you want to hear the details of my personal life?"

"Not really."

"Shame." Nonni forced herself to look down to the small triangle of skin that showed between the lapels of the detective's suit. The skin had a cold reptilian look, and there was nothing there for the living.

"What do you tell your husband," Pierceman said. "When you go out to this club?"

"I don't tell him anything."

"You must say something. That you are going out with friends, or maybe that you are going bowling or to play gin rummy."

"No, detective, you see, my husband comes with me."

"His name never appears on the register."

"A lot of couples do it that way."

"Why?"

When interrogators were concerned with ridiculous details it either meant that they had no clue what they were really after, or they were saving the accusations for later. The detective's cuffs were new, but unlinked. Her suit was drab, but not dowdy. Maybe it was easier just to give unto Caesar.

"Convenience. Parsimony. I'm not sure what you're getting at. Look, I don't know the fellow you're looking for. The club is quite up front about everything that goes on there. If you want a date sometime, well you're not really my type, but I'd be glad to have you along for an evening. I don't really know what else I can tell you. To the best of my knowledge there has never been anyone strangled to death at the club. That's the last thing we want there."

"I never said it was at the club."

"I'm lost now. A traffic intersection? Downtown Toronto? The middle of the Pre-Cambrian period. What's the connection?"

"Did you take Daniel home after the club?"

"Hardly," she said. "The young ones can't keep up with me and I don't have strangers into my house. Besides, I left with my husband. Ask anyone. Ask Gwen or Don. Heidi and Randle. The marathon couple. Can't remember their names. Both bi. Very hot. Very svelte, drinks. Try them. Why are you asking me all this?"

The index finger on the Blackfoot was then set at his pursed lips. One of his black eyebrows furrowed. Nonni thought for sure both hands had always been around his tobacco box. Perhaps she had said too little. Or not enough.

"A young man is dead," Pierceman said. "There was bondage paraphernalia at the scene."

"Half the bedrooms of the nation have stuff like that. Or the half that I've been to, anyway. Besides, the ones who kill themselves tend to be into the gadgets, don't they? I mean young men who asphyxiate themselves. They get sexually excited and strangle themselves while jerking off with clotheslines and pantyhose or apron strings from mail-order catalogues. If they find specialty equipment, then it's a bonus for them. I don't know what the figures are, but it must be dozens every year. Even young girls do it these days. I read about it in the newspaper. There was that young girl who strangled herself with a shower hose in the bathtub. I guess when you die in water you bloat up and the medical examiner needed a special instrument to extract the dildo."

The tobacco statue was proximal, then predominant. The extended cigar box touched her elbow. The walnut eyebrows now raised in mock surprise, as if it had discovered a new horrible secret behind a closed door that it wasn't sharing. Nonni gazed at the detective and thought of the different ways of taking her, bound naked to a bench with a clove-hitch gag in her mouth, pissing on her face through a plastic funnel, this poor pasty bitch that no one else would have.

"That was in Edmonton."

"Figures," Nonni said. "Really detective, why should the Onyx be any more responsible for this event than someone who sells nylon rope or tit clamps?"

"Because of the particular kind of club it is." The detective leaned forward in her seat. There was a devil in the details. "Because of the influence it can have on young men and women who don't know any better."

"They could find cruder stuff on the Internet."

"The Internet doesn't exert that kind of mass."

"Mass?" Nonni said. Like malediction or masquerade.

"Like bad gravity. Only people and places can do that."

"I don't think we have those kind of people at the Onyx."

"You mentioned Gwen and Don."

"The owners."

"You know them?"

"For years, even."

"What kind of people are they?"

"They're good, law-abiding people. They have jobs. They pay taxes. They might even vote Conservative."

"We'll drop by and talk to them," Pierceman said. She added a name to her notebook.

The menthol burned down to its end. Nonni felt the heat in her nail. She looked for a place to stuff the ash; a tray, a tin can, any open door, but of course there were none. A culvert or cathedral would have done the trick. The Blackfoot was not a foot away. His cigar box open and inviting. His wooden face sparse and unapologetic, as if he had been in this spot waiting to receive her debris all along.

"Detective, I may not be as smart as a lot of people," Nonni said. "I don't spend a lot of time reading books or legal papers like you, but I have read the newspapers. The Labaye case. It says you have no right going in there. It says the police have to leave us alone."

Pierceman gazed up at the ceiling and her eyes drifted back like she was reminiscing on an arrest made years before. "I'm glad you read the papers. Nonni, you're a fine-looking woman, and I know you're used to getting what you want. But I don't think you quite understand the situation. At the scene where we found Daniel, the floor was scraped and depressed. A great weight had sunk the hardwood. There was sawdust spewed on the bed and a smell of copper in the air. There was an imprint of a face on the wall. A person's features had been imprinted into the plaster, or else pushed out from the other side."

"Perhaps Worker's Compensation can help."

"This has nothing to do with lawyers or judges or the parliament, or a dozen philosophers or liberal free speech workers or the United Nations. We have to keep order in our dimension. One side of the wall clean from the other."

"Who exactly is this *we* you are referring to?"

"Do you know the story of the three hundred Spartans?"

"I like the version with Kirk Douglas."

"Then you would appreciate that there are people in our society who think they can party all night long and everything will be just wonderful when they wake up the next morning. They refuse to acknowledge that sacrifice must be made to keep them safe. They don't understand they are being used. They don't see what kind of machinations come out of the woodwork at a club like yours."

Machinations. Woodwork. Dimensions. How was it two people could use the same words and not be talking about the same subject, even the same universe? But Nonni didn't like the idea that this interloper would even have such words in her vocabulary, so she wished the wooden Indian could produce a hatchet from his tobacco box and end the interview promptly.

"You're quite the crusader," she said.

"These parties, as you call them, have resonance. Eventually you get uninvited visitors. I'm not talking about a few hookers, a domestic dispute, or even mass pornographic production. I'm talking about a very different kind of visitor. Look, we could have the Onyx shut down inside a moment. In a minute, we could have a dozen uniformed constables in there kicking down the doors. The club would close. Everyone who set foot inside there would be charged with being in a common bawdy house. It's still in the Criminal Code, go check. But that is not what we want. We want a special kind of solution for this special kind of problem. And I think you can help us with that."

"That sounds dirty," Nonni said. "But sorry. Not interested."

"Somebody will be." Pierceman gazed at the wooden Indian statue as if the two had been indifferent colleagues for a very long time. She felt in her pocket and pulled out another pen, but when she realized it was not a cigarette, she tossed it aside.

12.

Nonni sat back on the puffed couch in her living room and stared at the porcelain dolls in the mahogany hutch. There was a set from the nineteenth-century Hunan province that huddled in silence — blue and white poinsettia swirls of clay that never moved. She could make out eyes and lips in the patterns. They must have been lonely, trapped in that world of kiln blasted skulls and brittle flesh. The house settled in the evening cool. The glass hands touched and tinkled.

Her rubber suit didn't fit right. The ankles bagged and a crease formed under her breast. She had bought the suit in Amsterdam. It was supposed to be a black skin that covered her body like paint and reeked of need. Instead, the rubber was clammy. A flake of talcum powder balled in sweat, formed a paste, and rolled down her shoe.

Gerry came into the room. He had on a loose white shirt and sloppy black pants that looked like they had come off a peasant farmer in Renaissance Europe.

"Is that what you're wearing?" she said.

"It's the theme tonight."

"Right. The Depression-ist thing."

"Impressionist."

"Who are you supposed to be?"

"Van Gogh," Gerry said.

"What did he do?"

"He was a painter."

"I know he was a painter." She leaned forward in the chair and crossed her legs. "What did he do that was kinky?"

"He painted sunflowers, which was artistically subversive."

"That's not kinky."

"He cut off his ear."

"With a knife or a scalpel?"

"It's in the history books."

"Why did he do that?" she said.

"Over some woman."

"Did she cut it off?"

"He cut it off."

"It would have been better if she had cut it off. Why didn't he get her to cut it off?"

"I don't know, Non."

Sometimes people didn't get it. Doctors didn't get it, poets didn't get it, politicians didn't get it. Every once in a while, French aristocrats didn't get it and then they got their heads cut off. Nonni thought that might be exciting to watch, but nobody did that sort of thing anymore. Gerry unwrapped a batch of oil brushes and stuffed them into a satchel that was tied to his belt.

"What are you supposed to be?" he said.

"I'm a rubber suit."

"How is that impressionistic?"

"I'm an impressionistic rubber suit. I'm going to sit on someone's face and they'll get the impression they're suffocating."

Gerry went over and leaned against the fire place. He had a glass of Pinot Noir. He always had one five-ounce glass of Okanagan red before they went out to the club. "Nonni, talk to me."

Nonni rubbed Lycra oil down her thighs. The beads ran off her calves onto the carpet.

"Why?"

"Why not?"

"Because I don't want to talk tonight. I don't want to talk about relationships, and I don't want to talk about Impressionism, or urban social structure, or quantum physics, or the end of the Cretaceous Period. I don't really want to talk about anything unless it's dirty. I want to go to the club, find some slut, tie him up, and then do something that really, really hurts him."

The reflection of her face rippled in the glass hutch. The window was divided into panes, and her ghost features appeared in four different sections, each one fainter than the last. If there was a fifth pane, perhaps she would not exist.

"You sound different," Gerry said.

"How?"

"Guttural is the word that comes to mind. Like that woman who did radio propaganda during the war."

"Does it turn you on?"

He dropped his head against the mantel. The natural gas flame licked out of the hearth and curled up in the chimney. For the past decade, every time Gerry turned on the fire he rested his palm on the stack, expecting the heat to expand the brick, and explain the virtue of the universe to him. But this time he just tapped the mortar with his knuckle and turned away. "Something's happened," he said. "Or I guess it's better to say something isn't happening."

"And what isn't that?"

"We've been together nine years now." This sounded like it was going to be a long speech.

"Ten," she said.

"At first everything was different. Everything was exciting. It was an invitation to an intimate life. It was like by going out and doing these outrageous things we'd get to know each other better, or love each other more. But that hasn't happened."

"What did you expect?"

"Something more profound."

"What could be more profound than what we've got, except more of it?"

He stared down at the carpet. There was a point embedded in the threads, so far away that he had to strain to grasp it. Perhaps a molecule of iodine, iridium, or just irrationality. "Nonni, you're a beautiful woman. In fact, you're perfect. You're a fantasy come true, more than any man could ever ask for. I said that to myself the first time I saw you. And I know hundreds of people still say it today, but sometimes I wonder if there's anything else going on behind that gorgeous face of yours."

"I like going to the club," she said. Metaphysical points weren't worth talking about. Continuum propositions were a waste of time. They were the kind of thing people supposedly fought wars over decades ago and weren't worthwhile going through again.

"I like going to the club too," he said.

"So what's the problem?"

"How about we go and talk about painters. Or commune on the confines of our censorship laws. I don't know, maybe we swim in a vat of watercolours and experience new pigment perversion. But at least we can relate in some dimension other than the orgasm."

"You and Gwen can talk about that other dimension."

Gerry slumped against the wall and his fingers spread into a wide V across his forehead. Everyone was a sinner. Every time they had this conversation he had to bring up history: The Treaty of Versailles, Ghent, or some meteorological phenomenon from Pompeii. "Over the past ten years," he said. "We have played with over three hundred and sixty-eight couples. You have had sex with four hundred and ten people. I have been flogged by eight dozen dommes, tortured by twelve leather men, six transsexual mistresses, and performed a score of sacrifices to gods that you had no intention of believing in. Fidelity has never been an issue."

Nonni adjusted the bronze zipper on the ankle of her rubber leg. "Gerry, just go to the club and have a good time. Do your secessionist thing."

"Alone?"

"We have already talked about this. It was last July. A Tuesday. We were in the workshop, remember?"

There were bits of maple dust floating in the summer warmth and Gerry was working out an axle design on his lathe. It was twilight, and the moths had come out frantic and in a pollen frenzy.

"The agreement we had," she said. "Was that if one of us really wanted to go to the club and the other one really wanted to do something else then that's what we'd do, no hard feelings."

Gerry ran his hand along the mantel on the fireplace. There was a bronzed photo of the two of them standing on a fiord in Gros Morne National Park wearing pink raincoats. Her throat felt strange. A brass tube sending a clear message from a dank ancient seminary. "You asked me what I wanted and this is it. I want you to go to the Onyx Club and have a party with Gwen and Don. I want you to talk about the rise of nineteenth-century realism and its slide into Dadaism. I want you to compare the light of Monet and Klimt and decide finally, once and for all, which one is more secular. That sounds sensible to me. In fact, it sounds both intimate and sensible. It would be better for our relationship if you did that. Think of us as the left and right side of the brain. Together we form a whole. That has got to be the way it works."

Gerry stood silent against the fireplace. His eyes darted from her boots to her hair as if he was taking stock of a new object, species, or stigmata. The cat came up and brushed against his leg.

Nonni stood. Her rubber suit had warmed and melted around the curves of her hips. The wetness reflected in the flickering light of the fireplace. In her heels, she was over six feet. She could touch the ceiling if she wanted. Her mouth felt brilliant. Hard as polished chromium. "Don't look so glum, Gerry. Give me a call if you're going to be late. I'm going out."

"To where?"

"A young girl's house. Don't worry. She's eighteen. I met her in the gallery, remember?"

"No," he said.

"Aryan looking. University student." She walked over to the mirror above the fireplace and stared at her face. The skin was marble smooth and the lips ochre lust.

"Aryan?"

"Not right wing, Gerry, don't sweat it. She just looks like a direct import from Berlin, circa 1936."

"You sound sentimental."

"Have you ever wondered about that?" she said. "Why the concept of Fascism is so sexual, yet the legacy of Marxism is utterly platonic? They are both dictatorships, yet one fosters erotic experimentation and the other smothers it? Where do you think that came from?"

Gerry stared at her. The cat wandered away.

"What does she want?" he said finally.

"She's an archaeology student," Nonni shrugged. She found lipstick. "She either wants me to be a guarantor on her student loan, or else pierce her with bones. Not your cup of tea. Don't worry. I'll clean the bones first."

Gerry picked up his sack filled with brushes and his black felt hat and walked out the door. The handle on the stained oak cabinet in the foyer swung open, and then the copper knob ticked shut. She waited by the window with a palm on the sofa arm until his truck had rounded the corner and the red tail lights vanished in a grove of weeping birch. Then she found her cell phone and punched in the number. A young woman answered.

"Dietrich," she said.

"Nonni, is that you?" the girl said. Her voice was full of want, which was perfect for the occasion, and desperation, which would be better for the next.

"Of course it's me."

"I've been looking all over for you."

"Try answering your phone," Nonni said. She picked her keys off the hutch and walked to the garage entrance. The motor started up with a flick of an electronic button while she was still going down the stairs.

"I've been phoning the number you gave me and it didn't go through."

Nonni brushed the door of the convertible and checked a soap stain on the windshield. The glass squealed. "You must have copied it down wrong."

"I blanked out the last time we were together."

"You can make it up to me."

Through the phone, there was the sound of tavern glasses clinking, ping pong balls bouncing, and young people laughing with no clue how their lives would be at the end of a wasted evening.

"I can't believe what we did," Dietrich said.

"We didn't do anything my dear. You trespassed in a federal building, stole a priceless artifact from an academic institution, and then walked out on me without saying goodbye."

There was a rattle of fear through the lines, the milling of dust and conscience, neglect and musk. That gorgeous quick breath the panicked always take when they see their last plighted hope. A small patch of wax on the hood that hadn't been polished caught Nonni's attention, so she licked her finger and shined it up. Most likely it would only take that long before the poor girl figured out what she needed to ask.

"How can I make it up?" Dietrich said.

"We can talk about it when I pick you up."

"When?"

"Now, of course."

"You want to come out with me now?"

"In actually, darling. Your place. We can hardly discuss the chance of you going to jail for the next three years in a restaurant, can we?"

Dietrich exhaled. Her voice had no bottom. There was the sound of music and singing in the background and people who had no worries or cares in the world.

"Just keep it in a safe place until I find you," Nonni said. She got in the driver's seat and adjusted the mirror.

"I am at Troccu's Bar with tennis friends."

"They are not your friends. They laugh at you behind your back. I am your only friend right now. Start walking. What are you wearing?"

It took the facile mind of an infant hours to work through the easiest of equations and see their worth, but eventually she came around. "A blue dress, and pumps," she said. "I'm sitting on my rain coat."

"Gorgeous." Nonni hit the garage control and waited for the door to open. "Do not bother to say goodbye to your pals. Do not finish your pink Bellini. Do not tell anyone where you are going. Go into the washroom. Put your clothes in the trash can. Wear nothing but your slicker and pumps. Then get in a cab and meet me underneath the street lamp where I picked you up last time, like the little whore that you are. I'll pay the fare with my card on the phone right now. Go."

Nonni hung up. She found a credit card and dialed a cab. The lights of the city slid past in bars of yellow and neon orange and then vanished in her rear-view mirror. The air was dense. Red alder swayed in the sky and summer lightning erupted. The night, the night, always the night, Nonni thought, and her hand trembled on the steering wheel. She drove down Sixth Avenue in her black rubber suit. Everything was the night.

Dietrich waited on the deserted corner beneath the street light just like she was supposed to. Nervous, shaking, and dripping wet. Nonni stopped the car at the end of the block and watched the broken twig. She shifted her weight from one leg to the other and held the wet purse between two timid hands. Nonni thrust the car into gear and squealed around the corner. She came to a stop on the pavement and the girl's head snapped around to the lifeline of gravel.

She got in soaking wet, and there was no point in giving her any time to talk. Nonni drove away and slipped her hand in between the girl's thighs.

"I didn't think you'd come," Dietrich said.

"Of course I shall."

Dietrich lived just off-campus, in a drab condominium with a hallway that smelled of beer. The light in the foyer was out, and down the hall there was the subdued laughter of drunken graduate students talking Joyce. The inside of the suite was neat, sparse, and precisely ready. A fold-out bed, a desk of pressed wood, and a lonely bookcase whose texts would bear sole witness. There was a Blackfoot mask and a photograph of Albert Einstein. Nonni tossed an umbrella away and Dietrich slunk to the table.

"Do you have neighbours?"

"The walls are concrete," she said.

Nonni walked the perimeter of the room, examined a portrait, picked up a book, and flipped open the cover. "Do you study too much?"

Dietrich sat at the kitchen table with her hands folded. The colour had gone from her face. There was a blue hue in her thumbs. She followed the rubber suit around the room and winced when the heels touched the floor.

"Far too much."

"Do you have study friends?"

"No."

"But you play tennis?"

"They don't live on campus."

"Will they come around tonight?"

"They don't know where I live."

Her head listed against the cork board. A tack fell out and a photograph of the Bluenose followed it to the floor. A bead of water clung to the side of her nose.

"Which cupboard is the mask in?"

Dietrich pointed to a small locker that separated the kitchen from the living room. The mask had been hidden in white tissue and wrapped with twine. Nonni opened the package on the table. The wooden face was varnished with a thousand years of oily resin. The mouth was round and the eyes had rolled back in narrow delight.

"I can't even remember how I got it out," she said.

“Put it down as a gesture to love.”

“Wasn’t it?”

“Not really, darling, but it’s a good start.” Nonni sat in the plain wooden chair and crossed her legs. “And now the next step is for you to tell me you’re my filthy little bitch, drop those wet clothes to the floor, and get down on your knees.”

Dietrich twitched. Her hands cowered to the shoulders of her raincoat and the sopping garment flopped on the floor. So beautifully the innocence falls, Nonni thought. How stupid it was to be young. How stupid it was to be stupid. And then the girl sank down to her knees and drooped forward with her soaking wet hair dripping on the tile. Nonni cinched the girl’s hands behind her back with a belt from the raincoat and then found a computer cord on the desk. She wrapped it four times around her neck then yanked the loop up once. The girl’s head dropped sideways and her eyes went white.

“Do exactly what I tell you or I will choke you to death on the spot,” Nonni said.

Dietrich’s lids fluttered. A pearl of spit formed at the corner of her mouth in that perfect moment of aroused offence.

“I want you,” she said.

“Shut up. We all want something.”

Nonni knocked the plates off the wood table, then lifted Dietrich up with one arm. She was amazed at how strong intent had made her. How ribbed the muscle in her biceps had become. She could have pitched her poor victim across the room or out the window, but instead she dumped Dietrich supine over the table, and tied her wrists and ankles to the furniture with a pair of nylons.

“Now listen to me.” Nonni steepled her fingers and reflected favourably on the words of Sartre, Masoch, and even Hume. “It’s important you understand your position in the grand scheme of things. You're a thief and a slut who can't find a friend. But somehow you were lucky enough to be working in a museum bar when I came in. No one really knows or cares where you are right now."

Nonni touched Dietrich's tattoos. A dragon, a marmot, an ashtray filled with dust. Dietrich was afraid. That was good. The air in the room got jungle moist. There were branches snapping and strange birds calling, and the naked white girl tied to the desk gurgled in a swamp of need as Nonni struck her thighs with a ruler until they were welted, and the girl could cry no more.

Then Nonni took the stolen mask and held it up to the light. The wood smelled of academic papers and vaults where no one ever got laid and ivory professors fixated with atomic weight designations. So, she slipped the mask onto Dietrich face. The girl screamed and shook her head. But Nonni wrapped the duct tape around her temple until the wood formed a seal on her captive's head. The face reminded Nonni of a *Canadian Geographic* mummy in Bathurst Sound.

The sound of Dietrich weeping pleased Nonni, and so she walked to the bookshelf and thumbed through a few texts on talus slopes, Mayan civilization, and linear algebra. No books on SM, though, so she recalled with more pleasure the young girl taking the mask from the wall of the museum like a common criminal might have done in pre-industrial Britain.

A pool of sweat collected in Dietrich's navel. It smelled of cow parsnip seed. Her chest rose and fell in deep cycles. Her voice was muffled and far away.

"It's important you stay calm," Nonni lit a cigarette and watched a line of menthol rise up through the beads of the plastic chandelier. "Don't let panic over take arousal. Sustaining arousal is paramount. Besides, you don't want to use up all your oxygen right away."

Snot collected in the nostril of the mask. Amazing that mucus could travel so far. The girl's feet twitched in a syncopated fashion, and the inside of her thigh had become slick.

"I have to ask you a few questions before we proceed," Nonni said. She crossed her arms and smoked. As she walked around the table, the heels of her shoes clicked on the bare floor. "And you need to think about the answers carefully in your position, because one thing I won't tolerate from my toys is lying. Question number one: the young blond boy at the club. Do you know him?"

Dietrich calmed a little knowing that someone was still speaking to her and she hadn't been left alone. She spoke in a trebled mixture of terror and titillation through the wood.

"What boy?"

"Daniel."

"I don't know a Daniel."

"You've screwed him."

"I haven't screwed anybody."

"You are lying to me now," Nonni said.

"Please take the mask off."

"No, no."

"At least kiss me."

"I don't kiss."

"I don't like this game."

"That's because this is not a game. I guess you thought this was going to be sort of a lesbian bondage scene with silk scarves, lavender candles, and a lot of smoochie-smooch like you read about in the paperbacks," Nonni said. "Sorry, but that's not me either. Chantal, are you friends with her?"

"Who?"

"Daniel's friend."

"No."

"You've fucked her too, haven't you?"

"Why do you think I've fucked everybody?"

"Do you know what they did to people in the French Resistance when they wouldn't talk? They'd put a sheepskin bladder over their head, one taken from their own occupied fields, and let them drown in the urine if they wouldn't speak. The parallels to your predicament are obvious."

This was good. This was hot. This was historic. Nonni picked up a fistful of the girl's hair that flopped from behind the wood and moved the abacus bead of terror one inch down the rod. "Tell me everything."

"I don't know anything."

"Are you an agent?"

"A what?" Dietrich said.

"An agent? A saboteur? A malignant."

The girl thrashed from side to side and then she panicked. It was going to happen sooner or later. The table rocked back and forth. The legs struck the floor. But the cables were bound too tight and she could not escape. A wine glass fell off the shelf and shattered on the tile.

"Stop this."

"Everyone is having too much fun," Nonni said. "And although you can't know it, now, you are too."

Nonni squeezed the clump of hair so tight, water ran out between her knuckles. It smelled of cheap shampoo. There was a time for irony and for levity. For deception and horror. But a good commander also knew there was a moment when naked truth was the most potent weapon at hand.

"Here is the issue up front," she said. "I'm not going to stop until you tell me what I want to know. You know of fifth columnists and conspirators, and you will tell me everything about them. You will tell me every detail and give names and dates. Serial numbers and codes. Modus operandi is of prime importance. I'd hate to have you suffocate under that mask before you have a chance to service me, but that is the price of doing business in the sexual underground. You need to take a look at your position and decide whether you want to make me happy or frustrate me. I would give the matter severe reflection. Let's look at the facts. You have let a woman who you hardly know pick you up after only one date and take you home. She has stripped you naked and tied you to a table with a computer cord wrapped around your neck and a stolen mask taped to your face, and now she is asking you a series of bizarre, and quite frankly, disturbing questions. You have no friends, no relatives, no roommates, and I am assuming not one pen pal in the entire world who knows where you are right now. You don't know how many times I have done this before or if I never have. I could be an expert at neck knots or a complete beginner. I could have done three hits of Ecstasy before I met you, or I could have strangled a dozen girls and stuffed them in the trunk of my sports car, you just don't know."

"Red, red, red," Dietrich said. "I know the safe word. God, red, you crazy bitch, red."

"You know nothing." Nonni let the cord swing back and forth under the table and patted the forehead of the mask. "So you'd better start learning to accept the reality and play along. I am now going to ask you the most important question of the evening, and as my patience, and quite frankly my libido is running thin, you'd better answer it properly. Who commands you?"

"Fuck you," she said.

"In the museum. Behind the mask. In the wood. Every time you rub yourself in that dirty white little communal shower of yours thinking that some star quarterback is going to love you until your Canada Pension comes in, someone commands you. So, tell me now: who is it?"

And then Nonni stood upright and folded her arms, and a great flush of arousal made her hard as the Sphinx. "It's them, isn't it? It is the Woodenheads."

The silent mask turned towards Nonni, and beneath the knots she could see their empty hearts, hear the ancient drum of their pulse. She saw it then, the moment of possession, the second of revelation.

"Tell me about them." Nonni squatted down to table level. "Tell me what language they speak to you in. Is it ancient? Aramaic, Babylonian. Or does it come in pictograms or hieroglyphs? Sometimes, I know, it is not a language, it is a syllogism. It could just be a collection of milk bottles left on your porch, or a cumulus cloud forming in your backyard. It could be the names of boyfriends you have hated over the years. You think that kind of thing is random, but it's not. You have to keep track of these things. You have to keep records. I know you have. You're diligent. You're patient. Your type doesn't let these things go unrecorded. Where are they?"

"They aren't anywhere," Dietrich said. "I haven't been sent by anyone. Nonni, I want you. I love you."

"This is pointless."

Nonni went to the counter and pulled open a drawer. A miniature hammer and a box of polished finishing nails. How incredibly, impressionistically, perfect. Finishing nails for expedient home repair by the liberated gal who won't ring the service shop for help. She unrolled the box and put them on the table so through the eye holes of the mask Dietrich could see them glimmer too and she cried. The curtain ruffled in a wisp of heat from the vent.

"So now I am afraid we shall have to proceed directly to the experimental stage of our evening," Nonni said. "You see my dear. I believe that you are indeed an agent sent by the Woodenheads to do me harm. In fact, I believe that you are their flesh and blood incarnate, or wood and iron actually, for they have no flesh of their own. And I am going to prove this point directly to you now. I am going to puncture your pretty schoolgirl little teats with these chrome spikes. Now if your flesh remains pure, that is to say corporeal flesh of blood and veins and skin, then all is forgiven, and we can be the best of friends. Better than friends actually. Allies. But if not, if your eyes become glass and your mammary dense as oak, then we both shall know that you are one with them and have been lying all along. Sort of like the Anglo-Saxon ritual, trial by fire or water. Since you're the archeologist, I know you will appreciate both the irony and accuracy of our little endeavour."

Nonni licked the chrome nail. She perched it against Dietrich's nipple until the tip made a divot in her flesh. This was going to be a "chokecherry slow." But by then the breast hardened and calcified. The fat changed to alkaloid. The areola bore traces of gneiss. And then the body of this pathetic naked girl tied to a kitchen table, with a gallon of sweat pouring from every cleavage and cleft, was no longer soft nor human, but flat and worn. Smooth with age, dust again. There was chatter. The Monet on the wall trembled. A bargain was being struck. Computations made. A calculation was voiced in cuneiform, and Nonni came straw and confetti, and in a few moments she was walking between the leaves of an alder grove back to her sports car.

13.

The lights were on in the living room. They were on in the kitchen and the pantry and they were on in the hallway. They were bright and stark lights as if the house had been abandoned with the galley open and the hatch up.

Nonni parked the car in the underground garage and shut off the ignition. Then the voices filtered down the stairs. Unsettled marred voices, ones that bloated up from a deep well of trouble but Nonni rattled the keys in her pocket and went upstairs anyway.

Gerry sat with Gwen and Don at the kitchen table. Their hands were folded and they stared at a pile of crumpled pink papers on the slate table. They still had their costumes on, but they sagged, tired and disheveled in the sweat of a long night.

Nonni tossed her wallet on the counter and found a glass in the cabinet. The sweat on the inside of her rubber suit had cooled off and the neoprene creaked when she moved.

"What happened?" she said.

Gerry glanced up. He looked older. He shook his head and frowned. "The club got raided."

Gwen stared out the back window to the suburb of tall brick chimneys and green cottonwoods that rested securely in the middle-class dark.

"What do you mean, raided?" Nonni said.

"Busted," Gerry said. "Searched. Warranted. Broke up. Destroyed. They came. They saw. They interrogated. They made twenty-eight arrests and laid a total of seventy-nine charges."

Nonni drank the water that tasted of baking soda and then leaned against the granite counter. Her lips were salty and her palms were bruised. The inside of her suit was stiff.

"For what?" she said.

Gerry put on a pair of reading glasses and poked through the court papers that were marred with menacing stamps and signatures. He selected one and flattened the page out.

"Me, personally, for section 197.1 of the Criminal Code of Canada," he said. "Being in a common bawdy house without a lawful excuse. Also, section 173.1. Committing an indecent act. And a section 167. Appearing in an immoral theatrical performance. Whatever that is."

Nonni pulled her zipper down to her navel. The sweat ran over her thumb and trickled across her stomach. Specks of sawdust floated in the wash.

"What bawdy house?"

"The Onyx Club," he said.

"It's not a bawdy house."

"It is now."

"They can't do that."

Gerry shrugged. "They did."

"What about the bathhouse raid?" Nonni took the copper bracelet off her wrist and tossed it into the sink. "What about the Labaye case? What about the fucking Supreme Court? What about our great liberal nation, Gerry? You told me they couldn't do that kind of thing."

There was a tumbler of scotch by Gwen's wrist. She picked it up and put the glass to her lips so the ice cubes tinkled, but then just swirled the drink around.

"They arrested everybody inside the club," she said. "They arrested Jim and Susan who were dipping chocolate strawberries at the bar. Heidi and Randle, Shannon and Steve. They arrested a transvestite upstairs who was doing needlepoint. And I mean embroidery. They even waited in the parking lot and when Terri left early, they nabbed her and stuffed her in a district car."

A film of talcum powder had caked to Nonni's breast. She got a tea towel and scrubbed it off.

"They charged you too?" she said.

"Many times," Gwen said. "They even charged Don and I with a fire code violation, but that's provincial. They took us downtown and we had to sit in a stinky drunk cage for hours. We were in there with bandits and street robbers. I've never been so humiliated in my life."

Nonni slipped a red thumbnail between her teeth. Somewhere off in the edge of her vision, a wooden Indian curled his blue lips in exhalation. "This isn't possible," she said.

"It's now a historical fact," Don said. He put his hands in his pockets, walked over to the window, and stared out across the deck as if the shoreline was a long way off. "We got fingerprinted. We got stood up against a white brick wall and had our photographs taken."

"How did they get in?" Nonni said.

"Through the front door," Gwen drank the scotch and then pressed the glass to her forehead.

"Did they have a warrant?"

"Several," Don said. "It happened so fast. It was just a regular night. Shannon was doing Monet Masochism with her new friend. Heidi and Randle were covering each other with body paint. Then all of a sudden someone screamed. I can't remember who. Maybe that woman who came a couple of weeks ago dressed up like a domme. Then a dozen cops flooded up the stairs. They came in like army ants. Poor William. He was standing there counting bills. They bent him over the counter and handcuffed him before he knew what hit him. For a second, I think he thought it was game, like he was going to get do a cop-rape scene. But then all of us knew it was no game."

Nonni peeled lacquer off her fingernail. The table was quiet for a long time. The gold clock on the wall ticked over to four-thirty, and the first edge of light crept through the spruce trees in the alley making all of the world purple.

"So that was our night," Gerry said. "How was your date, Non?"

"She wouldn't put out."

"That's too bad." Gerry gazed down onto a speck of dust on the table top.

"So what happens now?" Nonni said.

"We have options." Don always had this strange look when he was thinking hard. His lips puckered in like a sphincter. A hundred years previous, he would have made the archetypal banker.

"They offered us a deal," Gerry said.

"Deal?"

"They said we were charged and that there was no way of undoing that. They said it would go to court and they would win. We would lose and we would all get criminal records. We could never be bonded, never leave the country, never get loans, or start companies. Or, and here's the option: we could get our lawyers to ask about something called alternate pathways."

"Alternative measures," Don said.

"Yes, that."

"It keeps it out of the court system," Don said. He had listened to the details carefully. "We do a day's community service, promise never to do it again, and then it's all over and forgotten. No records, no nothing."

"So do that," Nonni said.

Gerry fidgeted on his seat. He tapped his heel on the ground, over and over, and balled one fist up into the other palm. His knuckles went white. His lips got so narrow they vanished into his throat. And that wasn't good. That was trouble. The air in the kitchen got heavy and sour. Like lemons. The wallpaper sweated. There were balances being made, and computations being done, and none of them profitable. This was the rasping of people making life more complicated than it had to be and Nonni didn't like it one bit.

"I don't know," Gerry said.

"What is there not to know?" Nonni said. A tiny unicorn moth fluttered around the chandelier. "Let me get this straight. If you take this program, the police are out of it. We go on. It's over. No jail, no fine, no paperwork. If you don't take it then we have to go to court and stand in front of a repressed Mormon judge who is going to make his decision based on a dubious translation of the New Testament done in Utah."

"Basically."

"Remember what province we live in, Gerry."

"I know where we live."

Nonni went to the drawer and got a plastic scrubber. She flicked the lines of dried talcum off her shoulders and rubber thighs. The kitchen was unbearably white. The sun had come up to reveal all the leftovers of the night. The beer bottles in the alley, the dew on the eaves, and the wet newspaper draping over branches in manicured backyards.

"We can go somewhere else," Nonni said.

“This is a matter of principle.”

She threw the scrubber into the garbage bin. “You call spending the next two years of our lives in court a principle? We’ll start a new club. It doesn’t matter where or for how much. I helped finance Don and Gwen last time and I’ll do it again this time. I don’t care if I get a cash return.”

Don drew a circle in the condensation that formed on the sliding glass door. Outside, the last street lamp to stay lit made a strange pattern on an alder tree then went out. Nonni thought of a Magritte she had once seen but couldn’t remember which one.

“I won’t do it,” Gerry said.

“What?”

“No deals. I’ll fight.”

“Jesus,” Nonni said. In another five minutes there would be dried worms, drunken juveniles, and goblins on the sidewalk, too.

“I don’t care if I spend the rest of my life in court or in jail, I’m not going to let them do this.”

“They’re cops,” Nonni said. “They’ll always do it.”

“How long do we run and hide for? Do we sneak around from back alley to back alley like homosexuals in Victorian England, and put our dicks between our legs every time some detective gets a boner for a promotion? I say God bless Oscar Wilde.”

The two of them stared down at Gwen and waited for quorum. Gwen was the business woman. Gwen had the common sense. She’ll steer them right, Nonni thought.

“The lawyer fees alone will run us tens of thousands,” Gwen said. “We have club money. A few of our patrons will donate, but don’t count on them too much. That crowd is there for fucking, not fighting. Perhaps a strata of middle-class libertarians would give a small amount each if we go public. Just enough to satisfy their bragging rights at cocktail parties. Maybe bragging rights is what we want. Bragging means attention and attention means money and money needs mass."

She rested her chin on the tip of her folded fingers and counted one, two, three, four, and in a single silent nod the decision was made.

"Jesus fucking Christ on a stick," Nonni said.

Gerry took off his Van Gogh hat and put it in the middle of the table. He rolled it up, and then fastened the button. "This is larger than us. I don't know what the word is."

"Sublime," Nonni said. She pulled a black cord out of the hip of her rubber suit, then slid her boots off the edge of the basement step. There was no point in fighting this anymore. Outside the latticed window, it was dawn for sure. There was no denying it. Soon the newscasters would be revealing that the nation's treasury was built on glitz and not gold, that blood mingled at midnight was always a murder, and the poor worms drying on the sidewalk would forever miss the night. "It's a Romantic term used by nineteenth-century poets like Coleridge and Keats." Nonni picked up her pack of cigarettes from the counter and tucked them into her vest. "It's also stupid dawn, and I'm going to bed. Let's forget this now."

"I can't," Gerry said. "This is my country and my Constitution and I'm not going to let them do this to me. Goddamn it, where is Pierre Trudeau when you need him?"

"Trudeau is dead," she said and made her way up the stairs. "Pierre Elliot Trudeau is fucking dead, Gerry."

14.

A red waxy stamen, bulbous and engorged, waited in the corner of Dr. Sayer's office. The anthers stood erect in a deep pistil valley, inviting all living things into their pit of pollen. What was it with these plants, halfway between exhibition and stoicism? What did they want? Why did they care? Nonni sat in the baroque chair and stared at the flower.

"What do they aspire to?" she asked.

"Pardon?" Sayer said. He sat behind his desk and looked over his notes. He had a new pair of gold rimmed glasses that he moved back and forth on his nose. There was a new Group of Seven on his wall, but something was not pleasing him.

"Plants. What keeps them happy?"

"Pretty much what they told you in high school. Water. Sunlight. Nutrients. But then again, we're not plants, so it's hard to know."

The good doctor flipped back and forth between several pages of forms and prescriptions that were cajoled together with staples. Some of the pages were yellow. Others red. A few appeared to be constructed out of beeswax. The notion that anything of value might appear on white stationary was contradictory. Out of necessity Nonni saw that the seventh rectangle was her emergency admission form after the train ride.

"We can send a satellite to the far corner of the solar system," she said. "But we can't understand what makes a plant happy?"

Sayer rearranged his cufflink and contemplated a clipboard. He had on a purple pleated shirt with a black tie and platinum clip. Chopin drifted in from a stereo.

"Happiness is a human term, Nonni. So, let's give it a shot. Are you happy now?"

She adjusted a band of metal beneath her bra. She had twined it out on Gerry's lathe and felt much safer with it there, as if the alloy were keeping some secret in or some frightening thing out. One of the wires had punched into her rib and infected the cut. "Do you think there are other creatures looking down on us, wondering, sending us messages to find out if we are happy or not?"

"Unlikely."

"They'd have to decode our odd machinations first."

"The difficulty with the creatures you speak of is that they would be separated by a lot of time and space from us."

"Suppose they were here, living with us already?"

"Some people speculate that," Sayer said.

"What do you think?"

"I do medicine, not speculation." It was that simple. "And I have to tell you, Non, I am now looking at quite a few medical documents that concern me."

"Suppose they were trying to screw us and we didn't know that, either? If they had genitalia. Use us for erotic purposes, at least."

Sayer put his pen down. She couldn't imagine what he would look like without a pen. She couldn't recall what they had looked like when she had seen them first. Soldier, arsonist, refugee. On a dock at Port Said. In a back alley in Phnom Penh. They had to be foreigners. Outsiders at least. Probably parasites. That's what worried her most. That they were in her bloodstream unwelcomed. Unscreened. A minority parliament that ought not be sitting in this un-weeded garden.

"Where does this come from, Nonni?"

"Does it not sound like something I'd be capable of saying?"

"You usually think in a concrete manner, not in abstractions."

"Do I sound different?"

"Do you feel different?"

"I feel like shit."

"I think that's what you told the receptionist. Fill me in."

She fumbled for a menthol, pulled the lighter out of her pocket and flicked it over. "My lungs are atrophying."

"Could be the cigarettes," he said.

"I wish."

"Your chest looks bruised." He arranged his datebook on the desk as if it were a casual question.

"I did it in Gerry's workshop."

"Doing what?"

"Building a truss that's under my bra."

"What's the truss for?"

That much should have been obvious. These things were basic laws of the universe. Like gravitation or noble gasses. Why was it necessary to explain them to someone who already had a PhD?

"It's a metal guard," she said. "Some of it is made from wicker chairs from the basement. Gerry is going to kill me if he finds out. His mother gave them to us for an anniversary. Other parts of it are built from a bird cage. I have no idea where the bird went."

"Is this something for the club?"

"It's stopping the transformation."

Sayer nodded. The explanation was obvious. "What are the particulars of this transformation?"

A gem lock was missing from the strap on Nonni's purse. Perhaps she had used that as part of the truss. She had discovered that when she linked a titanium wire from her brassiere to her ear, a humming started in her temple then spread out in codices across her eyes.

"A guard," Sayer said. "Indicates you are building a barrier against something you fear. Do you fear being old?"

"No."

"Do you feel as if you are dirty, or unclean?"

"Hygiene isn't the problem."

"Then what?"

The notion of possession was for plebes. Schizophrenia was for sick people and Carl Jung was just too long-winded to contemplate. "I am being transformed from a living breathing creature into something that is inanimate."

"Inanimate in what way?"

"Un-living, unfeeling, un-fucking, and unlucky, that's for sure. It's not a condition of the mind. It is a condition of the body. Do you want to see?"

"No," Sayer said. He waved his hand across the desk and hit a button. "I can get a nurse in here for that. Just tell me about the changes. Tell me about what you are feeling."

"I feel a horrible sense of conflict."

Sayer sat up in his chair. Strange how you could get someone's attention by using one word over another. Nonni wished she didn't have to go through all this. It would be so much easier if her desires could just change the physical world instead of her having to explain her desires to those unfortunate enough to be physical.

"Conflicted that I am both basalt and breathing at the same time. But that's not possible, is it?"

"Everything that your mind does affects your body. The two can't really be separated. In that way we're not at all like plants. When we have deep-seated unresolved conflicts, they manifest themselves in exaggerated behaviours. It's called a neurosis. Hand washing, hair brushing, making sure our shoes are lined up before we go to bed. When we see characters do it in movies we think it's amusing. We say 'isn't that neurotic.' But of course when it happens to us, it's not so funny. And it doesn't help the initial problem."

"Then why do we do it?"

"To avoid the initial problem."

Nonni stared out to the pale green sea of skyscrapers below her. They too, looked like plants sprouting in a bleak desert of rich oil, waiting to be harvested. Or as sentinels, towering above all living creatures, deciding their fates.

"Vocalize the problem," he said.

"Gerry and I are having issues. Marriage issues, maybe. I don't know. It's deeper than that. It's like one of us is starting to live in another dimension. A few nights ago, Gerry and his friends ran into some trouble. Legal trouble. Insignificant actually. Not much more than a speeding ticket. There was an obvious way of dealing with it. A simple way. The only way. Yet he wouldn't do it. He wants to go through a tsunami of priggish hullabaloo and make it difficult for everyone for no reason. Nobody will get what they want. Everybody will end up frustrated. I can't understand what he's doing or why."

"Disagreements between couples happen for a number of reasons," Sayer said. "It might be that the two of you aren't really communicating what the issue is."

Nonni knew this speech: perhaps information is missing. Maybe one side is withholding information on purpose. Possibly the other side refuses to see what's there. A couple is out on a cruise. They are both playing cards. She likes cards. He doesn't. The boat hits a rock and starts to sink. The husband says that they have to flee. The wife is afraid of water. The wife has always been afraid of water. All she hears is that she has to leave the only safe place she knows.

"I don't think that's it."

"Then it could be that what is being done is far more important to one side or the other, but they haven't communicated that. The event is a great life symbol for one person and the other party sees it only as a passing fancy. That's a recipe for failure."

"I don't really understand the semantics."

The doctor put his pen in his mouth and leaned back in his chair. "Say for example that two people are out on a camping expedition. It gets a little cool and one person wants to burn a piece of cloth in the fire to get warm. The other person won't do it because that piece of cloth is their flag, say the flag of the nation or tribe that sent them on the expedition."

"Mm," Nonni said. "I don't get it."

"I think often you do get it, Nonni. I think you understand a lot more than you let on. You show remarkable insights. If you want to."

"Understanding takes work."

"Yes, it does." He sounded distant.

"We ran into trouble at the club."

"The swingers club?"

“It got closed down. God knows why. I wasn’t there.”

“Gerry went alone?”

On the doctor’s huge window there was a set of venetian blinds that came a quarter-way down the glass. They were cocked at a forty-degree angle, neither opened nor closed, and they vibrated in a way that made them sound like a cricket. A drone that rose and fell in pitch, as if any moment, they might attack. Nonni tried to think of the bug that that famous psychiatrist was always talking about when coincidences happened.

“I thought the two of you had a rule,” he said.

“Hardly matters now. The club is gone. Gerry refuses to accept any deals. Just like him, really. I said he should have gone with it. Give unto Caesar, I say. Now we have no play space for weeks, months, God knows, ever. I can’t bear the stupidity.”

“What does that tell you in light of what we’ve just said?”

Nonni held up her lighter and then slipped it between her teeth. “That Gerry is losing interest in sex and I’m not.”

Sayer pushed his chair against the wall and folded his hands behind his head. “Try again,” he said.

From the corner of the room, came the smell of old closets and polished maple. The kind of smell that would creep out of a hallway where the heat duct didn’t work and snatch the air from the living.

“I can’t.”

“You’re putting yourself under a lot of unnecessary stress.”

“Is there any that’s necessary?”

“Sometimes, a little, yes. Stress is self-produced in moral, thinking creatures and it is one of the greatest psychological phenomena in human history.”

The stress speech was not new either; stress can destroy us or make us accomplish incredible feats. Politicians thrive on it, sculptors carve it. Novelists write about it. But there's a downside. Too much stress can shut down our ability to think or see or hear completely. Especially our ability to hear those who are closest to us.

Nonni pushed a wrinkle out of the material on her rib. The inanimate world was closing in around her; the windows, the wood, the ferrous accoutrements that cluttered cuffs, cleft, and conscious. Why couldn't these creatures just come out and say what was on their minds?

"Look at the positive side," Sayer said. "Stress can also make us hypersensitive. It allows the human spirit to create works of unbelievable art and make superhuman sacrifices. It can make us see and hear things we normally never could. Languages, music. Sometimes people can hear radios from another room or conversations from other houses. Other times they put patterns in the stars or quarks in atoms that no one had ever thought of before. All genius, is to some degree, motivated by stress. What you must do is figure out how to put that part of your brain to work for you."

"This isn't stress. This is an outside intelligence."

Sayer blinked once and stared briefly up at the ceiling. A rotating fan with gold embroidery turned slowly in circles.

"What kind of outside intelligence?"

"The kind who are trying to communicate with me." Nonni slipped back in her chair. She wished she had her rubber suit. She wished the collar had grown into her clavicle. "But I don't understand what they want. I don't have a clue why they have picked me or when they'll appear next."

"When do they usually appear?"

"When I'm sexually excited."

The buzz of the venetian blinds grew. A mosquito, a murmur, a Messerschmitt. Sayer didn't seem to notice but Nonni knew the obvious: they were dropping hints just to let her know she was alone on this one.

"Not just sex," she said. "Not just screwing. I wouldn't want you to think that. Screwing is for animals. Screwing is for romance novels. They come when I'm aroused, enraptured, sublimated. I'm something else."

"There's a history of this kind of thing, in psychiatry," Sayer said.

"That's not what these are."

"What do you think they are then? A ghost? A spirit? A demon?"

"Demons are for children. They simply exist."

"That's not much of an explanation, is it?"

"They don't give out much biographical information. They just make me do things for them."

Doctor Sayer had two notebooks. One that he kept on his desk. That was for the two of them to see. The other, much smaller one, he kept on his computer keyboard that was on a ledger just below the desk. That one was occult. That one was coded. That one un-disclosable. He hardly ever wrote there. Without leaning over or even looking, he drew a single tick on one of the pages.

"What kind of things?" he said.

"I don't know what their idea of sex is. Maybe it's not sex. Maybe that's the only way they can talk to me. Maybe that's the only language they figure I'll understand. But I know I'll do what they want in the end."

"Why?"

The problem in dealing with scientists was that they always wanted truth. Bankers always money and clerics rarely compassion.

"These creatures," Sayer said. "Make you do things that you wouldn't otherwise do."

"That is the point."

"After you have done these things, do you regret them?"

"No," she said.

"No?" He appeared stumped. He was just about to play the winning hand in a game of psychiatric gin rummy and the cards had been snatched away from him.

"Sorry. Negative."

"Not the next day?"

"Not ever."

"But they frightened you?"

"Most things that are worthwhile do that the first time around, wouldn't you say, doctor?"

"Do these things ever want to make you hurt yourself?"

"A marathon runner knows that when he is training for a race, the curriculum might involve a little discomfort."

"Are you running a marathon, Nonni?"

"It was a metaphor."

"Let's put metaphors aside. Do other people get hurt when they ask you to do these things?"

Nonni's folded hands on her purse were still and cool. Hurting was a difficult concept. Who didn't like being hurt from time to time? Agamemnon? Lear? John Stuart Mills?

"When they come," Nonni said. "My body changes. My hands harden to teak. My face becomes brass. And my smile becomes an amalgam of things others are not."

The window shades trembled, and then all of the floor, and then perhaps her bladder too. Was that really a scarab on the glass? Nonni held the arms of the Baroque chair. The stitching was rough under her fingers. Two hundred years old and still rough with classical sterility. She breathed in and counted to ten, but then they were there in the room with her. In the corner, by Sayer's grandfather clock, they stood with their square box faces. She imagined what it might be like if they took over her entire body and all of her mind, too. Perhaps her soul would tremble just like the blinds.

"Why are you staring at the window?" Sayer asked.

Nonni's face was sweating, her hands were damp, and then her entire torso was wet. There was the sound of water splashing on the floor. She looked around to see if Sayer had spilled a cup of tea, but he only stared down in embarrassment. A large puddle of urine spread out across the floor in all directions. Somewhere there were children from her grade school mocking her. They were waiting in their short pants and white shirts, and they at least could hold their bladder until recess. Sayer's buzzer went off again and the nurse came through the good doctor's door.

15.

The term garden party really only meant one thing: that the party would start in the garden, but everybody would end up screwing in the living room or in the bedroom or in the shower or else down in the fruit cellar. You could always tell the couple that had sex in the cellar because they would come up wearing potato rinds on their ass.

Nonni parked her car outside Tom's house. She had on her black miniskirt, gold blouse, and red stilettos. No leather, no latex. This was a conservative crowd. That was the thing with swingers. Too puritanical. Doing your friend's husband on the billiard table while a dozen people watched was okay. But no bondage, no SM, and above all else no guy-on-guy action. That stuff was taboo. Tom was getting pierced by Terri, and Nonni wondered how he was going to get that act past his wife. Maybe that was the only reason she came. Probably he hadn't told her.

Tom and Wendy lived on a double boulevard street in Parkland. The neighbourhood had been built during the 1960s by the professional class that survived the Second World War. There were neighbourhoods like it in every city. The nation was filled with them. Big yards with well-manicured hedges and trees. Ranch-style houses with carpeted living rooms, finished basements, and granite tile. Everybody wanted a Robert Bateman painting in the den.

Nonni dropped her cigarette in the garden gnome's mouth and then walked up the steps. A BMW, a Jag, and a Lincoln were parked in the driveway. Tom liked rich friends.

"Hey, Nonni." Wendy was half-hearted to see her. She held open the door. Wendy was forty. Straw hair, freckles. She had been pretty once. She had on a maid outfit and held a gin fizz. "Where's Gerry?"

"He's not coming," Nonni said.

"You two are still together aren't you?"

"Oh yeah. I guess."

Wendy fiddled with the wedding ring on her finger. In the living room, there were two dozen people wearing see-through dressing gowns, Herringbone jackets, and skimpy skirts. They were talking hockey even though hockey season was over.

Tom leaned against the archway in the kitchen. Tom was funny, tall, and confident with a black trimmed beard. He knew physics, yachting, and Spanish, and was explaining most of it to a young blond in a negligee who was possibly old enough to be in grad school.

"Nonni, hello," he said and smiled.

She went over and kissed him on the side of the cheek.

"This is Deborah," he said.

"I've heard a lot about you." Deborah gave Nonni the once over and tried to smile.

"I've just told her the sordid bits," Tom said.

"That's all there is," Nonni said.

"Tom and I were just talking quantum theory," Deborah said.

Figured. Whenever two people were talking erudite at a party it meant one of them didn't want a third.

"When is the piercing?" Nonni said.

"Piercing?"

"Tom's getting a PA." Nonni took a glass of wine from a tray and looked Deborah over. She would do.

"What's a PA?"

"A Prince Albert."

"Which is?"

"A chrome cock piercing that can't get through airport security."

"I thought it was a concert hall in Great Britain."

Tom stirred the swizzle stick in his drink. He and Wendy always made their gin fizzes together.

"Really?" Deborah said. Her tan was studio, her blond hair dyed. But her skin was still tight and her smile said virgin pratt. Nonni could fix that, too.

"Thinking about it," Tom said.

"Won't that hurt?"

"That's the point." Nonni licked her index finger then put it on Tom's crotch. Something moved.

Deborah said, "What does Wendy think?"

"Oh, she's all for it," Tom said.

Wendy came over. Deborah raised her empty glass for everyone to see. Then she walked back to the bar that had been set up on the patio.

"What's with her?" Nonni said.

"She's young," Tom said.

"First time?"

"Maybe not."

Nonni watched the negligee twist out the sliding glass doors towards a steaming hot tub. The tart's half-life at the party was going to be about seventeen minutes.

"She came with Phil," Wendy said. "He's an orthodontist."

Wendy pursed her lips and stared out to the patio. A man with a goatee unzipped an older woman's dress. He had a square jaw and dark eyes, an excellent extract from a fashion magazine. A dimple on Wendy's cheek twitched. The algebra of swing parties wasn't that complicated.

"I know him," Nonni said.

"I don't think so," Wendy said.

"A couple of years ago. On his boat. In Howe Sound, remember? We went sailing, you know that time? It was an Eprise clipper. July, I think. He tied us both to the mast, remember?"

"Not really."

"He's hot."

"Gerry couldn't make it," Wendy said to Tom.

There was sort of a rule at Tom and Wendy's parties. You got invited as a couple. You came as a couple. The numbers had to square off. Definitely no single men allowed. Single women were all right as long as Tom said it was good, so the jury was stacked.

"When Terri comes I'll be her date," Nonni said.

"I don't think Terri is coming," Wendy said. "She had a pro-thing."

"Pro-thing?"

"Those things make us nervous. That's not our scene. Pro-stuff. I hope she's not on crack."

"She's not on crack," Tom said.

"I was looking forward to a piercing," Nonni said.

"This is a different crowd than you're used to, Nonni." Wendy had such a delicate voice.

"I see that."

"No hard SM. No flogging. No piercing."

"How about having sex with guys that already have piercings? Have you ever had a guy with a PA?"

"Have you?"

"Oh, sure."

"You can get prostate infections from those things," Wendy said. "I heard it on CBC."

There was a dissertation waiting in this. Nonni wondered why she had come. These people were boring. These people were tepid. Tom was making Wendy nervous just talking about PAs.

"Things are just getting going," Wendy said. "There's some new people so not everybody knows each other. After people have had a few drinks and the belly dancer is finished we're going to play boats in the hot tub."

Boats was a bourgeois swing game where people got into the hot tub and blew a big sail boat around. Whoever the boat touched had to take off their swimsuit. Nonni hated it.

Deborah came back with a new drink. The knot on her negligee had been retied in a double bow, so this one could go either way.

"Just so I'm clear," Nonni said. "Is this a closed door party or an open door party?"

"It's open door," Tom said.

Wendy put her hand on Nonni's arm and smiled. "Nonni," she said. "We need a quick word."

A clatter of cymbals exploded from the living room and then a barrage of pipe music attempted to charm snakes. The belly dancer's name was Trish. She was thirty, had Persian skin, and the kind of abs that said gym six times a week. Tom said she worked as a dental assistant.

Trish swirled in the room with a collection of silk wound around her body. There was a green emerald in her navel. The bracelets around her wrists and ankles jangled, and Nonni felt a creature with dark claws slide into the den.

"What do you think?" she said to Deborah.

The two leaned shoulder to shoulder against the wall. "Oh, she's good," Deborah said. "I like the dancing. I wish I could do that."

That was the thing about belly dancers, Nonni thought. They could look good. Men could look. Women could look. It didn't mean a damn thing.

"Those silks aren't coming off fast enough for my liking," Nonni said.

"Pardon?"

"Who did you come here with?"

"With Phil," she pointed to the far side of the room beneath a pastel archway.

"The orthodontist," Nonni said.

Phil was still standing by the sliding glass doors talking to the tall woman with short black hair, and Deborah still didn't like it. Same conversation as before, but now his shirt was open to expose his brutish chest hair.

"He's got two hundred patients," Deborah said.

"He seems to like that one's teeth."

"It's part of the trade. People want to know their doctor as a human being before they let him rip apart their face."

"What does he like to do?"

"Reconstruction work on incisors," Deborah said. "High end stuff. He does a lot of actors and politicians. No braces. Braces are out."

"I meant what do the two of you like to do?"

"We both like to spend a lot of time in Banff."

"No," Nonni said. "I mean what do the two of you like to do sexually?"

One side of Deborah's mouth turned up in a puzzled smile, and she had very perfect puffed lips.

"I am sorry, what?"

"Do you like swapping men or women?"

Deborah put a thumb to the strap of her negligee and twisted it clockwise. "I think Phil likes brunettes."

"I bet that one he's talking to now is shaved."

Deborah glanced over to the door again. Phil had his arm up over the brunette's head. His shirt hung open, his belt was undone. Deborah quivered and the muscles in her throat locked up. The belly dancer tossed the last sash onto the floor, but she was nowhere near naked.

"Relax," Nonni said. She recited the program: "It's a party. Don't get hung up on one person. There's always another option. That's what parties are for."

Deborah twisted her swizzle stick through some ice, but her eyes stayed fixed on Phil. A few hushed curse words pushed through her lips, and Nonni always liked the part when women got stupid with jealously. They'd do anything, really.

"You're in good shape," Nonni said.

"Thank you."

"Do you do a lot of ab work?"

"Pilates."

"Hot."

"These parties bore me," Deborah said.

"Let's find somewhere." Nonni took a rose from the den vase, and dropped the flower between her breasts. A bead of water ran down the stem and onto her pink flesh.

"Pardon?"

"Let's go somewhere."

The sun came up in a dark part of the woman's consciousness and for the shortest of moment there was light in the thicket. Then she put a finger to her lip and her face blanched.

"I'm not into that," Deborah said.

"Yes you are."

"How would you know?"

Nonni felt the great weight in the room beside her then and knew the party had yet another guest. The hardwood creaked with the mass of the visitor shuffling his granite limbs across the floor, and the chandelier tinkled too, so seeing into this sorry girl's past wasn't going to be so hard at all. The stone fist punched through her spine and yarded out a ribbon of pathetic affairs ending in tears, regrets, and even a bad attempt with a rusty razor blade.

"You did once outside the dorm at UBC," Nonni said. "There was a redhead beneath an ivy trestle, and the night smelled like tulips. She really wasn't worth the blood on your shoes, was she?"

Deborah's nose twitched. Then her lip quivered. Nonni was sure she could see the hair on the inside of her ear tremble as she reached deep into the red, turquoise, and purple recess of memory.

"Who told you that?"

"Just a friend."

"How would they know?"

"Omniscient viewpoint."

"Did Phil tell you that?"

"No."

"You people are sick," she said. Her eyebrows vexed. Her cheeks pouted.

"I know Phil. Intimately. He's game. How about the three of us go down to the pool table."

Deborah tossed her glass into the potted plant and walked out onto the patio. Her purse was sitting by the hot tub. She ripped it open and found a set of car keys.

"Good fucking night," she said to the closest three people, who had not a clue what she was talking about.

Tom walked over. Someone had smudged lipstick on his jaw and one of the dancer's sashes was stuffed in his pocket. He put his gin down on the plant pot.

"Sorry," Nonni said.

He stroked his beard. The music had changed over to European-techno. "To tell you the truth, I didn't think she was going to last anyway. She just came along with Phil on a whim." He glanced around the room and smiled at a yellow bra that was draped over the flat screen television. "Lucky Gerry didn't come. We're down a girl now and the numbers will match. Phil can find something."

"Maybe you can both do me after," Nonni said.

Tom bit his lip.

"He's bi isn't he?" Nonni folded her arms and glanced out to Phil on the veranda. His teeth glimmered in the evening sun. "I can always tell."

"How can you tell, Nonni?"

"I get instructions from another dimension."

"What is the other dimension telling you?"

"That Wendy is pissed and I could use two guys at once tonight."

"You could always use two guys." Tom had on a white pleated shirt, and when he swallowed his Adam's apple went up and down between the collar buttons.

"But it's not often that two hot ones are available."

"This isn't the forum to pursue that angle," he said.

Nonni looked over at Phil. His Mediterranean jaw always

looked tanned, like he spent most of his life on a boat.

"You want to," she said. "I bet it's huge. That Mediterranean look always means huge."

"I'm sure you have the stats somewhere on that."

Nonni let her head fall against the door frame. She played with the copper latch and gave her best don't-be-a-cuckold-fool stare.

"Oh, I'd go for it," Tom said. He put his drink down on the hutch.

"But. It sounds like there is a but."

"Wendy would freak." Tom shook his head, tucked in his shirt and gazed at his shoe. "We've had a few snags lately. She's been going to identity therapy."

"What the hell is that?"

"The concept is a bit baffling. They've been telling her swinging is bad for a relationship after thirty."

"After thirty what, thirty couples?"

"No, after middle age, middle class, Middle-earth, whatever."

"Bad in what way?"

Tom shrugged.

"What a load of horse shit," Nonni said.

"It's got something to do with interpersonal development. You have to have your doorways balanced or something."

"If she feels left out, let her join in. I'm happy with that. I've done Wendy before. At one of your autumn parties, remember? No, wait. That was with the chemist, Samantha. I went down on Sam, and Wendy was just necking with her."

"No, Wendy went down on you," Tom corrected. "And I think that's just something she wants to forget."

"Why is she pissed about your piercing? If she doesn't like it, you can take it out. Gerry has had three in and three out. His dick is like a revolving metal door."

Tom's eyes were out of focus, fixed on some point far away on an endless horizon of patios, spruce trees, and new Subarus. "She was all keen about the whole kinky thing. That was years ago. She was the one who made me go to the club in the first place. She found out pretty quick that she could have any guy she wanted. She could make them do whatever she liked. She'd always have this look on her face, kind of a 'see what I can do? So, you'd better be good to me' look. I didn't mind. In fact, I kind of liked it. I thought it was the dominatrix thing, although it really wasn't. One night, I talked her into going to the Onyx Club. You know, your club. We got down there and the place was closed. All shut up and dark. She took this as some kind of omen and said we shouldn't be going to places like that with unreliable business people who couldn't keep regular hours. So, that was the end of that. Now she's edgy about even swinging parties. Tomorrow morning is going to be hell."

On the far side of the room Phil was wearing a tie but no shirt. His fly was down. He didn't seem to be fazed that Deborah had gone. He glanced up once at Tom and raised his eyebrows.

"He's in," Nonni said.

The party got going when the belly dancer had packed it in and everybody went outside. On the cedar patio two sunken hot tubs steamed into the summer night. There were orange pumpkin lights and incense burning. The yard was surrounded by fir trees and the neighbours never complained, if they even knew. Tom flicked a switch, and the pools welled up with jets of white water that shimmered over blue strobes. Half of a successful swing party was convincing people that what they were about to do wasn't the practice of trailer trash. People wanted assurance. They wanted collateral. When they saw ten thousand dollar jets swirling the lit water, the bonds were deemed good. They changed into thongs and G-strings, and sat on the edge of the tub laughing and poking at anything that moved.

"I didn't bring a suit," Nonni said.

Wendy went into the cupboard and got her one.

Nonni found a Chardonnay, then got in the tub between Phil and Tom. The swimsuit was too big, but she didn't count on wearing it long. There was a ritual you had to go through just to get laid at these parties. First, you had to have the glass of wine. Next you had to acknowledge how beautiful and good everyone in the tub was, then condemn mainstream repressed society for the neurosis and stigmas it inflicted. After that, you established the rules of who could do what with whom in what order and what was verboten, insensitive, and très gauche. Then, only then, if the universe was copasetic and the I Ching had lined up with the Aurora Borealis, could you start to flirt. It was called filling the dance card, and Nonni thought it was a pain.

Beneath the champagne water, the rough muscles of Phil's leg rubbed against her thigh, and the moist air smelled of chlorine. There were ten people in the tub and the water bubbled around them half-disguising their arousal. The drinks floated in plastic life preservers.

Tom and Phil both had black hair over their chests, and kept making jokes about sailors. Phil's new friend was trying on pair after pair of Callisto shoes beside the tub, and Wendy sat on a deck chair with her clothes on, smoking coolly and contemplating a magpie on the garage.

"Aren't you coming in?" Nonni asked.

"I'm just a provocateur," she said. She watched the end of her cigarette burn down.

"Get the boat," Shannon said.

Nonni hadn't noticed Shannon was there. She remembered

her from the club, but she looked different out of leather. Tom put the red plastic boat in the middle of the tub and shut off the jets. It was a foot long and had a white sail on the top. Some kind of keel kept it circling around the centre of the tub. Everyone had to stay still with their shoulders against the side of the pool and blow at the sail. Shannon got dizzy. The red boat sputtered around in the middle of the pool for a few minutes, ambivalent about a port call. People giggled. Eventually the sail caught some air that smelled of Daiquiris and the boat drifted in between Shannon's breasts.

"You have to do what the captain commands," Tom said.

Shannon opened the hatch. A motorized voice barked out an order. "Stand up and take off your suit."

Shannon stood, peeled off her suit, and pitched it into the juniper bush. The people in the tub hooted.

"What's powering that?" Phil said.

"Batteries," Tom said. "It knows 143 commands."

Under the water Nonni ran her hand up the inside of Phil's knee. Deep in his grey eyes, Nonni saw the horrid rigidity of desire, the calcification from which there was no reason or return.

"Go again," a redhead shouted from the far side of the pool. Five more people got in the tub and shoulders formed a wall of flesh.

The boat set sail and made a few swerves away from people who shouted every time it got close. Finally, it bumped into Brian, a tall fellow with white skin and a smooth chest. Brian opened the hatch.

"Let your neighbour pull your nipple," the captain said.

Brian pushed his chest out and the redhead ran her palm against his smooth skin. She gave it a tiny twist, like Nonni thought you might see on a candy cartoon.

"It's set for light play," Tom shrugged. "Wendy wanted it that way."

Phil was staring straight ahead. He wasn't watching the boat anymore. He didn't care about the laughter. Nonni got her fingers inside his suit. Then she put her other hand on Tom's shoulder.

"Let's go," she said.

They got out of the pool. The chlorine water ran out of their suits and splashed on the tiles. There was a lineup of people to take their spots. Three couples were salsa dancing by the patio table with only their underwear on, and the music was turned up. Wendy was gone. No one noticed them leave. They went downstairs into the basement.

The rec room air was cool and smelled of potato sacks. The entire basement had been refinished with a carpet floor and teak paneled walls. There was a pool table, and a huge flat screen television played French softcore. In the middle of the room there was a duvet and a lamp shaped like an egg.

Nonni peeled off her swimsuit and pointed her marble set of toes towards the ceiling. No matter how you looked at it, the place was still basically a basement, and her feet were still gorgeous. Tom got down on his knees and took her whole set in his mouth. There were raspberries and whale tongues and everything was pink.

The Woodenheads stood in the room beside them. They did not speak, nor move nor touch nor breathe. Maybe they had come in through the door, or the fruit cupboard, or right through Tom's wall of ambivalence. Stonehenge figures, with eyes of quartz, it must have taken them centuries to blink. Perhaps that was the problem, Nonni thought, the world went by too fast for most people to know they even existed, and then a sea urchin of arousal rubbed against her instep.

She slapped Phil's face just because she liked doing it, then she took his neck and forced him to his knees with vice-grip fingers. She could break every cord in his vertebrae if she wanted to, but instead she just twisted him on target, and he made gurgling noises like there was something too big for him to swallow. The vibration of a universal joint rumbled through the room and Nonni flushed with joy because she knew her visitors were approving; waiting, watching, taking notes, with their flat wooden heads in the zebra paneled walls. They were everywhere. In the cracks in the plaster and in the nickel of the plumbing connections. And then the Woodenheads forced the two men into a bric-brac of one, until the room filled with mortal people watching, their eyes bubbling in champagne excitement. Then the split second when the omniscient visitors extracted all of Tom's fear and hopes, and squashed them out as dried leaves beneath a rolling pin for the world to see.

Wendy burst through the door. A magpie scream was caught in the spokes of a motorcycle. Chlorine water streamed from her hair and the towel wrapped around her waist wasn't stopping the water from splashing on the floor. Her face was red, wet, and distorted.

"Get out," she said.

"Jesus. Take it easy, Wendy," Tom said.

She pitched her glass across the room and it exploded on the fireplace. A splinter caught Nonni on the forehead, but only a bulb of clear resin bloomed on her ear and when she tasted it, she thought of pews, of oak and anger waiting in a dusty vestibule. Phil scrambled up. His cock purple and shriveling into the past. Wendy threw a cue ball. The marble chunk struck him in the temple. He fell backwards. His head hit the television and shattered the screen.

"Time to go," Nonni said.

Wendy smashed the light over Tom's back and an arc of purple electricity jumped to his elbow. Shannon wept. Wendy cried. Somewhere, Terri wept, too. Radio reception was interrupted, and people picked up what clothes they could salvage and headed for the door. The smell of burnt flesh lingered around the plant pot then rose to the lava light.

Nonni found a pair of sweats and tossed them to Phil. She put on a skirt and top, and pushed on a pair of pumps that might have fit, but who they actually belonged to was anyone's guess.

16.

Nonni waited in her convertible. Her cell phone was tucked between her legs and the idle on the transmission was running too high. She was parked outside the St Regis Hotel on the corner of Ninth Avenue and Fourth Street, and the only buildings in view were the Center of Hope, the Salvation Army, and a shop that built prosthetic legs for veterans. The morning was hot and the alcoholics from the night before were drying up on the black asphalt of day.

"I live in tombs," she said to no one in particular. But knew someone was probably listening anyway. "I am commanded by the dead. My lovers speak the psalm of sloth."

When she tried the cell phone again, Teddy's phone went off seven times before he answered.

"Where have you been?" she said.

"Getting things ready."

"Why in God's name here?"

"Here is the only place I can get enough electricity without blowing a circuit."

A tangle of black hydro wires ran across the alley into a creosoted transformer box, then slithered through a window on the second floor of the hotel.

"This place is a dump," she said.

"You're the one who said you needed help, Non." His voice was aloof.

"The people out here seep fluids."

"I don't doubt that."

She hung up the phone. The red tavern bricks that had been laid down in the First World War were sprayed with urine, and moss grew out of the mortar. A roll of dried thistle lighted on a fence post, and finally Teddy pushed open a fire exit.

"Don't leave me in a place like this again," she said.

"It's the place of the common man." He held the door open for her. His shirt was stained with sandwich spread.

"I hate common men."

"Don't leave your purse in the car."

Inside, a narrow hall was sullen with opaque light. A glazed window was cracked down the middle. The claret-red carpet sent threads of lint into the air and Nonni's breath condensed on the glass of an office wicket.

"It's always winter in here," Teddy shrugged.

Upstairs, a walnut banister ran around the landing. A row of black and white animal photographs rested above the wainscoting. Most of the rooms were empty. Some had the doors ripped off. In room twenty-seven, an iron bed frame was strapped against the wall. Teddy buttoned up his sweater.

"I'm pretty sure I can get an industrial load in here," he said. His desk had been set up beside the cupboard and was stacked with a heap of cables and a computer tower. Inside the cupboard, an ancient insulator cone snapped mosquito sparks off the bushing. At one time, the space might have been a laundry room because a row of drains pitted the floor.

"Why do you need an industrial load?" she said.

"For the set-up."

"Why do we need a set-up?"

"You called me," Teddy said. "You called me in the middle of the night, and you said that things were out of control. You said that they had come and ripped the constitutional family to barbarous shreds of contempt, whatever that meant. I don't really want to know. You intimated that you were hurting yourself and you said you would do anything to fix the issue. You kind of stressed the word anything."

Nonni couldn't recall if the police had come. She recalled railways. Screaming. An ambulance, too. Steel flying through her host's larynx and gravity having its way with party guests as the suburban landscape reeked self-glorious slaughter on its own kind. Tom had renounced the mortgage. Wendy had attempted suicide with an electric drill. Not that any of that mattered, but after, while repairing an imperceptible brow blemish in the mirror, Nonni watched her iris harden into olivine. As the tiny blue fibres in her lens stratified into silicate, she felt only a strange detachment, a distant farewell to a colleague she would hardly miss. And finally, after using tweezers to extract the ion orb, she set it on the counter, contemplated magnesium, then grew bored of the gaping black vacuum in her skull, and went to bed.

"Shut the door and lock it," Teddy said.

Nonni turned the key in the chamber. The lock rattled around then jammed up. A clump of wet dog hair had been stuffed into the keyhole. Teddy sorted the cables into three piles. The first was a silver coil with ragged clips on the end. The second, a mat of surgical spindles attached to needles, and the third a series of black industrial loops that were plugged into ballast boxes.

"Did you raid a grow op?" she said.

"That's for the transformer."

"What's the transformer going to do?"

Teddy hooked the silver wire into a grey tube that looked like a hair dryer. The sides were covered with grease. He put the tube down on a sheet of white paper. "We have to keep everything sterile."

Wedges of dust swirled over the cracked window. They loitered out of habit. Dried insect wings collected on the sill. The room smelled of carbolic soap.

"Why do you keep equipment out of the Industrial Revolution?" she said.

"Your eye looks like shit, Nonni. Go back to your shrink, if you want. Or maybe you can talk to your husband about your troubles." He flipped open the lid to his computer. A green screen flickered into life.

"You've changed."

"Stuff changes," he said. "You've changed. I've changed. Our relationship has changed."

"The tone in your voice has."

Teddy smiled. "From what you have told me, they too have changed. They have become more robust. More active. More powerful. I hate to be the bearer of bad news, Non, but if your pals are getting shredded by interdimensional entities at swing parties, the balance of power has shifted."

Teddy clipped a wire jaw onto a metal ring, and a yellow current jumped out to burn his wrist. His movements were lugubrious even in pain. He wrapped the wound in duct tape and stuck it into a glass of prune juice.

"You've been here before, haven't you?" she said.

A wisp of soot escaped the joint and the room smelled of cordite. Teddy licked his finger. His nails were purple.

"We have to try and fight them on a level playing field if we stand any chance of success, and this is one of the few places we can. They have substance in this world now. They have mass."

"I hate that word," she said.

"Why?"

"Everybody uses it."

"They require it, Nonni. You see, they have none of their own. No work can be done in a physical world without mass. Or energy, neither of which they have in their sphere, so they must acquire and transpose. Basic physics, really."

"And where do they get the mass from in our world, Teddy?"

Teddy looked up from a magnesium hitch and his nose bunched up into a red ball as if the universe were obvious. "They get it from you, Nonni."

"What do they want with me?"

"Want is just a human term," Teddy said. He looked vaguely puzzled that the question would even come up. "I know, again, not great news. But if I thought you wanted the sugar-coated version you'd be at home eating popcorn and reading *Popular Romance*. Somehow, I don't think that's your style."

"Can no one give me a discernible answer on this?"

"No one else is giving you the effort that I am, Non. I could make something up on the spur of the moment about what the symptomatic outcome will be — that they will consume you completely. That they will devour your conscience. That they will tear your libido inside out and turn you into a celibate nun who will never screw, drink, or adore sarcasm again. And while that would be more discernible, you'll have to ask yourself if it would help your situation."

Mass, alas, harass. Paternal discernible. *Memento merus hommo*. Nonni thought the words over. The room was cold, cruel, bleak, and dirty. It reminded her of a derelict hospital in Dresden she had seen with Gerry that was bombed during the Second World War. Mangled surgical instruments hung on the wall with no relation to anything but gravity, and somewhere down deep she found that exciting.

"I didn't think so." Teddy straightened his belt and lined up two Erlenmeyer flasks on the desk. When he poured the amber liquids together they turned red. Then he unpacked some cotton balls and dipped them in the liquid with tweezers. "Which is why we have to find out exactly what you can do for them. It's really your only chance, Nonni, finding out what your marketable product is and then delivering it. That's the purpose of our exercise here. I know it looks grotesque, but you'll have to trust me on this one."

Teddy rubbed his stubbled face. There was lint stuck to his ear and dandruff on his collar.

"Do you shave?" she said.

"Why?"

"Do you bathe?"

"Only when I have to."

"That's what I figured."

He bent over his desk and dribbled a red line of conducting fluid onto a chunk of arbutus. The liquid spread out in fractal curves, forming spiral branches. "Strange how that works. Swedish porn queen seeks advice from unhygienic cyber derelict in rancid hotel. The level of irony is intense."

"Suppose I don't want to find out what my most marketable product is. Suppose I just want to them to go away?"

"Probably a full-frontal lobotomy would work. Maybe you could do that Muslim thing where they cut out your clit."

She leaned back against the wall. A curl of mold was expanding out of the light switch. When she touched the pattern, a beetle sprouted out of the casing and fell to the floor. She let the creature make it halfway across a tile then crushed it beneath her shoe.

Teddy watched the act with indifference then peeled open a blue cellophane package and withdrew a set of diodes. He stuffed the cotton balls onto the ends of the diodes, and then lined them up on a strip of masking tape. The platinum wire got wrapped around the wooden block.

"This is creeping me out."

"We need to galvanize a baseline for the data."

"I don't want to galvanize a baseline."

"That's a nice set of tits you have there, Nonni." He pointed a screwdriver at her cleavage where a gash was exposed at the edge of her blouse. The injury gave him some sense of satisfaction. "Or was a nice pair until you got them all scarred up. I have to tell you, they look a little less pristine today. How much did a set like that run your husband, in Canadian dollars? Five, six thousand? What did you tell him, when he asked about his damaged investment? That you tried to fit them into a new Wonder Bra with a factory defect, or maybe you got them stuck in the Garburator? You don't strike me as the type that would spend a lot of time doing housework. Face the facts: the Woodenheads did it to you and now the collateral damage is starting to add up. In a moment of inaction, they punished you for your dereliction where they knew it would hurt most."

He reached out, pulled her shirt down, and examined the breast-like dime candy. She didn't bother to slap him away. The row of hieroglyphic scars that crossed over both nipples were an exotic touch, and she doubted Gerry would appreciate the semantics.

"Is that silicone or motor oil dripping out of there?" he said.

"Shut up."

"That language they've used to tag you with looks Greek," he said. He pressed the screwdriver to his dimple as he thought. "But that's a little classical for them. They usually prefer to write in a language that is utterly dead so only they can understand. Sumerian. Etruscan. It's a standard form of isolation technique. That's extra humiliating for the victim. The point is you have been numbered, branded, and coded just like a head of cattle so we had better get started."

"You keep saying victim."

"That's what you are, Nonni," he said. "Face it. You are a laboratory rat. And do you know what happens to laboratory rats when the experiment is done? The bad news is you actually think you're enjoying the experience. So shut up, listen to me, and do exactly as I say unless you want to live the rest of your life with the intellect of a fir stump."

He licked his thumb and opened his notebook. Appropriate notations had to be made. Then he pulled a voice recorder from his pocket and switched it on. He spoke her name and date and case number into the microphone, then adjusted the bass.

"Take off all of your clothes," he said. "Get down on your knees and face me."

"I don't sub."

"Then get out," he said. He made a stiff motion to the door with his head.

A black blowfly lighted on the window. She caught a quick image of a bondage model in black slacks circa 1955, and then she pulled off her shirt and pants. Her belt buckle struck the floor and a curl of dust rolled across the room. She got down on her knees.

"Spread them apart," Teddy said. He sat back in his chair. He typed a series of commands into his keyboard. "But don't touch yourself. Not yet. And wipe the blood off your nipples. You look like you work here."

Nonni spread her knees and her flesh made imprints on the slatted floor. Pieces of skin and hair haunted the space in between the timbers, and the dents were filled with nail clippings. She knew it then: the room, the hotel was a giant anemone, filtering out the brine and keeping all the small chunks of humanity to feed upon when the living had left.

"Point out each of your wounds and tell me how the transformation occurred." He spoke into the microphone as if he were reading from an instruction manual to a large audience.

She pointed to her left hand. "This one occurred first," she said. "I was involved in sadomasochistic play with a young boy at the club. Later I met him at his house. They came for the first time. My fingers became turgid, then classified, corrupted, and finally calcified."

"We will call that number one." Teddy scrawled a diagram in his book. He was left-handed and the ink kept smudging on the page. "Did they leave any instructions at the time?"

"Nothing."

"Next."

"I received these injuries during the second session." She held up her right breast in the sallow light of the window. A tiny wisp of spiderweb fell through the stale air and landed on her skin. "I was in a change room at a mall. The Woodenheads were trying to entice me into their dimension. The mall was being torn down. There was a knothole in the booth. It put its organ through the hole. I drifted halfway out in their sea."

"I've never seen an ocean."

"Often it's so foggy, you can't see anything. And then a

huge barge appears from nowhere at your bow. You realize how small your skiff is, and how easily you could be sucked into the wake and drowned."

"Very nautical."

"I used screws to anchor myself in this world."

"Did they help?"

Nonni dilated the cavern in her chest with perfectly manicured fingernails, and thought on the majesty of glaciers calving in the Baffin Bay. "I enjoyed limited success."

He rubbed the sweat from his palm to the knee of his purple corduroy pants and tried to sketch the injury. "We'll call that number two. Was there anything that was directly given to you by them? Did they give you any kind of tool to attach the screws with?"

"No."

"They must have left something."

"They didn't."

He shook his head. He found a red pen. He underlined a passage with a ruler. "Third," he said.

Nonni put her hand to her crotch. Number three was a winner. She had been given instructions. She had been confronted with an agent. Just like Teddy had said. An agent naïve. A young girl. A stupid girl. Picked up in the art gallery. Entangled her in crime. Then at the moment of consummation, Nonni's cervix had mineralized into the shell of a trilobite. Just as Teddy had foretold. "Of course, she knew nothing consciously, but I'm convinced she was given an agenda with political implications subtextually."

"Political?" Teddy sat up in his chair. His jaw tensed. His cock roused under his pants between two fat thighs.

"She was an archeologist. Aryan in both physique and conscience. She was convinced that all sex should be hierarchical, and that all forms of erotic arousal should be manipulated by a central terrifying figure masked by melancholy."

"Describe her to me."

"Twenty. Young. Blond." Nonni felt the room filling up with fog. There was the horn off in the distance. She couldn't feel her mouth moving anymore, but Teddy was still scribbling in his notepad. "Pretty in a sort of waifish way. What you'd expect Maria Braun to look like as an adolescent, but more gullible. Mole on her chin." No sooner had the next image of Dietrich formed in her mind than the silhouette bubbled in the wet wrinkles of the wallpaper and Teddy copied it down. "Easily seduced. Kidnapped. To her own house. Tied to her own table. Interrogated. Tortured. Mitigated. Refused to distillate."

The vessel drifted up to the starboard side of the hotel room and bumped against the wall. Teddy's letters turned into Braille, and when his pen punctured the paper the lock buckled against the door.

"Truth of the matter was," she said, "the Woodenheads tortured her. This dimension just supplied the stage. A stolen mask from the museum. Well, a *mensa et thoro*. We just got her to take possession temporarily. The true mission was to discover who her reichmeister was, but some inertia was protecting her. Giving her immunity. That's when it got dangerous to get close. In the middle of the torture scene, the mask exploded. And, alas, with it, the poor girl, too. The shrapnel mutilated everything in sight. My own uterus included. Theories of heliocentric violence abounded. That's how I sustained these injuries to the vulva you are now viewing."

"I can't see."

"It's not that difficult, Teddy. My pussy is shaved."

Teddy adjusted his glasses and leaned in. "Jesus," he said. "Did she just lie down and take it?"

"Her tits were nailed to the table."

Beneath the desk Teddy's hand flitted to his belt and a single finger extended to his crotch.

Nonni didn't mind the finger part. It was beguiling to watch a man try to jerk off and write his memoirs at the same time. Besides, the details were engrossing: two-inch finishing nails that had conveniently appeared in her cupboard to secure the nipples to an oak table. The hammer beating out high speed Morse code. For camouflage, the Woodenheads prefer the negative terminal to the right rib. Watch out for splinters.

"What did she do while all this was going on?" Teddy said.

"She screamed."

"What happened when you were done?"

"I left."

"Didn't she deliver anything to you?"

Of course not. Passive agents didn't deliver anything. They didn't come. They don't have dreams. But at the garden party, things had been different. A swing party of all places and the active agent was the host. Issuing instructions on a level that she didn't understand herself. Not through words but through a thousand desperate nights of headaches and excuses, balanced finance books, and memorized plots of sitcoms.

"Trans-metonymy," he said. "I've seen it before."

"They took her husband."

"You screwed him?"

That much happened all right. Nonni transmitted the coital details to a series of flickers in the hotel's shoddy lighting system. Teddy tried to uncramp his knuckles and knocked over a boiler flask. When Nonni moved to the topic of Tom's corporeal education at the hands of the Woodenheads, Teddy switched to shorthand and on the substantiating theory of the billiard room dismemberment he resorted to grade school diagrams. The final crushing soul into gravel scene appealed to him most. For here was the essence of a man broken down into his most ironic components — gladiolas, a red mailbox, and the come-stained mat in his basement — just as his wife stalked naked down the hall searching for an electric drill to put through her ear. And when Nonni got to the infliction part, the baseboards in the hotel hallway heaved inwards. A flake of plaster sifted off the ceiling and both of them knew exactly what waited on the other side. You've never known what real screwing is until you've been with them.

"I called you when I got home," she said.

"What instructions have they given you since?"

"None."

"They must have left some mark, some artifact."

"None that I've seen."

"It shouldn't be like this," he said. "We'd better proceed."

Teddy put on a pair of rubber gloves then pulled a length of cable from the table. "Lie down. They leave messages, codes. In your mind. We must extract them."

The floor was dirty and cold, and smelled of rancid feet. Teddy corralled the silver cable around her ankles then fastened her calves tight against a metal socket. On the ceiling there was an imitation Ming lantern that reminded Nonni of one she had seen at summer camp twenty years before. Teddy whispered the names of medieval saints and bound her wrists with duct tape. Then he gave the heavens a final unction and fixed the dyed cotton to her temple with circles of adhesive. The dye ran over her cheeks and dribbled on the floor, and soon the room smelled like a medical clinic. There were alligator clips fastened to both nipples. Two stringy wires that ran to a car battery, and a telegraph bar to complete the circuit. Last, he produced a chrome bridle from his suitcase and fitted the rubber bit into her mouth.

“I’m sorry about the horsey thing,” he said. “But I don’t want you biting your tongue off. Don’t worry, you’ll still be able to get the pertinent information out.”

Sucking in the room’s thin air, he stood and pulled once on the reins. Nonni’s ear burned against the floor. Teddy sat back on his chair and let his fingers flutter over the keys as if indecisive. He struck the space bar.

Nonni’s spine exploded in pain and a blue ball of light flashed in front of her face. She bit down on the rubber then buckled into a pretzel. Only the back of her skull and her heels touched the ground.

“Tell me what they have told you,” he said.

“Buck you.”

Teddy ran his fingers over the keys and waited. He gazed out the window. A cement truck passed. “I was a thin man once,” he said. “A handsome man.”

He touched the Q key. A flashbulb went off in the back of Nonni’s head. She flipped over on her stomach and her larynx rattled until it bled cicadas. There was a calendar on the wall she hadn’t noticed before. Bighorn Sheep on Mount Rundle. “But that was a long time ago,” he said. He folded his hands together and reminisced. “I never got the opportunities that you did. Although I worked for it. I pursued them. I begged them. I worshipped them for decades and all they did was ignore me. But for you, it just came easy. You flash your tits and paddle a few bottoms, and poof, they all line up.”

“Untie me.”

“You’re a very pretty lady. In fact, you’re the prettiest I’ve ever had. There have been others that were close. Sandra the secretary, Jillian an orthopedic surgeon, and then a young one that looked like a cheerleader. Christ, what was her name? All that hardly matters now. All that matters is that you tell me what the Woodenheads have instructed you to do.”

Nonni gagged on the bit and her eyes rolled over. There was a dead slater bug on the floor and no point in getting angry.

"Swallow the bit to the corners of your mouth," he said. "That way I can understand the consonants easier."

"Lick me."

"What do you think of the letter R?" He hit the key.

Deep in her eye socket, a pane of glass shattered into rose blossoms and then she pissed herself. The urine squirted out between her legs in a fountain of yellow and spattered on her ankles.

"I'm not really into that." Teddy watched the pool creep towards his desk. "But I know some people pay good money for it. You've never done it for money, have you, Nonni? No, I didn't think so. Not that you wouldn't use the cash, but I think the bottom line is that you figure no one could ever pay you enough."

"Callous witch."

"I think you mean bitch, but I know you can't say the letter B with that rubber thing in your mouth. Callous isn't my style, although I really think you should put more fluids in your diet. Your piss is the colour of a traffic light."

He waited until she slumped back onto the floor and a trail of spit drooled out of the corner of her mouth. Then he sighed and got a handkerchief from his pocket. He wiped the sweat from his brow and readjusted the pup tent in his pants.

"Sugar with your T?" His finger lingered over the pad before striking.

The sun is God, J.M.W. Turner had once said, and Nonni saw that sun too. Bubbling and boiling in its cornea of wiry orange pain, so bright in its loneliness that she cried. So bright that the tears streamed onto the floor and she cried again in long hiccups simply because she was lost and sad and then she cried some more in meandering wails because there was nothing else to do.

"I trust we have finished with the Neanderthal part of the interrogation and we can move onto a more transcendental plain," Teddy said. The toes of his shoes were round and scuffed, but still smelled of polish. "I'll give you one more opportunity to comply before I let my fingers do the dancing again, Nonni. Tell me the most salacious thing the Woodenheads have ever made you do."

"A mape."

"A maid?" he pulled the bit from her mouth.

"We had a maid."

Yes, of course. The Indonesian maid. With brown mendicant eyes. She was in on an expired visa. She had to work. Nonni didn't want to. She was desperate. Her skin was brown and tight. Her nipples black as beetle bugs. Perfect, really.

"And the manservant?"

Nonni had made him strip to clean the windows. Made him shave his pubes in Gerry's bathroom with a four-thousand-dollar iridium razor. He cried. He was Catholic. His family would never forgive him. That was the best part. Forcing him to worship graven images of Ferdinand Marcos with the visa papers in plain view on the hutch, then calling Immigration just when she got bored, with the Woodenheads issuing the instructions.

"Not bad for a start," Teddy said. "What else? More exotic this time, and with some historical context."

Maria Braun did not kill herself in the bunker. Cleopatra was vain. Macdonald didn't want a railway. A crescent of Nonni's blond hair rolled over the grit speckled floor, and her lips picked up a trace of lint. The bathhouse raid could have been avoided. The nation could still be saved. Nonni knew then that every man, woman, and mind of lethargy might be revealed.

"It would have to be for us," she said.

"For us then," Teddy said. He leaned forward with his fat pleading face and Nonni wasn't sure if there was an us, or if her mouth was moving, or if Teddy could even acoustically hear. But the message was then clearly imprinted on the cheap hotel wallpaper, and the Woodenheads were pounding at the door. Teddy turned off the machine. He got down on his knees, pulled her head up by the reins, and took the bit from her teeth. Red ink ran down her jaw. Teddy unzipped his fly. After the dye, it didn't taste that bad.

17.

Gerry sat at the living room table. He hunched over a stack of legal papers that were held down with a china seahorse. Stamps of lawyers and seals from courts were pressed into the pink documents. Some of the dye had come off on his palm. He wore his blue pinstripe suit and his pair of gold-rim reading glasses. Lines creased around his eyes and every few seconds he punched figures into a calculator. He glanced up when the front door closed.

"What happened to you?"

Nonni tossed her coat on the sofa. Her lip felt puffed. Her tongue was crustated and the great Odysseus knew no friendly fire.

"Nothing important," she said. She pushed his hand away and a button off her blouse rolled across the floor.

"I'm calling EMS."

"It's a bramble bush from the backyard."

"We don't have a bramble bush in the backyard." Gerry held up a shard of her shirt. The edges were singed. The bruises beneath the cotton on her ribs were angular.

"I fell."

"Where is your purse?"

She pulled the blouse back down. She'd have to make a trip to San Francisco to get another.

"It's gone too."

"Were you robbed?"

She sat down on the stairs and put her hands to her ears. "Gerry, can you do something for me?"

"What?"

"Turn the radio off."

Gerry glanced around the room. "It's not on."

"The signals interfere."

"I'm calling the police."

Gerry picked up the phone from the ivory night stand. Nonni's fist came down on the face. The dial exploded. The case split in half and blew over the couch. Gerry was left holding the receiver with a cord dangling in mid-air.

"No police," she said.

A transistor rattled out of the case and hit the carpet. "Let me take you to the doctor."

"This is not a physician's domain."

Gerry bit his lip. He pulled open her blouse. The collar had been shredded. Rectangular serrations rose around her neck like armour buckles. Along her ribs train track abrasions turned the skin purple. A series of dots and dashes had been punched into her thigh.

"Who did this to you?" Gerry folded his knuckles into his lips and sat back on the steps. He rocked back and forth, getting ready for the worst possible scenario.

"Nobody did this to me."

"You come home black and blue and look like you've been sucked through a sausage spinner and you say nobody did this? You're not making any sense. Just tell me the truth."

"I was out."

He touched the side of her calf and followed the bruises around her leg. "These aren't patterns." He put his glasses back on. "They are characters. This is writing."

"It could be a language. Etruscan was suggested to me. On the other hand it could be Aramaic. They are partial to those with Coptic associations."

"They who?"

"It was a figure of speech."

"It was not a figure of speech. You don't talk in figures of speech." He got off the stair, put his nose to her shoulder and smelled the flesh. "Nonni, did you get a branding?"

"A tattoo maybe."

"A single tattoo takes an hour. You have hundreds of them here." Gerry struck his head with a closed fist. Here was the man in defeat. "I should have been watching you. I should have been paying more attention. I thought you were out looking at sports cars, and instead you were out getting your skin microwaved."

"It's not microwaved. It is a physical encryption explaining how the physical world is dictated by desire. I have been given a set of instructions and I must follow them."

Gerry clasped his hands together. He looked older then. His hairline had receded some, and the tips of the hair were grey. "I know you are out playing with other people. I've known that for a long time. Months, maybe. It's all right. I have accepted that. I've also accepted the fact that I can't give you everything you want. No person can. I know there are things you have to do. Things only you understand. That's okay, too. I don't ask who your play partners are. I've never asked in the past. That was our deal. But this time it's different. This is outside the game. These people, whoever they might be, are crazy. You could have been turned into a snuff film or sold into white slavery. Tell me who they were."

"You wouldn't understand."

"Try me."

There was many rooms in the master's home and all of them worth deceit. "You were right at first, Gerry. It was a robbery. I was walking back out to the car in the East Village and I got robbed."

Gerry got down on his knees and examined the buckles on her thigh. He had studied Braille once and given lectures at the university.

"Didn't it hurt?"

"It hurt all right."

Outside the window a magpie lighted on the maple branch. The mahogany grandfather clock ticked over in the corner, and Nonni thought how painfully exquisite the moments in between the tocks could be.

"We've been together a long time," he said. "I'm not angry. I'm not jealous. But please don't shut me out. If it wasn't a robbery, was it self-inflicted?"

She tilted her head to one side and gazed down on her poor lost husband. She put a hand on his shoulder. "It wasn't self-inflicted. And no person did it to me. The Woodenheads did this."

"Who?"

"The Woodenheads, Gerry. I don't know what they call themselves. That's what I call them. They are beings comprised of wood or metal or stone or whatever they choose to use as a medium for the day."

"Are they a criminal gang or psychos?"

"They are not human. They come from another dimension. They control me and my free will."

Gerry bit on the end of his glasses. He blinked. Somewhere

behind his eyes, two dark stars collided. "Okay." He nodded. He fought to remember something distant from a psychology text. "Where are they now?"

"They are right here, beside us."

Gerry glanced around the living room. His eyes flicked from the staircase down to the dining room cabinet, the sterling candles and spoons all lined up on a felt rack.

"You can't see them, Gerry. I'm not trying to be condescending, but you won't ever be able to see them. You're a nice man, really. You are a good husband and a brilliant architect. But they won't ever come for you."

"All right." He stood up and walked across the room with a knuckle in his mouth. "All right. I accept that. What did Doctor Sayer think about them?"

"He didn't say anything."

"Did you tell him?"

"Not really."

"Why not?"

"He wouldn't understand."

"That's his job. That's what we pay him for."

"He's a psychiatrist," she said. "Not a physicist."

"We don't need a physicist. But we've got to get you in to see someone."

"I am seeing someone."

"Who?"

"An expert. Down in Chinatown. That's where I was today."

"What kind of expert?"

"More of a tradesman, really. He knows about them. He has files. I go to his place and he tells me about them. He has practical tools and instrumentation."

"Is he a professional?"

"He gives me advice and I suck his cock."

Gerry screamed. He struck his head against the mantel. A tiny bubble of spit formed at the corner of his mouth. On the table, a red rose that had been in a pearl vase shed a single petal.

"I do not believe this." He grabbed a fistful of hair and tried to pull some out, but it was too short. "Nonni, you can't ever go back to this guy again."

"You just finished telling me that no matter what I did, you would be with me."

"Nonni, this scam artist is using you."

"He never did any of this to me."

"Who did?"

"I've told you."

"Tell me where this animal is." Gerry shook his finger in the air and his chin vibrated in tremors. "I'll pound his brains in. Nonni he's got some kind of control over you. This isn't you talking."

"I know. I used to sound so simple and plain."

"This isn't you at all." It was not even an option. "Nonni, don't you see when you suffer, I do too? Don't you see that I can't stand to see you like this? You've got to tell me the truth. Are you taking your medication? Did the doctor change it?" He brushed back his hair, faced the picture window and then the judgement arrived, the storm had passed. "You're right. We are into something different now. I accept that, Nonni."

Gerry paced back and forth on the carpet. He arranged the legal papers on the table. He took hold of the chair and steadied himself to take the helm. "This Mr. Copperhead or whatever his name is. Are you going to go back to his place and play these games again?"

"I don't go to them. They come to me."

"They come to you? Of course. Yes. Where?"

"They can go anywhere."

"Are they going to come to the house? This house?"

Nonni looked around. The furniture sat on red felt dots that Gerry had installed on the floor with the interior decorator. An original Bernard Bennett acrylic painting hung on the wall and was dusted by the new maid who came in on Thursday. From the cellar came the faint smell of turpentine and precise blueprints of balanced conclusions. "I don't think they'll come here."

"You won't let them in?"

"They don't use the door."

"How about public places? Could they find you at a bus stop or in a library?"

"I suppose so. A library is unlikely."

"Okay, we're narrowing the geography down. What time are they most likely to come?"

"No particular time Gerry. I just have to be aroused."

"Yes, I guess that makes sense, doesn't it?" He spoke swiftly. He squeezed one fist with the other palm until his thumb went white. "They would come when you were excited. That would be the only time. I'm trying to figure out how to keep you safe while I make other arrangements."

"What other arrangements?"

"These next few weeks are going to be hectic." Gerry was in command of the fleet now. "Lawyers. Bankers, reporters. There's going to be a lot of them in the next little while. But we'll work it out. We always do." He walked around the table re-sorting the stack of letters that had already been placed in five different piles. "I can have Gwen and Don come down in the afternoons, but they're pretty much in the same boat I am. Terri is sympathetic. It's her brother that is going to be taking our case. We've got CCLA on our side, too. I know the director. He's an anthropologist. His daughter is all screwed up on the diet pills right now, but he's a believer in sexual discrimination suits. He'll want to talk to you."

"Why do we need a lawyer?"

"The case," Gerry looked up from the letters. This much should have been obvious. "Since we are all charged jointly, we are doing a class defence case."

Suddenly, the burns on the inside of Nonni's thigh hurt, her mouth tasted of tin, and the earth was a hard place to fall back on. "You said you were taking the alternative measures."

"I never said that. You said that."

"Let me get this straight. The prosecutor has said you could walk away for a forgiveness day in the food bank and you're not willing to play ball?"

"No," he said. "I'm not going to play ball. None of us are."

"None of us?"

"We voted on it."

"Voted. Great. Democratic stupidity. I didn't vote."

"You weren't there."

"Are you insane?" she said.

Gerry straightened his back and folded his hands together. He looked taller than she remembered him, and his face was flushed with blood and stolid like some kind of wartime leader she had seen in a school textbook. "No, Nonni. I am not insane. I am completely within my faculties. We are talking about two separate issues here and we must keep them distinct. One of them is your welfare. And I am concerned deeply about that. The other is a criminal persecution that we will not allow to be brushed under the carpet. And at trial time, if the Crown offers it to us again, we will refuse again. We want to go to trial. In fact, we will agitate to go to trial. We will make sure that this goes to trial and that it appears in the newspapers and television so that it must go to trial. We will have show after show at the club and get arrested again and insist to go to jail forever if we have to."

"In the name of all things that are holy, why?"

"Because it is the right thing to do."

"Finding a workable club is the right thing to do."

"We can't have the state breaking into our bedrooms night after night. Nonni, I didn't want to talk about this now, because I know you are having serious challenges and I respect that. But you also must respect what is important to me and if it means get thee to a nunnery for a while then you must do that. There's no other way around this."

"And you propose putting on a bunch of amateur theatre to ensure a longer prison sentence is the answer?"

"What do you propose, Nonni?"

Nonni felt her throat tighten up and her spine get cold. The last few moves on the chessboard were being sorted, and the bruises had sunk back into her bones. "I propose that I'm not left alone."

"You will not be alone," Gerry said. He spoke and the entire house was still the way houses got just before dawn. "I am here. You have me. You have your friends. You have a free country where you can talk to your neighbours when you like and walk down the street when you please and disagree with what is wrong when you wish. And that is just the point. That is not loneliness. That is intimacy."

"You are out of your mind." She snatched a coat off the foyer cabinet. The empty coat rack fell over. "If that club is gone, I will die."

"You won't die, Nonni."

"You're being co-opted, Gerry. Co-opted. Do you know what that means?"

"I know, Nonni."

"It's like you've volunteered to work in the soap factory in Auschwitz, and you think it's okay because with all that soap you'll have clean hands."

Gerry looked up. His eyes narrowed and some of the creases on his face smoothed over. "I didn't know you were up on the history of the Holocaust."

"Of course I'm up on it. I'm pissed off."

"You actually have your finest moments when you're angry, Non."

"Well this is me angry, Gerry. So get used to it."

Nonni seized a handful of the pink papers on the table and ripped them into shreds. Then she pushed all of the letters onto the floor and stepped on the calculator. After, she turned the table over, picked up Gerry's computer, threw it through the window, and walked out the door.

The light in Don's garage was on. A wedge of yellow shone across the pedicured grass of the Mount Royal lawn, and the hum of an electric tool echoed around a Roman fountain. Through a cluster of white birch came the sounds of someone working. Hammering and sawing, making the world a more ordered place than it had been before.

Nonni pushed the door open. Gwen was poised over the workbench with a drill in her hand. She wore her black evening dress with Italian stilettos and a pair of safety glasses. They had probably been out. Usually Moonlight on Thursdays. She gripped the tool awkwardly, attempting to twist back the rotation of the earth.

A black oil derrick slicked with creosote towered above her to the ceiling. Inside the rib cage of timbers, a monstrous silk phallus quivered with the air from a butane blower.

"Hello Gwen," Nonni said. She walked across the empty garage. There wasn't so much as an oil stain on the concrete.

The drill fell from Gwen's hand. The bit broke on the floor and the garage went silent.

"I didn't expect to see you here." Gwen locked her fingers together as if to pray and her lips trembled when she spoke. "Gerry's been looking for you."

Gwen pulled off her glasses. Her eyes darted down to the cell phone that sat on the buzz saw and then to the open window. Nonni hit the electric lock on the wall. Gwen was still a stunning woman for forty, and she wondered if there was time. Probably not. Swirls of wood and specks of resin spun beneath the work lamp. A line of armoured tools hung in an open closet.

"It's for the club," Gwen said.

"Let's just the two of us talk for a minute."

"There's nothing between Gerry and I."

On the corner of the workbench, an ancient box radio cackled Brahms, and Nonni wondered how many thousands of times misunderstandings like this had been played out in garages across the nation. "You and Gerry are not the issue."

"What is?"

"The issue is you and another dimension."

"What other dimension?"

"The one Gerry doesn't understand."

"Call him right now. He's worried sick about you."

Nonni ran her hand along the workbench and up the derrick to the bulging phallus inside. Because the pink silk quivered so quickly it was impossible to tell if it was every really in one place. What was the word for that: quorum, quantum, quixotic? There were a pair of needle-nose pliers by the vice grip. They might come in handy too. "What exactly is it supposed to do?"

"Shoot oil on the vice department."

"Normally, that would make me horny."

Gwen toyed with the string of white pearls that hung between her breasts and clung to them in case the boat went down.

"I know that over the past weeks things have been difficult," she said.

Nonni peered into the teeth of the pliers, then used the tool to bend over a galvanized nail that was held in the vice. She marvelled at how easy it was to bend even the hardest of irons when decision points got closer.

"Nonni, please put that down. You're making me nervous."

"I know I've not been very good to Gerry over the past few weeks. Past few years perhaps. Maybe I've never been good to him at all. But one thing I've accepted is that human affection is ephemeral. Not that it's a bad thing. Hell, it's a good thing for most people. It makes the world go round. This world, anyway. But there's another world. Another existence that I've connected with and that's the plain I have to work on. If Gerry is angry at me, I understand that. If he had an affair with you or a hundred other women, I'd have to understand that too. You and Don and him can settle down to a nice threesome and go on with your lives. Have a kitchen with granite counters and marble sinks. But the club you shall have to leave to me. It's more than a special place for parties. It is a device. A receiver. A transmitter. And you are going to have to let me do what needs be done."

Gwen nodded and went wide-eyed at the darkness that stood before her. It was strange to watch a woman with such perfect glistening teeth look so confused. Nonni wasn't sure if she was rambling. She wasn't sure if Gwen was listening. The woman, who for seven years had been the epitome of poise, was now trying to decide if she should use a power drill as a defensive weapon.

“You see Gwen, the message our club transmitted was so unique, so powerful, humans can’t recognize it. But others do. And those others came. They changed me, Gwen. They changed everything. I’m not trying to minimize anything you and your puerile civil libertarian pals want to do at the club, but once you’ve been with them. Well, anything else seems a little like treason.”

Gwen nodded and bit on her pearls. Her eyes darted to the car keys on the bench, to the fire alarm by the welding machine, and finally to the shovel by the door.

“I’m not angry at anyone,” Nonni said. “I just have to make sure things are done properly tonight. It may mean that some people will get hurt. Which is hard, because I’ve hurt so many people already.”

“Who have you hurt, Nonni?”

Nonni put a hand to her face. Her cheeks were rough as fir bark and cold, and in the crevice of age she could detect some heavy oil, perhaps a glyceride. “Where should I start? The list is rather lengthy. I think I hurt that waitress we met at the museum bar. What was her name? Sorry, can’t recall. There was Wendy and Tom. The piercing party. Phil and his tart got banged up at bit, too. And there still must be Teddy, David’s cousin. You don’t know him. Devious little prick. There were a few other sundry people that will probably show up on missing person reports soon enough and of course, yes, there was Daniel.”

“Daniel?”

“Club Daniel. Surfer boy, Daniel.”

“Oh my God, Nonni.” Gwen backed up against the oil derrick and the silk phallus inside chuckled to stiff attention. A box of nickel screws fell to the floor and rattled on the concrete.

“I didn’t mean to damage your feelings, or the reputation of your club, but this is part of a grand scheme in which we all play our little parts. Let me put it in a context that you'll understand: Karl Marx. To make an omelet — never mind. The point is, this had to be done. And I really wouldn't worry too much about Daniel, you see Gwen, he was an agent for them."

"Them who?"

"The Woodenheads. In fact he probably was one himself. Hard to tell an agent from a principal without a program."

"Nonni, I get it. I understand." Gwen pointed to her phone. "Let's call Gerry so he can understand, too. He can come over and pick up the prop and we can head off to the party. Everything will turn out."

"I'm sorry, no. It can't work that way."

"Why not? Listen, Nonni. We have to get to the club. You know how important this party is for Gerry, for me and Don and the club. The club was important to you, too. So let's get Don's truck, and go together."

"It's a very noble thing what you and Don are doing. But I can't let you finish it like that."

A small bead of sweat ran between Gwen's breasts. She reached for the door and snapped the string of pearls. The white beads danced across the floor, and Nonni thought about the song String of Pearls. And then about ions streaming over electric fields, and oil dancing on a frying pan, and then she thought of oils being osmotically transferred through bound naked bodies. And then she stopped herself from thinking and crossed the last few feet between them. Gwen's eyes expanded. She made a tiny chirping noise, like a black-capped chickadee and backed into the corner. One of the beads crushed beneath her foot. Nonni caught her by the collar and pitched her up against the tool rack. A plane saw tumbled from its hook. Gwen was left pinned up on the cork board kicking and flailing, the shoulder of her dress impaled on the spike. Nonni held her victim against the wall with one hand and ripped her dress off with the other. She spun the fabric into a coil and bound Gwen's wrists behind her back. For a woman of forty Gwen's skin was still amazingly tight. How they would like that.

There was a smell of industrial iron in the room. The windows in the workshop trembled and Nonni felt the sepulchral mass of the Woodenheads behind her. Then there was a gnostic choir singing, and the shadow of the visitors loomed across the wall and over Gwen's face.

Gwen cried out and Nonni thought how beautiful the moment was when terror was pure. And when it was obvious Gwen had seen them too, Nonni allowed her to crumple on the ground. She looked better that way, anyway. Nonni waited until the humming stopped and then she picked up Gwen and carried her to the tool lock and set her inside. She shut the door and pushed a tire iron through the handles so there was just enough air for her to breathe, but didn't worry too much because it was all for a good cause.

Nonni noticed then the veins on her arms stood out. Her muscles were tight as the scales on a garden hose and so she leaned against the workbench and lit a menthol. She dialed a familiar number on Gwen's phone.

"Hello, Nonni," the voice on the other end said.

"How did you know it was me, detective?"

"You're an easy person to recognize."

"This isn't even my phone number."

"It's your friend's number, isn't it?"

"You have a good memory."

"Where are Don and Gwen these days?"

"I was just speaking with them."

"And what is their tenor at this juncture?"

"Resolute," Nonni said.

"I'm sorry to hear that."

"So am I, detective. In fact, that's why I've called you."

"I like it when we see eye to eye, Nonni."

There was a pause at the other end of the phone. Then the sound of a chair joint squealing back and the leather stretching. The puffing of lips and the sticky curl of nicotine inhalation.

"You're smoking again, aren't you detective?" Nonni said.

"We both know where our habits reside."

"I got to thinking about habits. I did a lot of thinking, really. I decided that there's a time to be noble and then there's a time to be practical. There's a time to be immoral and then there's a time to be amoral. This is one of those times."

"To each thing, a season."

How fitting, Nonni thought. A little scripture for posterity. The detective always had such apt phrases. Come to think of it, their conversations had always been so apt, so intriguing, if not a little angular. Close even, on some issues, even if they had used different points of references.

"I know it's short notice, detective, but I wanted to keep you in the loop regarding one of those seasons."

"Which one?"

"The club."

"And when would this phenomenon be salient?"

"Contemporaneously."

"This is bad news."

"Depending on your perspective."

"What is it actually they have planned?"

"You've seen *Hamlet*?"

"I'm familiar with the plot," Pierceman said.

"I guess you could say this will be the epiphany scene."

"I'll come and pick you up, Nonni."

"I'll find my own transportation," Nonni said, and hung up. She walked across the garage and confronted the greased tower of pathos. The frail architecture made her feel melancholy in a fashion she knew was no longer workable. And so frame by frame she tore the beams apart with her hands. Nails flew out from the wood, absorbing into a furnace of intent before they even had a chance to strike the ground.

18.

Teddy walked down a back alley in Chinatown that was slicked with oil and smelled of tar. Nonni was waiting for him. The bag of groceries perched on his gut was in her crosshairs and the plan was simple: clutch, gas, impact. Redact him and his polo shirt to a red smear down the road, then relish on his slothful demise.

She had wedged her car in-between an ivy hedge and a brick wall. The rear tail light had come off in the process. When Teddy pushed open the garden gate to his backyard, the Mazda jumped the ditch and blew apart the fence. He didn't even see her coming. Pickets flew. His arms vanished beneath the grill. A potato went rolling across the alley. The bumper pinned his torso between the front wheel and the shed. The act was within a few inches of a decapitation, so Nonni felt champagne was in order to celebrate the precision, but facts be known, the miss was probably just an unfortunate coincidence.

Nonni sat back in the driver's seat. She revved the motor then popped the car out of gear. In the glove compartment sat an emergency pack of menthols. She knew if she sucked hard enough she could get dizzy. And dizzy meant horny which was always good.

"Help me," Teddy said. His hand wrapped around the hood ornament.

She rested the menthol in the ashtray, then pulled out her pair of leather racing gloves from under the seat. When they were secured on her fingers and laced at the wrist, she walked around the shattered pickets to the bumper. She thought then how much she loved the sound of broken pickets, of broken hoses and landslides and earthquakes and anything that made the earth rumble to celebrate the existence of chaos. She had just ruined the perfect trashy day in the life of a perfectly trashy member of the renting class, and she was proud of that. With his shoulder crammed under the bumper and his neck an inch from the wheel well, Teddy was not a comfortable sight. His blood pressure must have been up to the 150/80 level because his face was sunset red. The off-green tinge around his gills suggested that his hemoglobin count was low, too.

"Help me, Nonni."

"Why?" she said.

"Because I'm in pain."

"Excellent." She poked his belt buckle with the toe of her boot. She'd seen buckles like that in the window of a dollar store. "I hope that means you're in the mood. Because I sure am."

"Why have you run me over?"

"I haven't quite yet. You have at least an inch. I can get around to it promptly if you like."

"You're insane."

A possible topic. A pliable excuse. But somehow not worth the punctuation that would have to be expended therein. "I'm not sure on that one," she said. "I had an appointment with my psychiatrist today, but I missed it because, well, because I am here with you instead."

"Why?"

"Probably for the same reason you left me tied up with electrical tape in that filthy hotel, Teddy. With a circuit breaker shoved up my uterus. You liked it. It turned you on. It took me three hours to get out of that mess."

"It was part of the game. You wanted it, Nonni. You begged for it."

She stepped over a row of carrots that had been uprooted in the skid and stood between his legs. She picked up a garden hoe that had been flattened in the collision and twisted it into his crotch. Not quite the impregnable instrument it once had been. "How about this Teddy? Is this part of the game? Are you begging for it now?"

"No," he said.

"That's too bad because it's really working for me."

"Back up the car."

A Swainson's hawk flew across the blue plain sky. Nonni hadn't noticed that before. The animal fluttered down on to a carrier post by the railway that the CPR had been using for over a hundred years. All that history, all that grease, and she hadn't cared about that, either.

"I bought a new set of tires. Did you notice? They're supposed to have superior braking power. Something to do with alkaloid surfacing. I bet right about now you're glad I made the investment."

Teddy's face had gone jaundiced and a bubble of spit dried in the corner of his mouth. Nonni pushed the froth away with the end of the hoe then cast it aside. Teddy' lip quivered as if he were enduring an admonishment from a stern grammar teacher and falling into cataplexy.

“Back up the car, Nonni.”

“No. I’m going to drive it forward. I am going to run you over and squish your fat head like a watermelon, and watch all of your fat cranial juices flow over your fat stomach and laugh. I could come just thinking about that.”

“Please don’t.”

“Why not?”

“What do you want?”

“What do I want?” she said. Nonni squatted down and ran her gloved fingers over the spokes on her chrome rim, then over the dirt on the bumper panel and finally to the coarse stubble on Teddy’s shrunken chin. There wasn’t really much difference. “Let me think. My husband is going to jail. I have a lice infection from being tied up in filthy hotel, and my mind has been invaded by beings from another dimension, and you’re asking me what I want?”

“I don’t know anything about any of that.”

Beneath a mountain ash, a breeze ruffled the grass. The crimson berries on the tree shivered, and a compost of dried grass rotted with sweet simplicity under a white sun. How beyond pestilence the simple procession of seasons could be. How beautiful the glazed glass of azure sky was to hold. She stroked her jaw and knew the bone was as much gorgeous as it was marble.

“You know everything about that,” she said. “Take a good look at me. What do you see?”

“I’m bleeding.”

“At least you can still do that. Me, I’ve been turned into a supermodel of antiquity. A chunk of stone that people will gaze at in a museum for the next thousand years.”

“We fixed that. Remember the game? You’re better now.”

“We fixed nothing. And it’s not a game anymore.”

She turned, strode back to the car door, and put one foot on the gas. The motor shot up a thousand revs.

"Don't kill me, Nonni."

"Why not?"

"I'm going to scream. Everyone will hear. The police will come."

"Nobody will hear you. Nobody will come. This is a shitty alley in a shitty neighbourhood, and everybody here is on crack and they only care about their shitty little lives. They don't care about their neighbours and they certainly don't care about fat little you, and the only reason the police come here is to eat Chinese food."

"How do I help you?"

She peeled the filter off the next menthol before lighting it. "Louder. I can't hear you."

"Talk to me, Nonni. What is it you want to know?"

Nonni went back to the front of the car and knelt down. She picked a thistle out of his brow. Strands of matted black hair fell over his forehead. His collar was ripped. His shoulder was going blue. Cubes of oxtail soup were smeared on his neck. No wonder he always smelled funny.

"Do you see my face?" she said.

"Yes."

"Do you see it is turning into magnesium plated nickel?"

"No."

"What do you see?"

"I see marks."

"What kind of marks?"

"Scratch marks," he said.

"Exactly."

"What of it?"

"Horrible repeated scratch marks."

“So what?”

“Tell me what you see now.” She tossed her cigarette into the garden then peeled her blouse back to show a pair of nipples cleaved with screws. The blood had dried in dark red branches on top of a field of bruising.

“You’ve been pierced.” He closed his eyes. A short flutter of wind turned up his matted hair and the left edge of his lip wouldn’t stop ticking.

“Not pierced. Impossibly, terrestrially mutilated. Trans-provincially, Newtonian-expropriatedly-censured. And the reason they have been mutilated is because some creature that you have set loose on our dimension is feeding on me. Look at my eyes, Teddy. They are quartz. Look at my heart. It is mahogany. Who do you think did this to me?”

“Nobody did this to you, Nonni.”

“*They* did.”

“They?”

“Them. Who do you think?”

“Your pain is self-inflicted.”

She pushed a fresh menthol against his nose, then lit the cigarette up and stuck it into his ear. “I am turning into a conglomeration of insentient material. An entity that doesn’t feel or screw or come. They have done this to me and you are going to get them to stop.”

“I can’t do that.”

“Why not?”

“Because Nonni, there is no them. There is no other dimension. There are no creatures. It’s a fucking game and it’s gone far enough.” Teddy let his head fall onto the sidewalk. A slater bug stuck to his cheek. “I am just a horny man who can’t get any girls and spends too much time on the computer. I make it up. It’s a trick. I use it to get laid.”

Nonni held his jaw, ground his face against the tire, and twisted him sideways until a rubber stain smeared on his cheek. Then she took a soda cap and stuck it to his chin. He was a fat man. He was an ugly man. He was a plain man. And somehow in all that pathos, Nonni knew a little more pain would probably do him good. "If you have ever cared about anyone or anything, Teddy. Tell me what I want to know now, because I am going to die anyway, so running you over is no big deal. If you have seen what I have over the past few days you'd agree: I'm capable. And besides, you are now officially small potatoes. I've got heavy alloys for a clit, Teddy. Do you know what that means? The only thing that will get intimate with me is a compass. Or them. Of course, there's always them. Waiting in the cloak room. Hidden under the furnace vent. But now I'm tired of playing their game. You brought them here. You make them go away. Tell me what I have to do to beat them or I swear I will run you into the garage, leave the ignition on, and make it looked like you gassed yourself while you were jerking off to a horticulture magazine."

A line of cirrus clouds moved through the western sky. Their edges were turning pink, and over the crests of the Rocky Mountains, the deep valleys beyond, were already in darkness.

"You win," he said. "I'll tell you. But I have to be able to think straight."

"What do you need?' she said.

"Back the car up, for Christ sakes."

The glory of desperation. The despair of hope. Nonni let the emergency brake off and the convertible slid an inch. A gardenia got crunched. Teddy exhaled. Nonni sat on the hood.

"Go," she said.

Teddy's head slumped against the fender. His shoulder swelled up like a blimp. His gaze got lost on a roof. "The only way to pacify them is to do what they ask. They have already given you the instructions."

"They have told me nothing that makes sense."

"They play by their own rules."

"Explain their rules to me."

"You won't understand."

"I haven't lost it yet."

"Oh, you've lost it," he said. "There's no question about that. You're right off the deep edge. Don't you see, Non? That's why they picked you. They pick people because they stand out. Not because they're good or kind. Normal people don't have time for this kind of shit. Normal people don't even get their attention."

"I did."

"Because you're a horny, bent bitch of cosmic proportions." Teddy smiled and then his right leg seized up. "Think of yourself as a Phillips screwdriver, Non. A tool. For whatever reason, they use you. Who knows for what end, because along with horny you're also lazy, cheap, shallow, and selfish. Look at you: you've just spent the last couple of weeks sucking some fat guy's cock because you thought he would make a Jungian fantasy come true. Sometimes I wonder why they bother. If we're the best examples of what they see in humans, then our species is in bad shape."

"So they come to you, too."

Teddy pondered two creosote power poles that were lashed together with steel cables. His pupils drifted to the left, as if he were watching a river flow. He had the slightest dimple in his cheek that Nonni hadn't noticed before and when the pain let up it winced in Morse code delight.

"I accept the collateral profit. I get laid and tie chicks up. So far they haven't put a prohibition on that. I get an insight now and then. And I only get hurt a little."

He smiled again, but then his smile became cold, and then frostbitten, and finally fossilized. She thought of the wooden Indian in the tavern with Pierceman.

A voice came out of Teddy's throat although his larynx was still. His lips didn't move. The phlegm on his tongue dried out. Nonni wanted to hear a radio or television, but there was none. Just a bold oratory to an empty alley save an audience of one, so this was no place for the weak. She recognized the voice. It was Gerry's.

"I can't find her," Gerry's voice said. The noise buzzed through Teddy's vocal chords as a tinned telephone conversation, as if to stress she must have known already what Gerry was probably saying: "I looked all night, Dr. Sayer. You can't be married to someone for that long without knowing the difference between when they are having a moment and when their moments are over. She's changed. She's obsessed. I suppose a hundred years ago they would have had her committed to some kind of institution with nuns. Except it's more than just sex. Kinky isn't the word. Unearthly is precise. Then she got phone calls. Strange phone calls. In hushed voices that didn't make sense. She banged the car up a few times. She got into trouble with the authorities. She'd mention fantastic parties she'd been to or incredible dominatrixes who she'd met. Then I'd phone up those people and they'd say she wasn't there. Or else I'd check the pervert pages for the madams and find they didn't exist. We had the issue at the club. We had to do what was right, what was moral. For Nonni, it was like the Titanic was going down. She thought there were creatures from another dimension coming to kidnap her. Doctor, she put screws in her breasts and wrapped ropes around her neck, and lived in a world where she believed her actions had no consequence."

If those were the facts, then awake, arise, or be forever fallen.

People prayed for the end of the world only because they had no clue how bad things would get afterwards. Nonni pulled off her glove and put a hand on Teddy's cooling temple. His ceramic forehead was Edwardian as it was gorgeous and still. It had been a long time since she had seen such perfection in a man. Perhaps never at all. Utterly quiet. Completely content with fate, even if his hair smelled of malt. She felt his threadbare shirt, his bulging belly, and finally his split zipper. He had seen them. On this bleak oiled road, he had known their mind, and didn't plead insanity. Nonni put her hand to his fat thigh and her fingers clenched the blubber. Two vast and trunkless legs of stone didn't even notice. A pulpit of salty water splashed on Teddy's belt buckle and bled onto his torso.

Down the back alley, a line of children was led across the oiled gravel by a school teacher. They walked in a long row and held onto a blue string that kept them in place. The small ignorant faces bobbled up and down in laughter and their white teeth caught the sunlight. A boy with blond hair turned and gazed at the crashed car and the woman with high boots. His bright blue eyes were wide and round, utterly unknowing.

19.

Beside a peeled door, behind a scuffed window, and above a brass Buddha, the neon sign in the Onyx Club glowed a constant orange. The sign had hummed the same hue of twilight for over seven years and Nonni saw it as a symbol of youth and permanence. A party that would never end, a play scene without red words, an abolition of loneliness.

She stood on the pavement and listened to the gas cackle. Argon probably. An ugly gas. Like Freon or xenon, something that gargled away endlessly, serving no aesthetic purpose. Her leather boots were tied up at the knees and her rubber corset laced at the spine. A moth fluttered around the street lamp, and in the distance an arc light from a welding shop reflected off a tailings pond.

Inside the coliseum, the balconies were lit with gas lamps, and the chandelier sparkled amber. The air brooded in the nervous sweat of club goers, sticky in the second before collision. In a way, not much different than any other Friday night. Heidi and Randle drank cocktails at the bar and stared at the German porn movie that ran on its endless loop. Shannon and Steve oiled down a pair of leather crops. Upstairs, a tattered domme leaned against the ragged iron rack and smoked into Sunday morning. Her black dress fell off her hips just the way it was supposed to, and William polished a wine glass just the way he always had. Nonni couldn't decide if they were too beautiful to die or too stupid to know.

"What are you doing here?" Don came out from behind the bar. He had on a prison costume and jock strap. His face was blanched and his voice dried out.

"I've come for the party."

"You can't stay, Nonni."

"Why not?"

"Gwen told you."

"She didn't."

"Probably the police have already picked her up."

"I found Gwen."

"Where is she?"

"En route."

"What did she say?"

"That she'd be along with the props."

"Why didn't she call me?"

"She was working with fibreglass."

A wisp of resin floated off Nonni's shoulder. Don bent forward, but the tar was gelatinous and smelled septic so he didn't want to get too close. "Is that plastic coming out of your boob?"

"Foreshadowing."

"I thought you were going to see a doctor."

"You know, specialists." She picked at the string of plaster buried in her flesh and pulled out a thread. Only bloodied fibre at first, a long sinew of muscle, yet the more she pulled, the less it looked like herself.

"You're bleeding."

"That's stopped."

"People are going to jail."

"I like rough games."

Don had always been a compassionate man. A caring man. A man who went well out of his way to take diplomacy over dogma. But this time, he'd had enough. He twisted his wedding band around his finger and his eyes surveyed the club in search of one kind word in the balcony. The matter of discipline fell to his hands. "Let me put it a different way for you. I don't want you here anymore."

"I put a lot of money into this club."

"Nobody cares."

A trickle of creosote ran down from behind Nonni's ear then branched out over her jaw. People not caring about money missed the point. "You'll need me to deal with our visitors when they come."

"Don't fight with the police."

"Who's talking about the police?"

"Who are you talking about?"

"I negotiate with a higher authority."

"Whom?"

"I'll miss this place when it's over."

Don would have none of it. That was another flaw in his character, he couldn't deal with metaphor and getting angry made him stutter.

"Our members are frightened, Nonni."

Jim and Susan leaned over the fantasy room balcony with cruel fascination. Still beautiful, Susan stood in a garish rubber dress rattling her necklace with ageing knuckles.

"Fear is an aphrodisiac," Nonni said. "Which is what we need. Otherwise the collaborators will roll in. Alloys, alchemy, affection on Seventeenth Avenue, which would make the metonymy complete."

"I don't know if you're off your meds or if you've dropped too much peyote, and quite frankly I don't care. I'm tired of games, I'm sick of your life, and I'm done with your fantasy park. Now get out."

A beautiful blue glimmer flashed across Don's eyes like butane or a welding arc, and Nonni couldn't recall ever seeing a hue like that before. There had been a methane ball once over the pond at Lac Des Arcs, but that had been years ago.

"It's not time yet," she said.

"Do you have any idea what it is you've put Gerry through in the past few months?"

"Gerry is the least of my worries."

"That's your problem Nonni. You don't have any worries. You've never worried about anybody but yourself. Now go, before I physically throw you out."

"That's not physically possible, Don."

Don took her by the arm. His grip was firm. His muscles still conjured the strength of a man less his age, but it didn't matter. In pathos, Don was rather perfect: the sort of fellow who would avoid the apocalypse by being sensible. His resolution was only bureaucratic, and he was simply another piece of furniture that needed to be in the precise place at the correct time. His visage took on a melancholic look, like an Edvard Munch painting thinking on the lassitude of public good, or the association clause in the Charter, and so she let him go. When she was done, his fossilized effigy was all that was left, quartzite in form, calcite in structure, perfect in nature, but standing utterly inert at the centre of a dirty dance floor in a seedy club few people in the city could even find.

She might have lingered a moment, to stroke his hair, to

laugh about a party gone wrong or a piercing gone right, or maybe just to see if he would move at all in this new dimension, but the new dimension was already moving itself. A heavy figure rolled across the upstairs balcony and a line of sawdust sifted down from the roof. When the weight shifted to the rear of the fantasy room, the springs on the loveseat exploded, the light bulb filament above the stage blew, and a feather drifted up toward the ceiling fan.

A ball bearing bounced across the balcony, under the rail, then dropped down to the dance floor and came to rest by the cage. Someone had hung a seahorse bracelet over the lock. Nonni heard a laugh she didn't like, one she'd heard before, one that was too deep and too insincere.

The smell of a foreign cigarette lilted on the stairs and crept along the banister. She recognized the brand. She followed the scent upstairs and around the chain mail and past the flogging bench, and found Chantal standing in the corner of the fantasy room by the brick well. She flipped a penny through her fingers. Perhaps she was going to make a wish. Her eyelashes were done up cabaret style and her hair was curled like she had come from the opera. She was a gorgeously coy woman, with cheeks of cream and an ornately cut nose.

"Talking to someone?" Nonni said.

"No one you'd know."

"I didn't think Don would let you back in."

"Everybody here is acting rather stunned tonight. They're probably all stoned on poppers. Although there's not much of a crowd, either. I guess perverts don't have a lot of dedication."

Beside the bar, Heidi and Randal stood, pale face and still, clutching their leather aprons as if they were about to be scolded. Shannon and Steve cloistered in a snapshot with Jim and Susan at the cage, and Nonni could smell the perspiration running down their arms.

"You know nothing about perverts," she said.

"Where is Daniel, anyway?"

"That you should know."

"I don't associate with trash like that," Chantal said.

"I thought he was your trash."

"Hardly."

"Did you ever go looking for him?"

"He was a one-night stand," she shrugged. The young woman was both precipitously bored and immaculately composed. A figure that might appear in a wax museum, if she were old enough. "And who cares? I've got a dozen men lining up to take me out. Rich men. Important men. Men of substance. Just last week I had the CEO from Chevron Oil fly me to Montreal. The weekend before I was surfing in Tofino with a lawyer. Whatever happens tonight I can walk away from with one phone call. I can go wherever I want and take whoever I wish. One evening I was silly enough to come here with your beach bum pal and three days later he went AWOL. All right, I went to his house if that's what you mean. Nice place. Rich parents, probably. He certainly wasn't smart enough to make his own money. In Daniel's room the bed was made up. The cupboard was empty. A dozen coat hangers on a chrome pole. Everyone had moved out. Where he went or what he did after that, no clue."

Chantal checked her face in the mirror. There was a tiny imperfect spot on her chin and she made it go away with a single swab of her thumb.

"Did you talk to his parents?" Nonni said.

"He doesn't have any parents."

"How about his friends?"

"You should know he doesn't have those, either."

"Why did you bother to come back?"

A bronchial smell oozed out of the club's timbers, and from far down the alleyway, Nonni was sure she could hear a train approaching.

"I wanted to see what you would do next," Chantal said. She pulled a Winston from her purse. It was a Gucci. "I wanted to see what you would do in the end. In the checkmate position. I thought it would be fun to watch. I wanted to see what your kind does when they are forced into a pathetic finish like this. Actually, I'm glad to see you're all getting what you deserved. I'll enjoy seeing all your photos on the front page of the *National Post* and watching you rot in some provincial prison."

"Who do you take orders from?"

"I don't take orders from anyone," she said. "Unlike you, I'm not a slave to my clit."

Chantal stared at the embers of her cigarette. Somewhere deep inside the oxidizing leaves there was a complex variable to be worked out, and she almost had it resolved. "It's not so much what you do here that bothers me. It's what you don't do. You don't do anything. You're all so stupendously lazy. And monosyllabic. How anyone can even carry on a conversation with your crowd is a puzzle to me. I guess when it comes right down to it, you lack mass."

Nonni seized Chantal by the throat. She pushed the courtesan against the wall and the panels buckled in. The Winstons bounced off the sofa and a pink lighter rolled to the air duct. Three quick blows to Chantal's head matted her hair. Two seconds of strangulation dilated her pupils. The mortar of her flesh crumbled piece by piece about Nonni's feet.

Then there was nothing. Nobody to get angry at, no one to walk away from. Nothing left to break. A flake of gypsum spun earthward and a silver bracelet rocked on the floor.

"That sort of thing is still a crime," Pierceman said. She stood by the fantasy well the same way she stood by all things: ugly, awkward, and in complete command. She had on the same drab suit. The same flat hair. The same bureaucratic shoes. And the bureaucracy had seen everything, so there was no point in kicking anything out of the way.

Pierceman walked over and took the menthols out of Nonni's hip pocket. Being the type of woman who knew when she could take liberties, she toyed with Nonni's belt laces, and fondled her brass epaulet. When she finally got around to striking the pack of menthols against her wrist, two cigarettes fell out in perfect alignment. She lit one and a column of smoke shot up towards the fan.

"Are you going to arrest me?" Nonni said.

"Only if you want."

"But you're going to take everyone else."

"You could have your own club, Nonni. Your own rules. I promise you could do anything you wanted."

"Where's Gerry?"

"He's in jail."

"For what?"

"Does it matter?"

October, November, April, then winter again.

"You're going to make this just like the bathhouse raid, aren't you?"

"It is already," Pierceman said.

Already made sense to this woman. The order of history. The chaos of desire. She stared out the second storey window, where red and blue lights twinkled like Christmas trees in the parking lot, and hummed Lili Marlene. Nonni thought far back into her childhood with holly branches and luminescent bulbs of white pine, but of course it wasn't Christmas time and the forces marshalling outside the Onyx weren't bringing any cheer.

"I'll bail Gerry out," Nonni said.

"And the plebes at Goliath's will contest the law on appeal. Mercury will align with Mars. You and Gwen will go bowling. God knows, the two of us might even become close friends."

Pierceman's lips formed a perfect pucker. Those wet petals sweet as blue plums, and Nonni wondered what she had had against the old gal, the old regime, the old Moscow, Berlin, and the ancient laws of gravity that had deferred everything to this night.

The timid little Latin couple who had frequented the Onyx all this time with so little success congealed beside the cigarette machine. The machine sold eleven brands, but of course they weren't really sold, because that would be unlawful, so they were bought with club tokens that were doled out by William for quaint sexual amendments to the law. Juan had a thin moustache and smoked thin brown cigarettes and looked like thin paraffin wax, and Nonni had detested them always.

Pierceman went over to Juan and opened the fridge door of his chest. There wasn't much there, really. A mortgage, a half-creamed pot. The hinge squeaked. Maybe a quart of milk waiting in the morning, and a chance at the perverse come week's end. The man had actually written an academic paper on the role of the flint in Fraser Canyon brothels. Pierceman held everything there in her cold solvent hand and wasn't that impressed with what she saw.

"So you see, Nonni. It ends the way you always wanted it to. Friday night, eleven post-meridian time in perpetuum."

"I'll call them," Nonni said.

"Call whom?"

"Them, the Woodenheads."

“They’re not real, Nonni.”

“They are now.”

“Do you understand how many times I have heard that?”

“Never from me.”

“Do you realize how many times it has never come true?”

The foyer window broke in. The burglar alarm went off. Nonni had never heard a battering ram before and she wasn’t sure why the police were using one now, but no one in the club flinched, no one shouted, fought, or even cried. There were only the sad faces of the Friday night members she had known for all these years settling down as trilobites, silently down into a primordial sea, and then at last she was alone.

“Come kiss me, Nonni,” Pierceman said.

Jail was bad enough. Prison even worse. A brass spigot burst water over the counter. The power might soon be cut. She wondered what it would be like to stay in this world of kissing Pierceman. Living under her rule. From weekend nights of rubbled intention to Sunday mornings of respectable love. Then wandering the ash of old streets on Monday with older women, spreading out for miles into the wasteland, feeling nothing but lampposts in gravel or rail lines ending in brick. Waiting in queues for busses, taking orders from television, having affairs, divorcing spouses, diluting what feeling was left in the day to fill hot tubs that would be drained by midnight. And in the end, no mass, as if mass was good enough, or screwing, if that would even suffice, or loving, if that should ever fit — and it wouldn’t, and so she called them.

She called them through a copper wire that echoed through the air ducts of the Onyx, then curled around the mailbox at the end of the block, and stretched along the fiords of her concrete city. She wasn’t sure if they would answer. But when they came, they were the wood grain on the door. They smelled of sawdust, and sounded not drowned exactly, but as logs rising from underwater, marching in columns, a line of infantry on a hazy shore.

In the foyer. At the end of the hall. By the registrar. Then at the foot of the stairs gazing up. On the balcony, with their mouths open in mock surprise or their hands over their ears in dumb repose. There were a few of them, and then a few dozen, and finally they filled the room. Same wooden hats, same stiff wooden figures, same wooden heads. As expected, they hadn't barred the exits, but they had covered the clocks.

There were no more members of the living around: the last were paint smudges on the west wall or water marks on the wainscoting, and even William was no more than a sinew of cobweb between two glasses.

When the Woodenheads pressed shoulder to shoulder, a leaf snapped, a millstone ground down, and she knew they derived pleasure out of fear, delight out of dread, but she panicked anyway. They held the panic and passed it around as an ingot between beech palms, examining the worst moment of life with stumped fingers. This was the soul, this was the nation, this was the end. And the end was going to hurt, and the hurting would take a long time, and so she let them in before she got old.

At first they opened her chest, split her sternum, and Nonni recalled an adz opening a block of hemlock deep in her childhood. Then they took out a colon, a heart, some tendon sinew, and a spit of green spleen which reminded her of ferns on a wet Vancouver morning.

They broke her collarbone. They bent her ribs. They made her feel guilt about the times she had not voted, and the other times she had wanted freedom too much. A spandrel of pleura stretched pink and thinner under the blinking black-and-white porn loop, until it drifted up to the ceiling and vanished through the skylight. Nonni was sure she was screaming; she had no idea the inside of a human body could be filled with so much sound. The stroma crashed through her ears. Water pulsated down the porcelain sink. They pulled out her tongue, cleaved her teeth, and vitreous humour ran from her eye. Aztec, or impressionistic, the technique let life's liquid bubble down her arms in filigrees, until it burst the lava light by the exit sign.

Every time they crushed cartilage, the screws in doorknobs tightened, and the Onyx yawled to her command: the cribbing, the baseboards, the soffits. She discarded nostalgia to make room: five of her favourite photographs, a childhood necklace, and four vinyl records. Then, with no precision at all, they ripped out her intestines, and the bile pooled in a drain the club had installed years before. They separated her spine, and crushed what belief she had left into small discs and lay them as pennies in an offering box on the bar. Nonni smelled arsenic. Black gunpowder that clung to her ears when her scalp dried out. The unencumbered scuttling of mice between the thin walls of her skin. One of the Woodenheads had dried out a sheet of her flesh and held it up to the light to see if anything could be read. Apparently there was not much, so they took apart the last few blocks of her corpse because that was all there had ever been. As structures went, it wasn't a bad one she supposed. Deceitful, weak, angry, slovenly, and ill-founded, but still hers, and on a parapet, so next time she shouted, the fire alarm erupted. When she curled her fingers, the air conditioner snapped, and when she breathed, the tin vents in the basement expanded into the most distant realms of loneliness she could produce. She bled. She spoke, she lied, she cried. She did not know what to do with the detective, or Gerry, or her new nation at that moment. She would have to think of something.

ABOUT THE AUTHOR

Martin West was born in Victoria and spent his youth working and living in the Canadian west. He graduated from the University of British Columbia and has been published in magazines across the nation and twice in the Journey Prize anthology. His first collection of stories, *Cretecea & Other Stories from the Badlands* was published in 2016 and was the recipient of a Gold IPPY award (Independent Publisher Book Awards). His short story, "Miss Charlotte," will appear this fall in Best Canadian Stories.